The
Truth about
Lou

The
Truth about Lou

a (necessary) fiction

❧

ANGELA VON DER LIPPE

COUNTERPOINT
A Member of the Perseus Books Group
New York

Published by Counterpoint,
A Member of the Perseus Books Group

Counterpoint books are available at special discounts for bulk
purchases in the United States by corporations, institutions, and other
organizations. For more information, please contact the Special
Markets Department at the Perseus Books Group, 11 Cambridge
Center, Cambridge MA 02142, or call (617) 252-5298 or
(800) 255-1514, or e-mail special.markets@perseusbooks.com.

Designed by Brent Wilcox

Library of Congress Cataloging-in-Publication Data
Lippe, Angela von der.
    The Truth about Lou : a (necessary) fiction / Angela von der
Lippe.
        p.   cm.
    ISBN-13: 978-1-58243-358-5
    ISBN-10: 1-58243-358-5
    1. Andreas-Salomé, Lou, 1861–1937—Fiction.
    2. Psychologists—Fiction.   I. Title.
PS3612.I64T78 2006
813'.6—dc22

                                            2006023319

06 07 08 09/ 10 9 8 7 6 5 4 3 2 1

For my father,
John J. Harrington

With appreciation for
my publisher, Liz Maguire

All life is poetry. We live it day by day, but in its inviolable wholeness, it lives us, composes us. We are works of art but we are not the artist.

~ LOU ~

Contents

CONTENTS

Prelude

This book was inspired by a gift and a promise. The gift was a book my grandmother gave to me shortly before her death in the eighties some twenty years ago. It was a book of German verse by the great poet Rainer Maria Rilke that she had carried with her as a young woman fleeing her native Poland before the German invasion of September 1, 1939. The promise was one I made to her just before she died.

My grandmother was part of an imperiled band of ethnic Germans who inhabited a no-man's-land, German Pomerania with its cities of Zoppot and Danzig, that had ceded to Poland after World War One. Years later the ethnic German enclaves left there were suspected by the Nazi invaders of being traitors and by their own fellow Poles of being potential spies. With no other option, my grandmother made her escape to the New World, turning her sights to assimilating into a new culture with a new language, and she proceeded to hand down to my mother that same forward-looking view of life, with never the slightest inclination to entertain any nostalgia for the old country.

So it was a surprise indeed when shortly before she died, she entrusted a memento of her long-buried past to me, her granddaughter, partly because, she said, I could afford to look back, had in fact made a profession out of looking back as a scholar; and besides, she conceded, as the "writer in the family," I was the one most likely to appreciate this book and all it meant.

411 ✓

The book, I knew, was simply priceless, a first edition of Rilke's poetry collection, The Book of Hours (Das Stundenbuch, 1903), *bearing the author's intimate inscription:*

To Lou—In whose presence these words were formed and in whose hands they now live. —Your old Rainer

As my Oma lay sick, her strength waning in those last weeks, she seemed more willing than ever to speak of her childhood friends and family in Poland, to remember them all. It was almost as if she were taking one last count. So I'll never forget how, in pressing this little volume into my hands, she mused that, though she and of course the world had come to know the poet's verse, it had been the woman—this "Lou"—who had somehow eluded her.

"Well, you know, Oma, if this is the same Lou, I think it may be, it was Rilke's muse, the famous Lou Salomé." (I'd picked up that much in graduate school.) But how, I asked, had she come upon this small treasure? She smiled and lit up remembering, saying: "My mama, your great grandmother, Johanna Niemann, wanted me to have it, but she died too soon of influenza in 1918, and so it was Katya, my nurse, the face I will never forget from my childhood, who gave it to me just before I fled. Mama's close friend 'Lou' from Berlin had sent it to her with specific instructions that she was to give it to me when she saw fit. My Katya, too old to accompany me, did that for 'Mütti' at the last minute, when I was leaving . . .

"There was a note, I seem to remember, from this Lou to Mama with the salutation 'Dearest Johanna.' . . . Isn't it there anymore? Oh, I thought for sure I'd kept it. Perhaps with so much time elapsed and all the travels, it too has been lost, like so much else." And then, patting the volume in my clasp and gently letting go, she looked up wistfully. "I always thought I should somehow know her (what with Katya pressing this book, Mama's gift, her gift, into my hand at the very end), that

2

I'd missed her, this Lou, in some way, but I don't remember ever meeting her. I have no image of her. Not even a voice.

"So now the gift is yours, Julianna"—my name on her lips sounding so strangely old, the one I was born with but could never pronounce as a girl. "Yours, my dear Anja"—she whispered my nickname with a slight German inflection—"yours to make with what you will. Perhaps you can find out more about who she was. You can do that easily nowadays, can't you? I don't know why, I guess it may be loose ends, but I just think it would be good to know."

I didn't quite follow her or understand her need. And not long after that, death, her death, intervened, and then life, my life, intervened to send me to countless academic outposts in a nomadic search for a tenure-track position in literature and writing—eventually ending up years later at Skidmore College in upstate New York. On this vast, leafy campus at the foot of the Adirondacks, I'd been teaching comparative literature and conducting writing seminars in poetry, and now I faced the reward for all my labors—a sabbatical to finally write what I had always been putting off. For a writer, deciding just which topic will conquer one's procrastination is a terrifying prospect matched only by the one certain fate of any writer—the blank page.

But I didn't seem to have to choose; the topic seemed to choose me with the arrival of a package one afternoon in late spring as I was preparing my last classes before my long-awaited break. My mother, who was moving out of the family home into an independent care facility outside of Pittsburgh, had sent me an old hatbox full of Oma's personal papers. My eyes scanned the contents—a daybook, a dictionary, a postcard, a pearl hat pin, a dried corsage of white roses, the wedding certificate of one Cosima Niemann to Carl Lippe. Nothing before 1938, I thought, just the torn cloth arm of a doll with an exquisite porcelain hand. My fingers traced the perfectly formed old script and my mind worked its way back to that wandering child who in making the crossing had become my grandmother. And I remembered our last talk. Her gift and my promise to find Lou.

It was time, I thought. Over the years I had collected bits and pieces—an obscure monograph here, chapters from multiple biographies of her conquests—Nietzsche, Rilke and Freud—critical psychoanalytic essays and her own highly abstract, elusive, autobiographical prose. But all these were like shards in a mosaic that never fit. Forming no coherent image. No singular voice. Oma was right after all.

I resolved to write her story not as others saw her but in her own voice. To concentrate I decided to rent a remote camp in the North Country from an environmentalist friend, a Scotsman, who was off doing research for the year in the Arctic. He warned me that I'd be "having it lonely up there," he'd send postcards via carrier pigeon or musher, and that I'd know the winter ended when I heard the bear cubs falling out of the trees. But there was no better solitude, no more open space than that blank page of the Adirondack sky. In short, it was the perfect writer's retreat.

And so that is how this, Lou's story, began, with a hatbox of memories, the gift of a book and a deathbed wish to find the sender. As I came to hear her story, I could not predict how all those things would intersect. But she would tell me in time.

And as I came to discover, the genius of Lou was much more than physical. Her genius was her willful hold on the imagination. And indeed when I would stray away to the research and all the other voices, she would call me back with a clear voice to her story. She began her telling in the thirties, about the time when Oma was escaping Poland, and then she sank way, way back into the pillow of memory, to her mother and her Russian childhood. And she took me there and I listened. This muse to so many had now become my own. She spoke and I wrote.

This is her story, the truth about Lou.

—Anna Kane, Blue Ridge Camp, 2006

4

Improbable Beginnings: Reclaiming a Life

All the soarings of my mind begin in my blood.
—R.M. RILKE

The truth is, dear (and this may have been a fatal flaw of mine but one I was born with) . . . ever since I can remember I was drawn to the white flame of genius. As if genius possessed that necessary fire that would blaze open the floodgates of my small world to untold vistas and carry me down a raging river of thrills far beyond my native peasant Russia. I was a girl. I never thought to get stuck in the muck of some tributary. I never thought of an end to that adventure—smack into a delta. I was too young. Thank God for that!

Genius was, of course, not "genius" at all; it was something much more explosive, visceral. Oh yes, duplicitous. It promised spiritual flight and not incidentally, earthly pleasure—essential nutrients for my all-too-hungry body and willing soul. Restless girl that I was. I was like a darting goldfinch lighting but for a moment on some programmed path too deep and distant for my quivering body to know. So I tasted morsels of forbidden knowledge as they were shamelessly fed to me from the hand of these tutors of my experience and, well yes, then true to my nature, I took wing.

However bold, however quick to the challenge of these suitors I may have been, I was terrified too. But I must have loved the danger. Throughout my life I marveled at how the calm mind of genius could destroy and envision in the same moment a blueprint for resurrection. One man proclaimed the death of God in the middle of St. Peter's Basilica. He had another plan. Another cried the creation of the angel within the self-imposed exile of his dark dank Swiss tower. And still another mused on the sanctity of sexual desire, while stroking the austere head of one of his antiquities and quietly puffing a cigar way past midnight in the pristine consulting room of his Viennese home.

These encounters, when it comes right down to it, amounted to nothing less than erotic blasphemy. An undressing of the soul without ever having to disrobe. There was no stasis in the presence of these men. Something was always about to happen. The earth would literally shift beneath my feet and the only anchor that saved me from being dumped off the universe was the hand extended to steady my step and eyes that held me in rapt attention. So, yes, I gave myself over willingly, that is, to a point . . .

This is precisely how so many have regarded my life for all these years. In the relentless hold of genius. And I have not bothered to correct them, though it's never been my way to bask in reflected glory. I, Lou Salomé, have been viewed by fellow artists, the dearest friends and ardent critics alike, not the least of whom was my mother, as a mere appendage, an accessory to the crimes of genius, and that too, I fear, will be my legacy. My fiction—the wildfire of my imagination—the bloodletting of my passion—all but forgotten, I'm now known somewhat as a literary collector and visionary brooder.

No doubt my memoirs, my journals, my critical essays throughout the years have only contributed to the startling misconception of being serial muse to countless artists and by extension, midwife to some of the most sublime inventions of twentieth-century art and ideas. Vicarious interloper that I seemingly was.

If the truth be told, I think I was always more enamored of the art than the artist. As far back as I can remember I tended to value the message more than the messenger. I don't know its root cause. But I recall as a child spying the blue gentian flowers, the bluebells, along the roadside to our summer estate and naming them one by one—Sasha, Katarina, Misha—only to find myself crestfallen at the door. I'd picked them; I'd picked them all and there they were crushed in my small palm. I was ever distracted into remote corners of reverie. Hmmm, that was the artist in me perhaps. Incurably romantic, disturbingly unfeminine!

From the very beginning I lived in an imaginary world, often to the neglect of those around me. You see, it was the idea that transported me. The person did not, as dispensable as the body is to the soul. People might come and go but the flight of their words was enduring, my glint of eternity. Youth is so blissfully blind. And age, well, age is rueful and forgiving. I didn't know then what I do now, that their words would be all I was left with. No, back then their disembodied words became the lingua franca of my life's travels. The part of them I could take with me. . . . And so, though I surely let go of some friends too soon or may have let others down (I had my reasons), I never did forget them.

Especially not the poet. He wouldn't let me. His words held on. They *were* his soul. So he didn't leave this world, but lodged inside me, as if waiting to speak. No, I could never forget my Rainer, and neither will you, child. When you hear my story.

My life is the story of love's attraction and its puzzles with pieces missing. And though I always knew there was something magnetic drawing me to these luminous men, I knew too that they seemed to have been drawn to me. That's the part I've never understood. The me I couldn't face, the child I never saw. Can we ever know the muse?

I am old now. And for once in the looming eclipse of a crystal night when the world seems asleep to the throat-hold of fascism and the inaudible scream that will soon shatter glass on our orderly streets . . . Now when my body heals from the slicing assault on one breast and is no longer holding, I want for once to take leave of the gaze of my philosopher Friedrich, my poet love Rainer and my dear professor Sigmund that has so much defined me. (What would they say if they could of all the lies, the silly distortions of who we were?)

I want now to step into my own light before these eyes that have seen so much fail me. I finally want to know her. The one who's always been there but I could not bear to see—shy child, hands hidden in a mauve muff, worldly woman wrapped in the noose of a boa—the girl, nonetheless, who dared to stare into the eyes of genius. That girl was me, of course. But somehow I never knew her. Did they?

No matter. This afterthought is where my life truly begins. And though I cannot see her, I listen for her voice. Notes of an eluded presence. Like birdsong carrying me into my final dawn. The rest— the me—I can now imagine . . . *through you, my child*. Help me find her and draw her for others to see.

Listen, listen carefully. I can still hear the poet's words spoken like an oath in that cypress grove so very long ago: *"Let my heart beat through you,"* he said. Now, my dear, let me take you to her.

1

Child of Russia

"Mama, Mama—I wish you would drown, Mama!"

Like a graceful cormorant she dove from the perch on the far ledge of the lake into its darkest pool, disappearing with barely a splash into the deep. The late summer sun was hanging low, squinting its crimson through the trees. The water glimmered like diamonds on onyx and a wind shivered a beam of light across the water's surface in search of a scurrying presence. The birches leaning into the lake to find Mama sank into the black. She was gone. I was terrified by the power of my own words. Seized by a freedom almost mine. When just as quickly, it was plucked away when she resurfaced and, spewing an arc of water from her mouth, she offered the retort: "Then I would be dead, Louli." She wasn't. And I was still miserable.

Without a word she emerged at the shore and rejecting my hand reached for her cotton shawl and wrapping it tightly around her sinewy limbs stippling in the cold air, she let go a sigh of relief. Bending over and wildly shaking off the wetness, she tossed back a cascade of dark eely curls framing her heart-shaped face. The dark orbs of her lavender eyes stood out against almost translucent skin slightly blue from the freezing water.

Yes, my mother was disarmingly beautiful—with the pallor of a statue, smooth and unchanging, exuding a kind of brilliant glare. I could never get close to her; never see myself in her reflection. No, I was gaunt and ugly—ever wanting to shed my skin. I simmered inside to change who I was. But what I remember then is that I could not say I was sorry, could not speak the words, though I so needed her to touch me.

Her look registered the wickedness of my words that day but there amid the embrace of the lapping lake she didn't chastise me at all, and simply let it go instead. Her imperial way. Shunning shaming silence being a far more effective punishment for my misdeed. She had more on her mind.

So the death wish I had cast on my mother that August day did not succeed in its first attempt but ricocheted back, dropping like a stone into the turmoil of my adolescent soul and welling out far beyond that moment. Never again to be mentioned. That is, til now, of course, when the object of my murderous rage is long gone, no longer a threat, and through no fault of my own, she is finally dead.

I WAS born in 1861 into a turbulent Russia. No sooner had the serfs been freed and a two-year grace period of their liberation from slavery to tenancy expired, than I was born on the family estate in Peterhof—summer residence to the tsar and a host of imperial officers, of which my father was one. Coincident with my arrival, a disquieting sense of a larger social project gone wrong and impending breakdown just outside the gate was beginning to spread like an errant rumor across the land.

I was the sixth child in a long line of boys—my sex a distinct disappointment to my mother. I never quite fathomed her aversion to girls—only that one does not fear what one does not know. And she would meet in me all her fears and then some—the spirit unleashed that she had tried so hard throughout her lifetime to constrain.

Though mother had always thrilled to displays of small rebellion—outfitting the domestics of my childhood with her cast-off finery and insisting in her dotage on being carried in St. Petersburg's streets dur-

ing the workers' uprising—my mother could never stand her own freedom. She drew the line at that. (She was a serf to her own class.) No,
that was as unnatural for her as a spirit escaping from its own body,
denied a true end, ever questing after imagined origins. All that was as
unnatural for her as a daughter—the daughter I most regrettably was.

*Strange how destinies, large and small, intertwine. In those years
when the serfs were free to reclaim ownership of their own bodies, I was
struggling to free myself from my own private bondage—the clutches of
my mother. This almost physical need to break free and seize control
would follow me for years, flaring up in new relationships, free spirit
that I became. But the sensation triggered a strange distrust of my own
body. I was uncomfortable in my own skin.*

*So, you see, my mother never did leave me. She may have wanted to
own my body, but her real hold for all those years was on my soul. I
gave her that boldly, mirroring an abandon she wished to disown. The
daughter she couldn't bring herself to touch.*

THAT late summer afternoon we walked the lake road back to the
house through a tangle of huge plain trees and the filigreed canopy
of delicate birches. We passed the gazebo playhouse at the corner of
the walled garden—a hexagonal structure with two doors, one opening into the colorful ménage of exotics and cultivated flowers within
our magic garden, and the other leading out to the gray phalanx of
birches and gnarled wood beyond its protective walls.

This little house on the edge of the garden was the sanctuary of my
youth—the place where I was safe in my fantasy. I rarely touched the
dolls and stuffed animals that lined the window seats (though their
locks were often shorn and various appendages torn), but it was here
where I created the fantasy of me and the characters and companions
that would then keep me company throughout my day of chores,
lessons, meals and religious observances. It was a sacred space and I
allowed no one to enter it, except for my brother. Evgeny was two

years older, but an altogether much more nurturing playmate to the dolls and animals, whom he looked after and ordered, assigning them each individual pillowed surfaces, while I, in turn, looked after Evgeny who with each year seemed only to get weaker. A weakness he never outgrew til one day he traded the brief high fevers of childhood for the chronic consumption that would never leave him, til life did.

That day the gazebo seemed almost transparent in its emptiness—bereft of the fantasy friends I had invented there so long ago. My mother was worried about Evgeny's persistent cough that now left blood on his handkerchief. She was also furious with me for being cited for insolence during religious instruction—a matter the local pastor had chosen to bring to her attention.

I was sixteen and preparing to be confirmed in the German Reformed Evangelical Church—the pietism that embraced our small foreign enclave of officers and servants of the Imperial Crown in St. Petersburg. My transgression in short was my "insolent" response to our pastor Reverend Dalton's pronouncement that there was no place imaginable where God was not. First thinking of my gazebo, I thought again and blurted: "Oh yes there is, Hell."

The good reverend blanched and with eyes squinting like pincers about to extract the thorn of my verbal assault he ordered me to write over and over again in my notebook lines from St. Paul's first letter to the Corinthians in which Paul, the thunderstruck disciple, quotes the damning admonition of Isaiah: "I will destroy the wisdom of the wise and the cleverness of the clever I will thwart." Had that angry prophet been outwitted too?

But that wasn't all. Lest the lesson be lost on me, I was forced to stand before my classmates and to recite Paul's lame interpretation of Isaiah: "For the foolishness of God is wiser than men and the weakness of God is stronger than men." Scripture interpreted, the lesson was delivered. I would never go back there again and that was my mother's frustration.

Next day my mother, preoccupied with my brother's illness, entrusted me to my father for a stern talking-to. My father, wanting as much as I to get away from the nervous confusion of my mother's accusatory gaze, took me into Peterhof where we walked among the high-pitched tents of a touring circus. I thought of my vacant gazebo and the lives that lay dormant under those still sheets. Here among the tightrope dancers, the jugglers and the bears on leashes I imagined escaping with my father to join the caravan and live a life filled with roasted chestnuts, harmonicas and the dancing tunes of gap-toothed gypsies.

I didn't know then that this tall fair-haired man with emerging paunch, this man whose slate-gray eyes, full lips and lopsided mouth that looked happy and sad at the same time I had inherited, would not live out the year. That his heart would soon give out—from what I in my girlish way thought was a superabundance of life—playful hugs and a hearty laughter that began somewhere in his belly and rumbled through his chest with gentle intensity. Bursting through life's pretenses.

Though a military man and a strict observer of tradition, my father was never one to stand on ceremony. He had seen too much death on the battlefield and squalor out in the countryside to take too seriously the charge of his daughter's heresy. So giving no credence to my crime but merely to its consequences, he counseled a practical approach: "Louli, listen my dear Louli. Try not to upset your mother." Such was my punishment. The rest—how I would keep the peace—was for me to decide.

My father was earthly to the core—he gave me my freedom. And I idolized him for that. And though he left me too soon, he let go with a firm squeeze of my shoulders, implanting a quick kiss on my forehead—the conspiratorial yes that I would never forget.

FATHER would never learn of my solution. A year later when he was taken from us, I remember a sound inappropriate and frantically merry—the squealing of the sleigh carrying his coffin through St. Petersburg's black iced streets. I breathed a wish, the word "Papa"—warming the frozen tears on the ice-encrusted windows of our carriage that followed in procession—and spying a flickering succession of houses aglow and people drawn to hearths within, I breezed forward. I would never know them.

Yet I had been harboring a secret fire of my own for some time, ever since Aunt Jutta suggested I attend the Dutch Reformed Chapel on the Zogorodny Prospekt not too far from my home. It was there I would see him. That instant those eyes seared slowly into memory and I knew he'd become my beacon. I did not breathe a word to anyone.

This little chapel with its triangular roof and modest spire seeming like two hands folded in prayer stood dwarfed in the shadow of the massive onion-domed Vladimir Cathedral with its huge vaulted stained-glass windows. It had become a popular venue for the restless seekers, followers and leaders alike, and so its shelter provided a breathing space, like a caesura in scriptural law, for the more radical preachers of our church, known to the youth who hungered for their progressive message.

My widowed aunt was advanced in all ways of life and I trusted her implicitly. She had lost her husband early in life and now lived independent of any social expectation. That is, her widowhood had released her of a certain social bondage, and not as fate but as part of the vagaries of life she could now enjoy being a spinster if she wanted.

Jutta was always making fine distinctions between a woman's "freedom" (finding freedom in a man she could "snuggle up to physically and intellectually and finally adore!"—hardly sounded like freedom to me) and a woman's "independence" (which seemed the opposite to me, a lonely, self-satisfied lot of having a mind of one's own). Submitting or settling seemed a dismal choice, but I nodded and listened nonetheless. There was definitely some freedom in

Jutta's lot though—for she told me she accommodated her independence by satisfying what she called her "wild urges," without ever giving me the details.

Jutta had a life of her own in Berlin. But she knew that for her young niece to escape the narrow confines of St. Petersburg's imperial court, I would have to undergo certain prescribed rites of passage—and above all, stay on the straight and narrow. I would need quite literally the passport of confirmation in the Reformed Evangelical Church, for without proof of these papers conferred through this Christian rite I could neither travel nor pursue studies abroad. And what with my heresy and my public humiliation setting me at odds with my family, I was at an impasse.

Mine would surely be a difficult course, but Jutta, my confidante from afar (though she came to us for father's funeral), would be a trusted guide, experienced in social diplomacy and that sleight-of-hand psychological strategy of getting what she wanted no matter what.

Jutta knew all of the significant stumbling blocks, the hidden family ghosts that lay in the path to my freedom. She knew for instance that her father, a butcher and draft dodger in Germany turned sugar-refinery magnate in Russia, had spent his very last years closeted in a back room, off the pantry of their family residence, under the watchful gaze of the cook, butler and countless dispensable maidservants.

Apparently in a fit of obvious religious hysteria, my grandfather had taken a knife to his own son's throat, following instructions from on high to kill all the survivors of the Neva flood. "As God is my witness, I must take you, my son." A mere teen herself, Jutta came upon the scene of my grandfather out back by the water trough, cuffing his young son by the neck, about to butcher him with the same deliberate speed that he sectioned the wild boar and drained its blood each year for Christmas dinner. According to Jutta, my mother—just twelve—cowered paralyzed in the woodshed, unable to do anything or even utter a sound, watching her father about to do the unimaginable.

Jutta, always fleet of mind, screamed at the top of her lungs that he stop listening to demons and invoked a controversial article of our pietist faith—that he "could not impress God with idle action" but "should 'know' he need only believe." She grabbed the knife from her father's hand and the livery men came running to restrain him. And though God did not need my grandfather's good work or any of our efforts for salvation for that matter, my uncle did definitely benefit from my aunt's quick-thinking action that day.

The family decided to closet "Opa" under full watch in that small back room looking out to the stables, where the Neva's constant overflowing would never provoke him to act again. There he sat alone with his faith for the rest of his days, receiving daily messages from a wife who no longer visited him, who would remarry and send word of her deed in the same dutiful way. He took in none of this. There he sat with furrowed brow and the bewildered look of one who has lost his moorings and forgotten the tether, the why or the wherefore. And through no effort of his own, he slipped into a curious bliss of forgetting, absolving him of all his transgressions.

I remembered this man I never knew, my lost grandfather, many years later when the great philosopher Nietzsche delivered to me an apt description, "Blessed are the forgetful, for they get the better of their infirmities."

⁓

My grandfather's aberration was never to be mentioned again, til one blizzard-swept night during winter holiday in Peterhof when he wandered away from his kitchen refuge through an open door and the next morning was found frozen in a snow bank on the path to the gazebo. So like the snowman of my youth melting away outside my playhouse into the oblivion, was he real, was he not? No matter. My family with their wits about them consigned my very real grandfather to a similar fate.

Just how my mother derived from that trauma her favoring of boys (out of protective guilt, perhaps), I do not know. And still how after that incident my family professed an even deeper pietistic faith is simply beyond my understanding. Faith alone might save them. From their own fear perhaps. But the menace of life was another matter. The meaning of that violent event was closeted away as swiftly and surely as my grandfather had been, into some forgotten corner of the mind, made harmless by virtue of its neglect. It was just another locked door. But how many stood between me and my mother, I didn't even question. I just knew I was shut out.

My mother had learned to look away quite early. And much later she would give herself into the protective custody of my father—a military officer no less. But Jutta was not one to let fear get the better of her. Just as she back in their childhood had saved her sister and brother from harm's way, years later she would become once again a guardian angel, this time negotiating my safe passage through the second coming of the flood, having nothing to do with the tides of the Neva but the moods of my headstrong adolescence. And while Jutta would become the navigator, commanding the vessel that delivered me to the safe port of my independence, the pastor Hendrik Gillot would become my very own savior, redeeming me from my loneliness—heaven and earth in one—my man-God. Or so I thought.

INTERLUDE

She lost her father too early. I lost mine so late, lived most of my adult life with him so indomitably there. Never get used to him being a memory. But to have lived so much of life with only a memory of a father—indomitably not there—as Lou did, well, that seems hardly imaginable. Did she look for him everywhere, every step of the way—that man who in his prime fell from his horse—her real toy soldier? Did she think she could find him, resurrect him again, all those years searching for the spirit of a memory no mortal man could embody? Like a prayer to an idol.

There's that old cardinal at the feeder again—dad's favorite bird. . . . Huh, blood red, tufted rust crown, a real loner always surveying his landscape, sends the tits and goldfinches aflutter, stranger to these parts though, regal, commanding, expanding into space.

2

First Love

Dear Honorable Pastor Gillot,

This letter to you is a first and last appeal. (For you do not know me.) The person who writes this letter is a sixteen-year-old girl who is in the throes of a crisis of identity, which threatens to sever all ties to family, church and community. I have lost my faith, dear Reverend, and I fear I am losing myself as well, falling into an ever-deepening cavern of isolation and despair.

I am a congregant of the German Evangelical Church here in St. Petersburg and it is there that my questions have been unfairly singled out for their heretical content. This perilous and painful state of affairs will, I fear, result in my failure to be confirmed in my family church. The truth is, Reverend, among my peers I am courteous but not at all sincere and how could I be, without betraying the questioning authentic person I know myself to be. You cannot imagine what it is like for me to be constantly holding back, unable to join in the laughter and social gatherings of the other girls, unable to voice my mind's spirit for fear it will be broken. Pastor, I hunger for knowledge and learning, for the courage to uncover the God I know to be in my heart. But if my questioning be blasphemy, then I am truly damned forever and you need not read one more word.

I have heard you speak from the pulpit: "True faith renews and makes the whole man alive in Christ." I wish so much to know more and to be made whole, to be led into the light. And I am willing now to live without answers. But I need someone to take me into his tutelage, so that my heart can be quieted in knowing my questions have at least been heard. So I appeal to you to be that person, and if you will only have me, I promise to respond with a determined mind and every fiber of my being.

Yours sincerely,
Louise Salomé

I know there is love at first sight. But at second sight there is always time to reconsider and love is more of a gamble. As I stood there in the anteroom of the modest gabled house that Pastor Gillot called home, I held in my mind the image of the flaxen-haired pastor in peasant shirt and sash, up there behind the roster, with an inextinguishable almost eerie light emanating from his eyes, speaking words that floated out over the congregation drawing them in with the tidal force of an undertow. As I stoically waited for reality to dash my dreams, the rote words of my letter catapulted me into a panic. I trembled and I bit my lip in anticipation. Crumpled in my gloved hand was the only real evidence of his answer—the slight hope of his intentions penned in a perfunctory reply to my letter: "Miss Salomé, come to my home next Tuesday at four o'clock and we shall discuss your dilemma."

A maid emerged and with downcast eyes led me up three flights of stairs to Pastor Gillot's garret study. Opening the door she motioned me in and just as quickly disappeared. I stepped into this small room and the first thing I noticed was my letter with its hastily scrawled signature, scattered amongst a stack of other papers on a small desk, an open inkwell and a breviary. The attic room was itself spartan—desk and chair, a simple cot by the wall to my left, a hearth to the right, a few pen and ink drawings (a couple of Dürers), Lucas Cranach's *Luther* above the desk, and a small telescope by the dormer window.

Pastor Gillot was seated on a high stool with his back to me looking out the window as if anticipating some other arrival. He turned, and with a penetrating gaze that looked as if it originated in the most faraway recesses of mind, he gestured to me and said in a soft but matter-of-fact tone: "So Miss Salomé, be seated and tell me your trouble."

I sat in the desk chair, and without so much as removing my crocheted gloves, I began to rattle off my transgressions as if to a confessor and I added the admission that both my parents but some teachers too were disturbed by my unchecked habit of making up stories from the whole cloth of my imagination and then trying them out as truth on my unsuspecting family and classmates. I questioned my faith in God by invoking the world of lived experience and I questioned reality by conjuring a made-up world. I couldn't find my peace in either world and that was my problem, I couldn't <u>win</u>. — Bewhole /

Oh yes, that world-weary sixteen-year-old was me all right, always so ahead of myself, thinking I could edit my story, preempt the surprises, write my life, as what I wanted to believe, wanted others to believe too. Running so fast from all I knew, oblivious to the fact that I was moving at all.

Pastor Gillot moved toward me from his perch at the window and laying a hand on my shoulder said: "My child, you are not alone in your questions. Are you prepared now to learn the story of man's attempt to fathom the mystery of God's creation? That is the history of science and philosophy, seeking knowledge, and I can tell you that story. Are you also prepared to learn the history of the world's great religions? Because that is the story of our quest for spirit. History and story. Story and history. This is all simply the struggle between body and soul, between what we know and what we desire to know. If you, child, are willing to learn, you will become truly wise and 'educated' in the original sense of the word. You will be led out of this darkness that surrounds you."

He fell silent, and then holding my gloved hands in his large grasp, he went on: "But you, young lady, must do your part to make yourself ready. You must promise me that each time we meet, you will let go of all of the foolish fantasies that possess you—and tell me everything that clutters your troubled mind and spirit, sparing nothing. And your mind will soon be cleared to let a tree of knowledge take root . . . your heart will be open to receive the wisdom of the spirit that you so desire." With this, he let go instantly and I felt faint and at sea. It sounded pontifical, more suited to the echo chamber of a chapel than this dank attic room.

Of course, I said yes. What it meant for sure, I could not know. But what I felt at that moment was the hold on my shoulder. A physical trust. And I thought of my father. I didn't know I would soon lose him. But I believed beyond a doubt I'd met his worthy successor and I was blessed. I was suddenly filled with a blissful expectation mixed with a hint of impending betrayal. A betrayal I had willed, indeed wanted.

At first blush you don't see first love for what it is, you don't even question. Because it's the only love, everything. You've lost control. Your whole life depends on it being true, and there it is, your life delivered into someone else's hands. For me what could be safer, more blessed? That someone was a pastor. To make it all right. And loyal to the last, first love stayed with me, long after it was over, never really letting go, holding me in the unspoken suspicion that regardless of him, I, I had willed it to happen.

We began that spring with two hours a week, usually meeting late in the afternoon, sometimes going beyond the hour which left me racing home defiant in my girlish euphoria, determined to keep my secret, but just as fearful that I would miss the evening meal and be caught out. I remember starting each session, sometimes sitting at the desk with Gillot in the high stool at the window or other times, particularly when I was upset with something gone wrong at home, sitting on the edge of the cot. Occasionally I leaned back onto the pillow while Gillot remained at his desk. I would begin by closing my eyes and relate to him all the stories and fantasies that had intruded on my days since our last meeting.

When I think back on those early days, this truly naïve invention of ours—what Gillot called our "Märchenstunden" was not unlike analytic inquiry today. Our "fantasy hours"—unscientific and spontaneous as they were—were all part of a game within which I could speak my foolish fantasies freely, without fear of reprisals.

The idea for me was to "relieve myself" of my menacing fantasies, to get rid of whatever impelled me to make them up, but what Gillot's presence actually caused me to do was to embellish them with new twists and turns occurring in the moment. I did this because in dramatic moments I opened my eyes for a second and saw a faint smile on his forgiving face. He was intrigued by my creations. They clearly pleased him, as his full sensuous lips curled and parted as if waiting for the next breath of my story. So I did all I could to prolong the fantasy part of our lessons, if only to delay what followed: our actual studies.

Gillot would embark on longwinded discussions of the history of philosophy—man's notion of what God might be—the one true god—and the history of religion—which as far as I could see was God's notion of what men should be—the one true people. But how many gods and how many chosen people? The only common ground of these multiple faiths seemed to be in the claim of being special—one and only.

Gillot was translating a history of religion from his native Dutch into German and I struggled fiercely to teach myself Dutch on off-hours and during the two-month summer recess when my family retired to our summer home in Peterhof. My job during our lessons was to help him find the precise German rendering, as he worked himself through the original Dutch text. A drudgery I couldn't quite follow, because it seemed so predicated on a literal interpretation of the word.

It seemed to me disingenuous—God's word having been handed down through countless generations in multiple tongues, no telling how many translators being just like me, each one unable to curb their inclination to add a little here and there, to satisfy their lost spirits. Their lives were dull enough and here was diversion. And if Gillot's exactitude was typical of a scholar's formal precision, what then of the Luther-inspired personal God with a written word and scripture, which the faithful seeker not only had complete access to, but could even interpret and make his own, indeed improve upon? What of the words that truly spoke to the soul?

Oh we displaced all that passion percolating just below the surface into exacting God's word. Silly as it sounds, we did. Only much later would we have words for it—"repress," "sublimate." I couldn't begin to question what happened in that space. He, my confessor and I, I, his . . . ? And another word, "dissociate," for what would later happen. "First love" masking feelings, untranslatable.

So in returning from two months of pent-up fantasies under the accusatory gaze of my mother, I yearned to resume our "studies" and I burst into Gillot's study with an urgency to tell the truth, *my* truth, to the one person in the world who would understand and believe me. With that unmentionable incident by the lake last summer and my wish for my mother to drown, for my father and me to escape with the circus, and hoping beyond hope for my dear brother, please God, not to die, I had more than enough stories to fill the fantasy part of our lessons. And enough vivacity to improve on reality for Gillot's meticulous scholarly translation.

I had begun to feel feverishly desperate in the weeks of our separation. I needed more than his counsel or his spiritual care. I needed his physical presence, that protective warmth of being seen for the first time, for who I was. I was determined to preserve our conversations and never to lose this kinship that I had never before experienced, so I would go to any lengths to confess to Gillot the sins of my fantasies, those black stones weighing down on my "lost soul," and to pretend a devotion to his religious instruction that I did in fact not have. If only to perpetuate the intoxicating hold of disclosure, this feeling of desire I had for him, I gave myself over freely to my stories, sifting through the embellishments, searching for the one lie that would speak the truth of me to him. That he would believe. That would move him to respond. . . .

MEMORY, *what is it? I dreamt of my mother emerging from a flooding of water naked and her body, surrounded by the black snake-like curls I knew so well, was barely pubescent with young buoyant breasts and nipples that looked like sand dollars—she was smiling not shamed at all by her nakedness or struck by my alarm . . . she did not seem to recognize me but lifted both arms and then with aplomb reached with her left hand to deliver into mine her right hand severed from an arm that fell limp at her side like a complacent tired doll. The water around her was a ruby red but no blood drained from her body. And the hand I held in my hand was that of an old woman, with blue veins mapping traces of deep riverbeds. But to which there was no delta. And I stood there, with her detached hand held in mine, and reached for a water lily to wrap the hand in, and pulling it from its root I looked into the heart of the flower to see a face with eyes so like Evgeny but somehow not his at all, how could it be, and I let it go to float away in the pink river . . . away from me, from my grasp. . . . And I felt the full surge of a scream that was inaudible. Though I tried, I could not be heard. And then I awoke, holding nothing but the memory of a dream.*

What is dream but a distorted creation? What is memory—but a created distortion? Then if memory is at once remembering and inventing at the same time, what can reality be? An invention?

And why does it frighten me so? . . . I asked Gillot when I returned to him that fall and our "fairy tale hours" became more fraught with emotion, sometimes to the point of precipitating a fainting spell. Far more than missing Gillot, I found that the tension around those secret meetings (a tension that seemed to escalate with each questioning look of my mother, trustful pat from my father and stoic accepting smile of my brother, as I made my exit) began to overtake me. I no longer spun my tales to exert control but my tales began to spin me.

Gillot seemed to soften with each telling of my emotional distress and I interpreted that to mean he had also cared and had missed me. He was no longer the stern patronizing analyst of my foolish stories. Seeing that they terrified me to the point of tears, he took me on his lap, caressed my hair and face, and whispered tenderly, "Girl, you must let it all out. I am here. No one can hurt you."

Could I have really been so blind, so breathlessly naïve? Was he simply obtuse to what we were doing or mercurial, calculating? I question now what I couldn't then, no not for a moment.

I tried to reason out the torture of my dream—my childlike mother, the Neva floods of family lore, my brother—no, her brother—swirling down a river of generations of blood in the innocent hold of a water lily and the culprit who was responsible for this family misfortune that spilled into my sleep, where was he? The sly one was nowhere in my night's creation. He stood somewhere beyond the grasp of sleep.

Could I find him if I was vigilant enough and pieced together the story I remembered of the Neva flood with the details of my dream? What had happened to my mother that day so long ago? And why did she forever fear me, her girl-child? And who in God's name was the culprit—my grandfather?—or was it perhaps me for imagining these torturous things—for suspecting something I could not see . . .

I was dreaming the unspeakable—sexual betrayal, my mother's, of course, never mine. . . . No, push it away. And he, well, uncertain now but still so comforting, deliberate in wanting to continue.

Intuiting that this relentless questing for meaning left me sleepless, losing weight and filled with more questions than useful answers, Gillot began to focus our studies on a neutral subject—a space neither too real nor too divine. He set about teaching me about the heavens and its stars.

He arranged for us to meet that winter for one hour a week coinciding with the evening vespers service followed by a social gathering at our church, so that the evening hour would not be questioned by my family. During these sessions I would stand at the garret window and he was seated just behind me on the stool with his hand around my waist. In this way he would guide my line of vision and instruct me to look through the telescope and observe some of the most distant mysteries of the night sky.

I remember feeling a warm sensation at his touch of my waist and a tingling sense of playful apprehension as he held both my temples from behind and tried to position my gaze through the instrument. Pointing at some object in the heavens, his hand would open as if to release some energy of his own to the night sky. "Look at the world beyond us, Lou," he would say, "the universe beyond you and your family, beyond you and me. The universe we're just beginning to know—we're all a part of. See those stars, Lou. They float way out there in the chill of the heavens just like us. But we feel them. They are burning."

I remember feeling a perplexed thrill at Gillot's words, as I was pulled out of my troubled self, the world I knew, and delivered in the simplest way to the distant orbit of the stars. I looked forward to this one evening per week when he would hold me in his arms and I would be transported for once to a world I had not created. He gave me a running commentary of celestial objects infinite distances away from us and yet we could know them intimately by observing the course of their travels, the intensity of their light. Venus, the brightest star in the sky, commanding the stage of day's beginning and end as the morning star and the evening star. And he marveled at the distant planets and their discoverers—that poor heretical creature (who had his own run-in with the church hierarchy) Galileo Galilei who beyond challenging the conventional wisdom of our place in the universe had also discovered Jupiter. Jupiter with its swirling red spot and its many moons, invisible to the human eye and barely visible to our telescope, seemed to live in a huge world of its own, a Goliath rivaling solar system to our very own David earth and its one lone moon.

What fascinated me about Gillot's excursions into the stars was that the inhabitants of these heavens bore no Christian names at all but something more original and primitive. These heavenly objects were the namesakes of mythical gods who carried the legends of some enduring "all-too-human" behavior.

I remember Gillot telling me about Io (one of Jupiter's moons), the "other woman" in ancient myth who for loving Jupiter (sometimes known as Jove), a married man, was turned by his vengeful wife, Juno, into a cow. And while Jupiter could assume at will all forms, in this case, that of a bull to be with his bovine paramour, Juno would not be made a fool. Though Io might be saved by a peacock named Argus, Juno the wife managed still to lure her husband back. Not only that, but she commended Io forever to a pasture where unbeknownst to Jupiter a gadfly would forever sting Io in the hide. "Hell hath indeed no fury like a woman scorned, or a goddess no less."

Stories of such ancient and familiar vengeance sent us both reeling in giddy laughter, for though I was young, the age of Gillot's daughters, and he himself was settling into the dawn of middle age, I could feel the undeniable visceral attraction directing my every word toward him and his approval—as natural a part of me as the gravitational pull of the earth around the sun.

Imagining another world drawing us together, keeping us in balance, denying all the while the real gravity of the world we lived in.

Yet too, I knew from our forays into myth that there were harsh consequences for even the most natural behavior. This was made clear to me when one evening as Gillot hovered over me at the telescope, his daughter Katarina burst in, and blurting an apology, "Papa, forgive me—I didn't know," she frowned, hesitating, her hand to her mouth, checking her words. And as Gillot, letting his hand drop instantly from my side, cried "Dear," his daughter quickly disappeared.

It was done. We were as exposed as those stars in the heavens, suddenly spied by other eyes. We never spoke of that moment openly but the hand that let go that day was an admission of intentions Gillot could not reconcile within himself. The neutral territory of our celestial studies had suddenly turned perilous and Gillot wished to return to the safe terrain of our confessional pietist studies. Yet I in my naïve girlish and inexperienced way would not be cast out of his orbit. I tried to make light of our attraction, thinking that we could forever hold desire in the balance in the same way that heavenly bodies might never touch though were forever joined by huge distances of intimacy.

My dear Pastor Gillot,
QUOD LICET JOVI
NON LICET BOVI
> *Don't talk to me*
> *of civilization*
> *and its decline.*
> *The gods still reign.*

> *Day follows loyally*
> *on the heels of night*
> *and Argus pierces through*

31

the blue black gloom of solitude
and guides a lover to a mate.

Somewhere in a wooded glade
a nymph succumbs to a god,
is discovered by a wife,
and all hell breaks loose,

when out of the dark
struts a peacock,
splaying the eyes of a giant,
fanning his prey before the kill,
dancing a tune no longer
melodious—he will, he will.

Her beauty regained, but never the same,
She is pure and proven form.
Io is strong and she knows,
Io knows, so much the wiser now,
what Jove is allowed
is never permitted the cow.

—Yours ever, Lou

I wanted him to laugh. I wanted to be taken absolutely seriously. I tried my hand at poems I sent to him and began to write down my stories. What I discovered to my surprise was that my lying that was censored everywhere else found its appropriate true form in writing. The written story could be untrue, a lie; it could be fanciful, as long as it had its effect. And it did.

A smile from ear to ear when that afternoon Gillot opened his study door. He loved the strutting peacock and in a moment of levity he said he wished that we had such a dutiful protector for our trysts. But in our case, he told me, "God would have to do." I found myself ever so slightly taken aback by this hint of sacrilege and by some vestige of faith deep within myself—a faith I would never have admitted to. I tucked the hurt away, didn't want to know.

Many years later, when the great philosopher Nietzsche was discussing the nature of laughter (its tendency to implode on itself) for a book of aphorisms he was working on, I was reminded of this particular period with Gillot, when he would almost hold his joy in check at our tender meetings. Fritz had said that "Laughter" was the full release of hope into the joy of the moment, that being only momentary, must dissipate into nothingness. And I guess that was true. But I was annoyed at the philosopher's presumption, that he could arrogantly declare someone's happiness, our happiness, people he had never known, fatally doomed and yet he, sage messenger that he was, escaped unscathed. What really bothered me though was being reminded of this shaky, all too brief time with Gillot when all our intense joy would take its natural course and evaporate. (The philosopher was right after all.) First love in hindsight had become a cruel joke.

That autumn Gillot's demeanor toward me, his young tutorial charge, seemed to soften and become tinged with a distanced acquiescence. He surrendered to the reality of our affection within that garret study, as he accepted too its absolute censure outside those walls. A kind of quiet reserve overtook him. He seemed less an authority, and was disturbingly weaker to me. Though I know he delighted in my stories and my bold attempts to unmask the prophet Isaiah and Paul for the mere mortals they were, and to be au courant with the philosopher-saints of the day—Spinoza and Kierkegaard—I would catch him looking at me from time to time with a sad smile. Like one who knows an end for which there are no words. . . .

Abandoning celestial science and our evening hour, we returned to meeting each Tuesday and Thursday at four o'clock and took up once again our religious studies, moving to the Passions of Christ. It was a lugubrious time in our lessons. I felt precipitously thrown from heaven to earth. But I did not question Gillot's decision, for he seemed to be questing for some answers of his own. I sat and listened, transfixed by the painful endurance of this man Jesus whom so many would come to call savior—who in his final hour called out to his heavenly father "Father, why have you forsaken me?" and then simply died. Without an answer. He was the first great questioner of his faith and of his family and given my doubts about my own mother, I felt a kinship with this man Christ. Gillot was right. I wasn't alone in my disbelief after all.

Gillot explained how the disciples bereft of their leader were driven in their grief to create a community of their own that would wait for their brother to be reborn and to return. That this hereafter—the belief in the resurrection—was the linchpin of faith. A wish born of our own mortality. A wish to know the future that we could not know. A wish to know that we would live in that future unfettered by pain and sickness and the losses of love. All very human, I thought.

But the reality of faith, Gillot went on, was something much more personal. Faith was now as it was back then, as our pietist faith instructed. Faith was not souls floating in a netherworld or a church, with the insurance of tithes and indulgences. "Faith is, my dear Lou, no more or no less than a hereafter of the heart." A kind of memory, I thought, of what has passed, what happened, what died. . . . He said this looking distractedly out the window and his eyes seemed to well with water.

I didn't quite connect with Gillot's sadness at that moment. I didn't want to. I was relieved just to know that my belief was not so far from the truth. But I found myself disturbed for reasons I couldn't fathom to learn that there was no certain resurrection of the flesh.

The afterworld in which all wrongs were righted, all suffering redeemed . . . no, that was a creation. Fiction. And like all good fictions it found acceptance in its written form—and became the lie that told a truth to so many people, including myself. A fiction we needed.

But in the end, in the end, all we had in Gillot's gentle tentative words, as if spooning out a bitter medicine to me, was "the hereafter of the heart." I thought of my long-dead crazy grandfather, of Evgeny who was ill, and of all the questions I could never answer. And I wondered how a father could not help a son crucified for unjust reasons and how another father generations later could take a knife to his son's throat in the name of that original negligent father. All the suffering, all the human pain. Small wonder then that that first idea of a resurrection caught on so long ago. But no, "God is in us," Gillot said almost inaudibly, "each and every one of us, and all we have for sure, all we were left with is the 'hereafter of the heart.'" Even then I thought Gillot was telling me something else, something much more personal, not about God, but about us.

I was to understand those words with a loss, an eclipse of my heart, the first. That winter my father suffered a heart attack while taking the cadets through their early morning exercises in the large courtyard beside the Winter Palace. I imagined him in the full splendor of his uniform, performing his duties to the moment of death and then falling in a heap from his horse, his loyal Lipizzaner "Mir," suddenly disoriented and loosed of the ballast of his secure weight. And then others whose names I would never know realizing what had happened rushing to hold the hand of this fine magisterial general in his final moment. "The hereafter of the heart . . . " I would whisper again and again, ever perplexed by its meaning.

With the funeral and its aftermath of family visits, I did not return to Gillot's garret study for over a month. When I did that February afternoon, I was disconsolate. Gillot rocked me in his arms and I wailed like a keening peasant my loss that could no sooner be erased than the silence, the absence, my cries sought to fill.

As he placed another log on the hearth and stoked the fire, I watched as the birch bark peeled like the ancient scroll of an unread letter into the faint glow of the embers and finally dissolved in white ash. All the answers I would never have. I began to sob and confessed to him what I felt to be a betrayal. I had wished to tell my father of our "lessons"—but it was a wish that I could not fulfill without breaking my promise to him never again to upset my mother. It was a necessary betrayal in life, but in death, one I couldn't bear.

Gillot cupped my hands in his, and then moving to his desk he dipped his pen in the inkwell and began to pen a note of introduction to my mother. I protested. He kissed my hand and said, "No, my dearest Lou. This is the only way. Now more than ever you must proceed with your initiation into Christ and go on with your studies. Your mother must know now that I am here to help you through your confirmation. We mustn't forsake your father any longer. We'll both feel redeemed in knowing that we have not betrayed your father's trust—that he lives in the 'hereafter of our hearts.'"

That phrase again. That damnable phrase I never understood. I couldn't follow the direction of his words. I wanted everything to stop. I wanted to be held in his affection.

But Gillot sealed the note in wax and said with uncharacteristic assurance, as someone committed to a course: "Now, Lou, the father of your flesh is departed and it's time for me to take up his mantle and become the father of your soul. Out there in the open."

I could only imagine how my mother would greet Gillot's proposition. Though as always I welcomed him as sire of my spirit, I wondered what was to become of the tender touch I'd come to depend on? And if my innocent flesh was not willing to give him up, what about him, this wiser more experienced believer? In silencing the torment in his heart, what was he doing, if not sacrificing our happiness and me?

3

∽

An All-Too-Human Savior

I never learned to dance. I could never have mastered the steps. It wasn't so much the rhythms that were as inscribed in my young mind's catalogue of quadrilles, mazurkas and waltzes as the exquisite parquet pattern that glistened beneath my slippers. No, the worst was the music itself coursing my body and invading all the senses like a stealth fever that rages til it suddenly crests into a calm cold silence.

Music's abandon—its commanding hold and release—simply scared me as if I were being thrown off a runaway horse. That harmony of body and soul whirling through the maze of the dance floor never quite whispered the ease of its flight to my feet. I was too grounded. Too confused by the noise. Too cerebrally stuck. I tripped but never the light fantastic. To my father's dismay who was himself an unstoppable dancer.

I remember as a small child crouching beneath the piano as it hammered the frenzy of Chopin's "Polonaise Fantasie" with all the guests transported in wonder and then, joined by deeper more soulful strings, the piano would swoon into the cradle of one of Strauss's worn waltzes that sent them all and my father too, more frequently than not without my mother but with one of the unsuspecting ladies, careening out onto the ballroom floor. On one such evening, I squealed when ash from his cigar left precariously in an ashtray on the piano fell onto my arm. Spying me in my hideout, he pulled me out, covering my arm with kisses, and we floated out to the regal notes of a waltz. Giving in to his body's rhythm, I could do it. I could do anything in my father's embrace.

Imagining all the coy expectancy and dutifully joyful steps that had once graced this grand room, I stood there in the stillness, encircled by multiple gilded mirrors reflecting an infinity of absences with no true entrances or exits. I smiled to think of the dancers' delusions of being everywhere one looked and their horror at never being able to leave. These balls, these dances could get out of hand, could last forever, far worse than my fantasies. But now all the mirth, the rogue life, and my father too had somehow found their way out of this room and moved on.

I was aware of the French silk curtains of old that no longer whispered in the breeze of imminent comings and goings but hung stiffly, drawn against buttoned-down pocket windows between the rose-veined marble columns that outlined the majestic perimeter of the room. The multitiered crystal chandelier, once illuminated like a birthday cake, hung like an exquisite ice sculpture, precariously suspended in the blue darkness of late afternoon.

Every object here stood in regal silent witness to those who had come and gone. Somehow now I was the only one left in the room— there as if awaiting a sentence. Too tall to hide under the concert grand, I moved toward the adjacent parlor door and listened to the furor raging inside, far more cacophonous than anything ever heard before in these rooms.

Gillot had come to present his case. Spying through the keyhole, I saw my mother, more animated and articulate than she ever was with me, accuse him of seeing her daughter in private without her permission. Gillot was seated in formal dress, in waistcoat no less, on a sage-green velvet sofa before the raging hearth, and my mother in a chair opposite him that she ascended from in her apoplexy to declare that all further studies would be purely catechistic. That she could not abide by the lies of her daughter's fantasies and he was not to encourage them.

"She must be confirmed. If you are the one to accomplish that, then so be it," she paused. "But I do not trust your intentions, Pastor Gillot. Given this year of clandestine meetings and what I know of my daughter's wild imagination, I can only question in the name of her dear departed father your proposition."

Gillot rose from the sofa and holding her in his mesmerizing gaze and extending his hands for hers to fall into (I must say, I was annoyed by this), he said in a gesture of utter peace: "Madame Salomé, Louisa is but a child. I want to have her in my tutelage only through her confirmation. Your child is now mine." My mother's hands that had rested in his but for a second now thrust him off and she announced: "Pastor Gillot, hear me out. It is my daughter's soul you will shepherd and nothing more." She knew it all. She knew and yet she let go. Again.

Seized by a sense of sad elation, I fell back into the center of the room and found myself looking at a painting. Amongst the iconic faces of archdukes, princesses and imperial guardsmen claiming space on these walls was the one face not immediately known to me, and as fate would have it, the only one to whom I was related. The matronly looking woman in the portrait, braced with an Elizabethan collar and a restrained smile, was my father's mother—frozen in the eloquent silent stare of the dead, the painted dead who never look at you but only through you.

I wondered what she thought of her son's choice back then—my mother—and what she would think of that daughter-in-law's choice now. My mother's "yes" had been so unlike my father's.

Hers, even when she was giving in, was full of bitter recrimination and I found myself wishing for anything, yes, even for music itself, to drown her out.

﹌

There is an old Russian saying that goes: *Liubov' ne kartoshka, ne vykinesh' za okoshko*—"Love isn't a potato. You can't throw it out the window." And I used to delight in imparting this bit of wisdom to friends who viewed it as evidence of the essential peasant core of the Russian soul.

Who knows, maybe there was some truth to that. But if so, this particular measure for calibrating the affairs of the heart, with its raw, common taste, had also found its way into the ranks of the imperial aristocracy, for whom a potato was slang for a sexual adventure with no consequences. It was known even to those of us who lived in the outermost circumference of the crown's inner circle that "potatoes" had become a staple not only of the archdukes' but indeed the emperor's diet. Fresh from "potato parties" in the country they would return to their palaces along the Nevsky Prospekt, to the royal ties that truly bound, and they approached their prescribed mates with the same knowledgeable palate they brought to a good vintage wine. There was bouquet, age, nose, and certainly aftertaste to that consecrated union but never the mundane pleasurable moment of the potato.

Our emperor Alexander II, known within the family as Sasha, was a chief offender in this regard but I liked him nonetheless. As a child, I used to think that his silver mustached tusks actually meant that he had been sired by a white elephant. Supreme animal. Supreme man. Our emperor would oddly sacrifice his life trying to reconcile these polar sides of his character, his peasant desires with his imperial duty.

This man who in his public life had freed the serfs and then flirted with the anarchy of a constitution had in his private life installed his mistress (Ekaterina, the nameless one) and three illegitimate children in a palace apartment just above that of his wife, the empress Maria Alexandrovna. He wanted to bring the outside inside, to bring the hidden out into the open. He was famous for having said: "We must liberate from above before they liberate themselves from below." And he tried to do this in his own household; he tried to contain two rivaling forces—mind and heart, duty and passion, wife and mistress—and though these women could not abide one another, he forced them to live under each other's noses, thereby neutralizing any threat to life and limb that might be hatched from their private plots of revenge.

In the end, though, it was the bigger contradiction that proved his downfall. He could not reconcile the folk with the crown. Sasha the indomitable, Sasha the fallible, would fall victim of his own magnanimous heart. And as fate would have it, it ended up exploding on him literally, when one day in an excursion outside the palace grounds he was attacked with a grenade thrown by one of the very subjects he had tried to free.

VIOLATING moral standards, in the Orthodox or Lutheran traditions, was a nasty business but not hard to do in my native Russia. After all, what was it to be Russian, if not to rise above or fall below? And just who the ultimate arbiter was, was a moving target: the god of the land or the god of the imperial altar.

There was some pull fomenting in those years to declare one's allegiance to Mother Russia, to embrace the distant expanse of the tundra as well as the crown. And that requirement sent my mother into fits of anxiety. As a widow now she was feeling the social pressure to withdraw from the cosmopolitan circles of St. Petersburg and retire to the countryside surrounded by the mystical alchemy of the masses—a prospect that was clearly out of the question and far too Russian for her.

She had already seen my cousin Emma fall prey to just such fateful choices. Emma, who was my age and my father's sister's daughter, had as a young girl fallen under the treacherous spell of religious orthodoxy, the mighty Russian church. As she relinquished her doubting Lutheran pietist faith, she gave herself over completely to the mystical séances and visionary practices of that special brand of orthodoxy festering in the countryside. Coincident with her spiritual conversion, my cousin fell in love with a young Russian cadet in the corps whom she would later marry and thereby surrender both body and soul to Mother Russia.

Poor Emma—she was the only girlfriend I had in those days—she was robust in every way, full bodied, and I envied her for that. In fact her physical maturity made me painfully aware of my lanky late-blooming boyish build that I compensated for by stuffing handkerchiefs under my modest breasts to give them the lift and curvature that were the style of the day.

Emma knew of my private lessons with Gillot (she had covered for me with my family more than a few times) and I knew of her flirtation with mysticism from her frequent excursions to the countryside. I also knew enough not to inquire and kept mum. But I didn't understand the full extent of her conversion until one day in a history of religion class in the English Private School that we both attended, Emma rose from her desk to have her say in the middle of a lesson on the cleric Martin Luther and his many reforms, not the least of which was the insistence on the right of each and every one of us to interpret scripture.

And Emma, my sweet ordinary cousin, stood there with eyes unblinking and a look of terror contorting her face, one fist tightly grabbing the side of her skirt, as if trying to hold down whatever was agitating her, and the other hand, outstretched, pointing to the park outside our classroom window. Bells began tolling from the onion dome of the nearby cathedral as if enunciating this moment and Emma declared she saw him burning out there by the linden tree.

While the girls hovered around her and a teacher ran to calm her, I peered out the window and saw not so much as a brush fire. But Emma screamed that he, that he was burning—he was burning—that his body slathered with animal fat was propped up on a pike and suspended over hot coals that toasted him slowly to a crisp black—that a lion lay inert in death's sleep beside him with a crown of fire raging around him, fueled by ancient scrolls, books and his beloved scripture. It was all going up in smoke.

Alas it wasn't Luther, thank God for that, and it certainly was not a Grigory or a Basil too close to the Russian heart. No, it was poor Jerome, that saint of old in ragtag frock and bald pate. The one who cooked himself, flagellated his flesh and beat out his lustful thoughts in the desert, the one whose learning Augustine revered and said was not to be surpassed. "What Jerome is ignorant of, no man has ever known." Actually he was neither prophet nor seer. He was simply a scholar who was as much at a loss as any of us to predict our Emma's wild imaginings.

As patron saint of translators, Jerome was the one who got it all started, translating the stories, collecting the tales from all and sundry tongues into one coherent story, into the one true Vulgate Bible, written in the one dead tongue that no one questioned, not to mention, even spoke. Til centuries later, a monk equally penitent from a colder, more punishing climate would challenge it all again in theses nailed to a cathedral door, declaring the people's need to know their God, to speak to him in their own tongue, to determine for themselves what they meant when they spoke about God.

And so in our unending quest to get to the bottom of the one who truly knew the answer, who after all declared himself our "alpha and omega, the beginning and end," a grand unraveling proceeded through the centuries from the wizened old Jerome to the defiant young man Luther and now to poor hysterical Emma and the mystical incantations spreading like plague itself throughout Russia. And it didn't end there, no, no. It would flare up throughout my lifetime in the pronouncements of the great philosopher, the aching predictions of my dear Professor and the ranting of the monster himself. Because the truth, unspeakable as it was, was that there was no ending, no beginning, and no one true truth that we could all know. (And what comfort could there possibly be in that?)

And what I remember about that afternoon was that everyone in that classroom, whether Orthodox, Lutheran or Roman, seemed to accept some part of Emma's vision as true, that she saw what they could not—without so much as a grain of proof, simply because they needed to. They needed to believe in what we could not know. In sharp contrast to my stories, I might add, whose characters and plotlines always had more than a smidgen of truth, and whose ties to the world we know were as obvious as the light of day. Yet my tales, my "visions" of reality were subjected to the scrutiny and summary censorship accorded nothing less than a latter-day heretic.

And so Emma and her delusions were allowed to recede quite unnoticed into life in the countryside where she would bear several children, within the blinding isolation and rampant superstition of Russia's white nights—open, empty. She did not find the eternity she had sought. But she did find drink, like others, to still her fears of that endless unknown.

❧

"Russia is awash with holy men, surpassed only by its numbers of wanton women," my mother used to say. "Our tsarina and her royal entourage lend their ears to the former, while our tsar and his archdukes lend their swords to the latter."

My mother was no poet. Subtlety was never her forte. Mother never plumbed a deep inner meaning when she could pluck from within reach a sterling matter of fact. She was a willful practitioner who compromised means to a desired end. And she viewed her pact with Gillot as just that. Three more months—four at most—of private preparation for my confirmation was merely the means, the compromise, to the larger end of my de-Russification (my papers and release to study abroad) and, not coincidentally, as chaperone my mother would then be spared the dismal fate of inner exile to the Russian countryside.

Volga

Even from afar, it's you I see.
Even from afar, you who remain with me.
Like a present that cannot dissipate,
Like a landscape holding me in its embrace.

And had my feet never on your shores rested,
I still think I would know your distances.
As if each wave of all my dreams had crested
on those unfathomable and lonely vistas.

Poetry is a wonderful thing. It says one, two and sometimes three things at the same time and still manages to pierce through the ambiguity to the heart of the matter. I wrote this poem, ostensibly to the Volga, the lifeblood of the Russian countryside. I barely traveled her expanses as a child but now on the cusp of leaving that childhood and my homeland behind, I wanted to claim that Russian soulfulness as my own.

The poem was for him, of course. The one who would immediately feel its dimensions. And that late afternoon just a week after his meeting with my mother, he closed the door of his garret study and clasped both my hands in his, saying, "Lou, dear Lou, you're back, you're back. We're together."

Gillot was looking a bit disheveled—hair askew, a tattered sweater—as if he had been sleeping in his clothes. He seemed slightly undone to me. Gone was the command of his pulpit and the tutorial magic I'd come to know. He paced distractedly, caged like one who would be here and there at the same time and did not know his own mind. His eyes finally met mine and rested with the look of a wincing pain.

Removing my cape, I pulled a folded sheet of paper from my pocket and said: "Pastor Gillot, Hendrik (the first time I had spoken his Christian name), I have written something here." As he reached for his glasses I motioned to him: "No, you needn't. Please let me speak it to you."

I recited the lines by heart from my heart, and as he listened, the notes of my poem dropped like my own tears into his eyes. He pressed his lips to my cold hands and then let go in defeat. Composing himself he said in a steady tone: "Let's sit down now, dear Lou, we must, and continue our lessons."

Poetry does that. It promises life as it delivers endings. It can do no less. And so it was for us. I had arrived the year before with his summons crumpled in my hand, "We will discuss your dilemma," and I returned that day with my own penned rendering of a much larger dilemma: the "unfathomable vistas" of our impending separation.

Acknowledging imminent endings has a way of putting all other things, all people, and all events into curious relief. Gillot's imminent absence loomed large. I obsessed about it. It was almost palpable. Compared with this enormous reality before us, everything became very small and inert, like the dolls of my playhouse. And I felt small too, as if I had been reduced to a grain of sand in a huge hourglass whose sole function was to mark the moments toward a passage through which I would slip and beyond which time would literally stop.

There was something so stifling and joyless about those months I thought I must squeeze the heartbeat out of every moment. But where was that heartbeat? As we abandoned our tutorial pretense of my fantasy or his philosophy, the play of our relationship, which had made him at once the most divine and the most sensual of men, both teacher and lover, all but vanished. It was buried in what could now no longer be spoken.

The secret of us, if never spoken, might over time be forgotten, might become the lingering ache of some irretrievable yet undeniable loss. I worried the feeling had stopped. I worried because love, after all, like story and so much else, needs to be created, to play with what it is not, if it is to survive. Without love's lie, its ruse, its cover, we were lost.

As everything around us became focused on the endpoint of my confirmation, I felt more vulnerable and oddly exposed as never before. Our lessons that had once been ignored were now subject to countless intrusions.

I'd hear a female voice in distressed heightened pitch from the parlor just off Gillot's entryway as I was led up to his study. His daughters would arrive unannounced to fetch a book from their father's study or to deliver an unexpected pot of tea. I was suffocating under the burden of palpable suspicion. My reaction was physical. I held things in, as if literally holding my breath; I began losing weight again and sank into lethargy. Mother viewed my sullen demeanor as proof of my chronic obstinate ingratitude.

Gillot responded by immersing himself more and more in detail. My part of the work completed, he would continue to refine his translation alone. We had covered the history of religion and the provocative flights of contemporary philosophers. Now we focused on the commandments, Psalms, Revelation and fashioning a program for my confirmation—no room for dream, and much worse no room for the fanciful embellishments of our unfolding story.

47

We sat together through those first sessions not questioning our conspicuous silence, not questioning the supplicant voice of Psalms or the mad paranoia of John that rose from the page, as if waiting for a revelation of our own. He was steeped in his translation and I left to the drudgery of my catechistic study.

Heaven came crashing to earth. Io was no longer a moon or mythical creation. Io was me and I felt the sting of my mother's instructions, his daughters' intrusion and his wife's complaints that seemed to trumpet my every arrival to their household. All of a sudden I was that cow now aimlessly grazing in his pasture.

I plucked up my courage. Complaining to Gillot, I protested the choice of texts. I could not connect the Psalms' plaintive plea for surrender to the damning threat of Revelation to triumph over all the unworthy infidels—of which I thought myself possibly one. There was violence in salvation. There were no stories to these books. Where on earth were the people?

There were only symbols and ominous numbers—seven seals, twelve candlesticks, five stars, dragons, lambs, harlots and brides—and all of these things stood for something whose meaning was known only to the prophet. And a plague on him or her, who added to this prophecy, embellished that text. She would be visited by pestilence for the rest of time right here, the prophet said, writhing in an everlasting world of death, mourning, weeping and pain (fair warning). I knew better than to tempt fate (heresy, defying the known, was bad enough, but defying prophecy, the unquestionable unknown, now that was pushing God's limit). I knew which lot I would end up with.

Gillot didn't know what to make of my distress. But he urged me to return to the safe territory of the older stories. "These last books are part of received wisdom, Lou, a prophecy yet to be revealed. They seek the beyond, a resurrection and reunion with a lost brother. They were grieving. Go back to the older stories and write what they tell you. There you can express your fantasies through the hurt of earthly people battling to know an earthly savior. You see, my child, they were seeking a man. Theirs was a clearly human story."

I took his advice. I discovered that through writing I could begin to create my own prophecies and in no small measure save myself, create my own word, in short, chart my own way. Little did I know the gift Gillot had given me that day by directing me to seek solace in the old stories and counsel from a savior within. So I set about looking for something remotely familiar, for a sign in the scripture of old that would beckon, would guide me, and not surprisingly perhaps, I found my way to my namesake.

The Truth about Salome

The truth is she loved to dance. She was only a girl growing into her own body when she learned that the flowing lines of her nubile form sculpting curves of a simple rhythm could send men into a frenzy. A girl with hoops in her ears and spangles on her wrists who saw herself as she whirled and whirled seized by an unending ring of blazing mirrors—their rapt eyes. She was everywhere when she danced, she was all theirs in the room of their body but as she peered through the gauze of her veils, seven veils no less, and felt the caress of eyes from afar, the undulating spasm of her hip, the kiss of air upon her belly, a moist dew forming between her lips, she let her silken scarves drop one by one, and feeling herself disappearing, disappearing ever so slowly, she stopped, becoming nothing before the fiery gaze, the claws, the fangs of the nameless one who would devour her.

The truth is she danced not for them but for the favor of her mother—a woman for whom there was no natural favor—no thing taken for which she did not extract revenge and no thing given for which she did not exact a price. Her mother had used her daughter, as parents are wont to do. So in this way Salome became the thing given to Herod to satisfy her mother's revenge, her stepfather's lust, in exchange for the head of the one man who had seen through her mother's treachery—the one holy man who could have saved her. Saved her from her own aching need, from that silent cry for her mother's embrace, from the insatiable grasp of anonymous men and from becoming the unwitting instrument of her own destruction. Alas, it was not meant to be.

And whirling through the centuries, through a veritable cult of Judiths and Lucretias who cultivated the baser instincts, killed for good or bad, collected heads nonetheless, a holy man here, a tyrant there—Salome would whirl and whirl enduring centuries of luscious desire and highhanded derision, til it ended with another Salome who knew her mother's manipulation all too well, who loved that one holy man and who thankfully never learned to dance. She wanted only to be lifted in his divine gaze, and delivering to him the sword the others had used to decapitate so many, so indiscriminately, she gave him the strength he needed to consummate this, their holy union. And breaking the spell and anointing her his own in Christ, this Salome was reborn as "Lou."

I wanted him to smile at least and he did through tears. His ageless cool northern command suddenly gave way to the fluid uncertainty of the moment. He seemed to be caressing the beads of a broken chain in his palm. He said in a soft considered tone, as if having worked his way to a conclusion: "But the difference, dear Lou, the difference with this Salomé is the man who finds himself blessed to be reflected in those soulful eyes of hers."

I always knew I loved him but now I was sure that love was returned. Gillot had responded not to phantom palpitations of the heart but to the inscribed voice of my own words and I felt emboldened and protected by that.

Holding my face in both quivering hands, he drew me toward him in a long protracted kiss and as I sank onto his lap on the cot his hands began to travel up and down my vertebrae, as if playing a stringed instrument. My skirt. My breasts. And falling into him, I felt his loins stiffen.

It was a wild grasping of bodies as we seemed to swim into each other, clutching for some hold, some release. And feeling the full weight of his body on my chest smothering me, into me, I pulled free and sank to his knees and began to weep. I did not want to see his face. That would be too close to my shame.

I remember looking up to the distracted gaze of Cranach's *Luther* and then lighting on a crucifix on the wall, on that ray of light, the clot of blood from his pierced side, the last droplets of a life that no longer flowed in him. And at that moment what came to mind was that among the witnesses of that long ago event with Mary and Magdalena was a Salomé too.

Gillot sat hovering over me and kissing my head said over and over again: "Dear Lou, dear Lou, no, no please don't. Please don't, it's not you. I have been struggling with this for so long. I must talk to Katya [his wife], to your mother. There must be some future for us."

As much as I wanted to believe, I could not. My mentor was a man, nothing more. And his savior had died—an icon on the wall. As changed as he became for me from that moment on, still I knew I would come back, but never the same. The lie, that promised now no future, but only an end, was back for only us to know, but never to be spoken of again.

EXCEPT of course until we would speak our final leave-taking. Two months later in a ceremony in Sandpoort, Holland, his birthplace, in the presence of my mother, Gillot presided over my confirmation. We had prepared a program deliberately in Dutch, a language my mother did not understand, but which we secretly devised as our lifelong nuptials. Drawing from Isaiah (the angry prophet who had descried my youthful heresy—not my choice),

Gillot summoned me to Christ with the words: "Fear not. For I have chosen you. I have called you by name. You are mine." And facing him feeling only the hold of impending death and not rebirth at all I responded: "You have blessed me. For I do not have you." First love when lost is the lie that tells the truth—the one that haunts you forever, like a phantom limb always there but not, and so it was with me.

As the train made its chugging labored way across the Dutch flatlands through their glorious quilt of blooming flowers, I thought of Sandpoort, its vaulted cathedral at its center now empty, its neat cobblestone streets with everywhere squinting windows, mirrors allowing the eye within, lost in the glare, to observe the comings and goings on the street below. Did anyone recognize that day the grasping of hands between celebrant and confirmand on the steps before the closed cathedral doors as the rueful farewell of lovers? And if they did, would they not expunge the thought at once in a clean righteous sweep of what life should be? Not ours.

I left him there in the security of his earliest childhood memories, his birthplace, and set out under the pesky eye of my mother into the great unknown. We would travel south through the secular godless towns of Switzerland while Gillot would eventually make his way back to St. Petersburg and beyond to rescue souls from that infinity of solitude—the Russian countryside.

Mother Russia never tired of her holy men. They were legion, good men and bad men, no matter. Russia was not discriminating and always needed redeeming.

Mother wrote to me years later of one in particular—one who had raped the countryside and penetrated the inner sanctum of the imperial court to "cure" a child. Finally he took as his lover another young prince, only to get himself murdered by his royal paramour three times over—poisoned, shot and dumped into the Neva River. All this treachery to no avail—he couldn't seem to die and his legend prevailed with the force of folk sainthood. Grigory Rasputin became the Russian symbol of evil incarnate and oddly of a certain peasant resourcefulness. It was a powerfully dangerous precedent for others who would follow.

As I set out on untold adventures, I didn't know that I would not see Gillot for many years to come—and only then under the most ironic of circumstances. This man who had given me so much and confirmed me in Christ would preside over my real nuptials. The one who had taken my innocence was forced to bear witness, indeed to give me away to my intended and how many others to follow. It was a curious closure to the body of my whole childhood irretrievably lost and yet still casting about like the soul of "first love" itself seeking the safe harbor of his blessing. I did not know what lay before me, but I had already discounted the beneficence of any love equaling the one that lay behind me. I was faithful.

From this side, I am told that when I died—that hunched over nearly blind woman, that famous writer in the large stucco house with the vineyard garden up on the hillside road—they burst into my apartment—the ones whose heels clopped brilliantly and in unison against the sun-bleached cobblestones—their hollow insurgency coming, and they emptied all my bookshelves into a huge heap out on the street. One of the brown-suited soldiers paging through a volume of poetry here, of prose there, addressed his officer: "Who was she?" he asked. "Her name was Salomé." "Oh, like the one who danced," he quipped. "Yes, only this one was not young and nubile. She was a wizened old hag who danced with swine. With Jews."
Death has some dignity and that is to free one of life's indignities. I am told that one of the soldiers became distracted by one volume and

pocketed an inscribed edition of Rainer's verse, dropping a match that instantly went out, as he left without so much as turning around to see if their work was completed.

So indeed many of those inscribed words did survive. Those that did not survive the countless other burnings survived the mind. Not unlike the childhood etched in memory. Not unlike the faith etched in the heart. Or the name he had given me in life, because he could not pronounce "Louisa" in Russian, so he christened me with a nickname that sounded like the Russian root word for "love." The name I carried throughout my lifetime and translated me in death, to be spoken in so many tongues: "Lou."

BUT I am getting ahead of myself as I was always wont to do. And though I left behind the things of a child—her form, her virtue, her first love, her faith, the girl in the mauve muff—I took with me something I could not squelch. It was a cry that sometimes woke me from sleep, a cry I recognized as my own but could not reach, could not calm. The cry, almost like a waking lullaby of who I was not, could never hope to be. Eventually it was muted and my pain gave way to that slow dance of the heart that beat and beat past my father and Gillot far into the future toward the dark grace of the one, with hand extended, the one true one, whose eyes would light my way . . .

INTERLUDE

A cold mother fearful of her only daughter, a crazy grandfather closeted away, a dashing tutor, a pastor no less abusing his influence. Familiar story. But still such a believer! A spunky girl, wanting to get out from under. A little girl who cries and cries, but doesn't break . . . wants to keep it distant, order it all, push it away. Hide it.

I laid my head down into my pillows, safe in my North Country cabin, lit a candle on the night table by my bed, breathing in its citrus melon scents, staring into the flicker of flame as I did nights after writing, spying the light for the next word, glimmering feeling, some odd cranny releasing me into dream.

My God, what a shroud of secrets enveloped her. How could she, just a child, have found her way through that? All the unspoken deeds, the broken promises. What a stranglehold of secrets. "Don't be so sanctimonious, girl. You probably have your own safely under wraps, ones you wouldn't tell anyone, ones you've yet to discover. . . . You think writing can control them?" Quiet now, I'm the one writing this book. "You are, my dear, but not without me." True, Lou, but I give up. Okay, so maybe it's our story. Just not now . . . tomorrow. Those secrets—they'll keep. Enough already. I need to sleep.

I blew out the flame, the voice inside my head, all those knots in pine walls blinked into dark and turning with a woomf I buried myself in the down comforter, dropping into a deep snore. Dar, my beagle's sighing snorting body like a fur hat curled into the pillow above my head. Puppy love. Gotta cure him of that. Well, maybe later . . .

4

Delivered to a

Superman

*Have you heard the story about the madman who ran with a lit
lantern through the marketplace in broad daylight, shouting,
"Where's God? Where's God gone? Has he lost his way, wandered
off like a child? Has he emigrated like a citizen of the world?"*

A madman writing about a madman on a train hurtling along the
Italian coast inward into a blaze of ever more languorous heat closing in on the day, closing in on the man one late afternoon in April
of 1882.

*"God is dead. Dead. Is it already forgotten? The deed. Our deed?
Has it already slipped our minds? What we have done . . . "*

The train, making countless stops, collecting more and more pas-
sengers, bursts of garrulous laughter, heads peeking out the windows, arms flailing to the conductor, a train wending its way,
gathering more and more delays. When will they move on? When
will they stop . . . the noise stop? Peace of mind. A prayer too late.
Time a furious confusion—cacophony of dwindling space. His time,

not theirs. His too little, impatient. Theirs too long, lingering. Never on time. The station clocks don't work. He needs to make time for time. Impossible to find the space. As towns slip away as indiscriminately as wisps of dream, comings become goings, pink and golden villages, whole societies sucked away to a vanishing point on the horizon. Escaping into nothingness of what is to come. Facing the back, he too had wanted to be ahead of all parting.

When all of a sudden a diminutive man with withered face crowned by a fedora and a large woman in black bandanna drawn around a smiling face with glimmering gold tooth and two wriggling children descend upon his no-longer-empty compartment, claiming their seats like squatters, spreading their belongings, their luggage, their screams and pulling out from a large wicker basket the eating utensils, the bread, the wine, the bloodwurst, the stinking Limburger cheese, and eating and eating with abandon they settle in like the immovable feast that they undoubtedly are.

"Have we inhaled the heavens? Swallowed the oceans in one gulp? Who gave us the sponge to rub out the entire horizon? Where is the 'beyond'? I must get my bearings. What were we thinking when we unchained the earth from the sun? Drifting as we are into black space of tumbling stars. . . . Where is the heart of our universe, our up, down, backwards, forwards? We are in freefall."

By now his head is throbbing and the notebook in which he frantically scribbles his thoughts is obscured by an inner glare and sporadic bolts of houndstooth-like lightning sending a relentless blinding pain to his temples. He grasps to pull the shade, to shield his eyes, to the loud protest of his traveling companions. The stately woman of obvious rank, svelte figure and indeterminate age in the peacock-feathered hat with net over her eyes who claimed the seat opposite him at the last stop seems to recognize him, the man's distress, and motions the others to silence. They jeer, "No, we need the light to eat. The children need to see where we are going."

"Do they not smell the putrefaction? Divine putrefaction. Have they forgotten? Who will absolve us of our deed? Who will we resurrect, if not ourselves, to worship in his stead? This God who is dead." And the ungrateful survivors, will they celebrate themselves?

The man who is the creation of the real madman with eyes closed, still jotting his notes in his corner seat, is, in stark contrast to his ailing creator, a free man. Loosed to the page he warns of a wisdom traveling through deep space that will burst forth in a thunderous clap. And he declares something not wholly original: *"I have come too soon."* Not soon enough, mutters the madman, writing.

The words. The words, he believes, *his* words will someday be heard. The train slows down. The boy jumps to his feet and scrambles to the window, grabbing the man's knee, releasing the shade in a snap: "Mama, mama, we're here. We're here." A slim volume of Heine's philosophical and religious ruminations slips from the writer's lap. It is the same poet who just fifty years before in the throes of his last days, when every muscle in his body had atrophied leaving him unable to even open his eyes, had prophesied death to the old Jehovah—the God who could not save him.

The dignified lady, now overcoming her reserve, gestures for his attention and says demurely: "My dear sir, I believe I made your acquaintance a few years ago at a dinner in Bayreuth. How good to see you again." He nods and winces speechless at the memory—the still resonating crescendo of loss, the megalomaniacal conductor, kinship that could not be sustained, the enduring friendship of pain. The madman reaches for his notebook and, closing it, scrawls on a title sheet *"The Joyful Wisdom."* No more godly gloom, he says to himself. The lie that speaks the truth. He wills his words to be heard. His "joyful wisdom" of mind. The words that breathe desire into his paltry experience.

The great philosopher, gripping his notebook in one hand and bag in the other, disembarks onto the platform and walks with halting steps, sidling his way like a penguin into the station to deliver himself into an awaiting carriage and convalescence at the Villa Mattei on the Via della Polveriera with his patroness, the beloved "Aunt Malwida."

Some arrivals are more portentous than others and mine was definitely the latter. I had arrived in Rome just a couple of months before Friedrich Nietzsche, with only a few unmemorable poems that had served as my introduction to Malwida von Meysenbug's literary salon, and nothing much more in my head than the urge to shake my mother's constant guard. I had convinced her to come down from Switzerland to celebrate the "independence" of my twenty-first birthday in Rome.

I had the wan birthday wish that she would tire of our extended travels and want to return home to visit my brothers in St. Petersburg. Alas, my mother became even more tenacious in unfamiliar environs, as was made clear to me when she leaned over to blow out the birthday candles on my cake before a bemused assembly of literati in the beautifully appointed parlor of Malwida's villa.

Malwida, recognizing my embarrassment, gave my hand a protective pat and, diverting the others from my mother's momentary indulgence, introduced me to her circle as a young poet with an exquisite potential for realizing Malwida's brand of "practical idealism." I was a young student brought to her attention by her good friend the Swiss art historian Franz Overbeck whose classes I had audited in Zurich. But while I might be a ripe disciple for her philosophy, there was no better embodiment of the visionary dreams and the real defeats of practical idealism than the founder herself, the author of the tremendously popular *Memoirs of an Idealist*, the venerable Malwida von Meysenbug.

This aging patron of the arts had begun her life as the daughter of a wealthy industrialist from Kassel. As is often the case with children of privilege, her station in life afforded her the freedom to consider radically altering the status quo, while leaving the means by which she might reach those conclusions relatively unscathed. When just slightly older than my tender age, Malwida had thrust herself into the thick of revolutionary fervor in late forties Germany. Working at various girls' schools in Hamburg she won a reputation for championing educational freedom for women so vociferously in fact that she found herself a few years after the failed rebellion of '48 having to flee along with Garibaldi, Kinkel and other radicals to the safe festering haven of London. There she took a position tutoring the two motherless daughters of the great Russian revolutionary and founder of socialism, Alexander Herzen. Upon his untimely death, she adopted the girls, and then promptly dropped all political work to retreat to Rome to raise them.

Malwida had never become a mother herself, never had the time or the place, since she was part of a wandering citizenry of European intellectuals touring the cosmopolitan cities of London, Paris and Rome, sponsoring salons of intellectual exchange, fanning rebellion and heralding everything shockingly new, and deposing the old. Their time had not yet come. Or if it had, it trafficked now in ideas, like germs of a disease yet to be realized.

Malwida took on multiple murky roles within these circles but she was, if nothing else, a sure maternal confidante to Herzen, Baudelaire, Wagner, Nietzsche. Presumably she too had taken a number of lovers in her day, certainly implied by the freewheeling discourse of her circle. But talk of one's romantic exploits was always to Malwida unbecoming.

Anyway, by the time I met Malwida she was an elderly woman, a surrogate mother for the arts, a mother to so many artists and philosophers that the only sire of such a lineage would have to have been God himself. And so I too became her adoptee, though I often wondered if ever, in looking back, she had doubted her practical idealism, for what she had given up—for the chance to bear a child of her own—and for the settled life that she had perhaps unknowingly passed by.

That evening with the warm breath of Roman spring wafting the scent of jasmine in from the veranda, I sat mortified by my mother's display but mollified by Malwida's gracious way of focusing attention on the real reason for our simple celebration. There seated on a simple settee in her mauve dress with a tiny whimsical black silk veil atop her head, she drew from the leather case on her desk one of the poems I had sent her from Zurich. Handing it to me, she beckoned me to recite the verses before the half dozen captive souls.

"So my dear ladies and gentlemen, join me in welcoming to our salon a new fresh voice that comes to us from the intimate unstoppable heart of Russia."

I hadn't known which verses might appeal to Malwida's freedom-fighting practical spirit and was completely dumbfounded at her selection. With the hindsight of age, those lines seem boldly histrionic in a way that only youth could write them, brashly seizing the moment and daring to own the future or be undone. Sweet youth that abides no compromises. That poem was aptly and solemnly entitled "Prayer to Life":

> I love you with all your menace
> and even if you might destroy me cold,
> I would tear myself from that sentence,
> as a friend recoiling from your breast's hold.

With all my strength I embrace what's yours.
Let your flames set me afire.
And in the glow of that last war
May I still fathom the depths I so desire.

Oh, to live on for centuries. To ponder.
Fold me into your arms again.
And if you have no more joy to squander,
So be it. Then give me your pain.

L.S.

There is nothing like an unfamiliar audience of various literati to fortify one's notion of poetry as a solitary pursuit. You are judged by the silences. The words may fall on deaf ears. And you are free to fall on your own sword. What with the long interminable pause and the darting scrutiny of eyes, it seemed my embarrassment that evening had only been compounded.

Following the requisite sighs, the clearing of throats, "Who was it? Who was it for?" they asked. "For Russia, of course," my cutting retort. I could not tell them. I couldn't tell myself. They seemed vaguely satisfied but not convinced. The poem had failed. Abstraction burying the real thing. The pain. The pain inflicted. The pain I had to bear and could not face. The pain I folded into words to make it go away. But it just didn't. It lay there like the large curling ache of a question mark in the heart of my poem. That was enough. I was exposed and resolved then to give up these verses for good and return to true life, to the lie of the story.

Little did I know how hard that would be—harder even than escaping from my mother's clutches. As fate would have it, those words that should have been left for dead strangely survived for decades immortalized in Fritz's song, "Hymn to Life," while the one saving grace was that my name was eventually absolved of attribution. And my words became part of the irrepressible reserve of that most prolific of poets, "Anonymous."

A single clapping from behind us cut through the bracing silence and I turned to see a tall lanky man with deep eyes and melancholy smile, in full rumpled dress suit, leaning gamely against the parlor door. There was a commotion beyond him in the entryway and Trina, Malwida's trusted servant, came instantly to whisper something urgent to her mistress. Looking up, Malwida's face lighted up with a youthful blush of a young girl, as she exclaimed: "Paul, Paul, how lovely to see you. To what do we owe this pleasant surprise?"

"Malwida," he said sheepishly, "I'm so sorry to intrude unannounced on your soiree with such obvious talent in your midst. May I be so impertinent as to join you but I wonder if I might first have a word with you."

As if responding on cue, Malwida nodded to the shy diminutive woman with pince nez seated across from me to proceed with the reading and then drew some bank notes from her desk drawer before disappearing into the anteroom. There was a release of laughter, as the livery man returned to his carriage and the sound of the door latch closed out the night. As they reentered the room, hovering over his hostess with his arm firmly around her shoulder, the man said with a slight chuckle: "Malwida, you have saved me again. You would truly be my angel, if ever I believed in them."

"My dear ladies and gentlemen, if I may interrupt your reading, let me introduce my dear friend—someone who would truly be my son, were I so blessed, Paul Ree. As you may know, Paul is the author of that most provocative book *Psychological Investigations* and, as if carried here on the sirocco winds, Paul has just blown in from Monte Carlo."

There were some raised brows amid telling smiles and furtive whisperings ("Psychological, my word!"), as Paul Ree took a seat in our circle. The reading had been Baudelaire, I think, or some florid French writer beyond reproach, though my eavesdropping on events in the entryway had broken my concentration. I was distracted by his eyes which seeking a neutral focus seemed to settle on me.

Mother sensing danger suggested it was time to make our farewells, as we did not wish to inconvenience Signora Falcone at the Pension St. Anselmo where we were staying. Taking the opportunity to see me to the door, Paul Ree calmly remarked that he "did not quite believe that bit about Russia" but had a lifelong passion to someday travel to my homeland. "Perhaps then, Fräulein Salomé, Malwida will arrange a time for us to meet and continue this conversation."

❧

Malwida's intervention was a mere formality and hardly necessary, for from the very first Paul Ree and I knew we were bound—bound by our youthful curiosity to get to the root of an attraction, an attraction with no clear path but the conventional one we deliberately wanted to stray from. In those early days, our conversations were endless extending into the wee hours of the morning, when arm in arm, Paul and I would wend our way back from Malwida's soirees through Rome's ageless streets making up theater all the way, here a Roman statesman orating from the coliseum steps and there a wolf baying senselessly at the moon.

One pitch dark night, Paul and I stole away to the eerie ruins of the Roman Forum. He plucked some branches from a bush and wound them in a garland about his head and racing into the temple of Caesar, he leapt onto the boulder of its altar and intoned:

"You blocks, you stones, you less than senseless things!. . .
Oh, ye hardened hearts, ye cruel men of Rome, remember you
*   not Pompei.*

Watch your fool head or she'll take it home. I bring you Lou Salomé."

Screeching out from the black, a cat sent Paul tumbling from his promontory. Picking himself up, both of us laughing, he dusted himself off and kissed my forehead: "Caesar has spoken, Lou, or was that your mother? Time to go." We got back at daybreak. Signora Falcone had long since left the watch. My mother was fit to be tied.

Such flouting of mores was not to be tolerated but it was the first time that I noticed a reluctance on my mother's part to speak the charge, for fear, I think, of the likelihood that her daughter might have already crossed the line and gone too far. Mother no sooner wished to face that possibility than to be returned unceremoniously with her delinquent daughter to the Russian countryside. So she resolved to keep me on a tight leash, to engage Paul Ree's confidence which he surely could not betray and to enlist others to drive a wedge between me and my newfound gentleman friend.

But despite the anxiety surrounding my apparent suitor's intentions, Paul Ree was never a direct threat to my virtue, not then or for the subsequent years we spent together, and I loved him for that. He was too mired in his own complexity, too involved in chasing down his own shadow to question mine. He stood close and never tried to dominate me.

I loved his contradictory nature, self-effacing yet so accepting of all that I myself might want to be. The consummate friend—Paul never asked too much but stood ready to give all.

Paul was several years older, a published intellectual, and he seemed a maverick to me. He had a way of anticipating all life's disappointments and making light of them before they caught him by surprise. And so I delighted in his mischievous "ennui" and did not recognize that relentless drive toward irony as a force that would one day overcome him.

I was young then and looking for a kindred spirit to squire me through Europe's sophisticated literary circles. I could not imagine having anything to offer him. And Paul was at once a handsome connoisseur of those circles and an enfant terrible—a philosopher who had the ear of great minds within the academy—and a gambler wed to the roulette table, whose future and fortune might be squandered on a whim, one last crazy gamble, to tempt fate to save him from himself.

But I didn't know his darker side then, nor did I think him a suitor. His worldly experience so outweighed my own it was hard to imagine he might really need anything from me. I was simply seduced by his daring—his upping the ante on all human exchanges (whether it be persuading the Monte Carlo croupier to lend him the train fare to Rome or subjecting my stunned mother to a premature postmortem of the Romanov dynasty or enlisting Cosima Wagner to feign interest in the estranged philosopher's infatuation with Bizet while coaxing Fritz to attend the debut of *Parsifal* in Bayreuth). Paul would do these things for the sheer thrill of seeing what would happen.

He was one of those people who either truly didn't care what happened (but that would have been too depressing) or felt specially favored by chance—by all the bets and wagers he had taken, accrued and survived! Now, this was the Paul I chose to know.

So Paul, my dangerous protector, became my teacher in the art of pushing the envelope a little further in all social exchanges. From the first I saw him as an unrepentant literary roué, but I soon discovered Paul was a gambling philosopher too. Voraciously unsentimental, he was no more possessive of his ideas than he was of money, but saw their usefulness in their value as currency. And he traded.

A staunch disciple of Darwin, Paul denied the existence of any spiritual creator and saw our customs, laws, beliefs, the very fiber of our culture, as the mere outgrowth of a naturally selected dynamic of survival. So our morals are as naturally protective as the coloration of the simple blue jay whose blue camouflages it from predators in flight while its white shields it when feeding in the snowy exposure below. Or so went the speculation.

"We are all working with an elaborately constructed legacy of camouflage to insure our survival, Lou. Yes, you and I."

"Well, what about our higher moral sentiments—belief in a greater good, compassion for the poor and sick, and what about that feeling of unqualified love we can have for another person . . . What about all that, Paul?" He replied, "You haven't lived enough, Lou. . . . It all boils down to the base instinct for survival in a natural hierarchy of dominance and submission. Let's face it. It's a dog-eat-dog world."

Then his eyes softened and he broke into laughter. His joking drawing me in, but always a little disturbing, as if the joke were on me, on us all.

"That moral armor of yours will prove, like everything else, to have outlived its usefulness. . . . And that human armor, love between two people, that too has its time and its place, its moment and then not. . . . But look here, Lou. You are my one and only, my salvation, and I love you . . . At least for now."

His steely blue eyes would smile out from under the crying slant of his brow. I had known no one who could give so much and ask so little. And I seized his moment as my tomorrow.

For those first months, Paul and I spent all our waking moments together frequenting Rome's many salons, its eating establishments, its tourist haunts. As our friendship intensified, it seemed all the more impossible in the larger scheme of things. Through it all were his fleeting gestures of an arm firmly around my shoulder guiding me aimlessly through the serpentine alleys, stopping to caress my head against his chest under one of the many arches (saying "It's not that I want you Lou, it's that I never want to let you go") or planting a kiss on my virgin ring finger, as if dropping a gauntlet, as we said goodnight before my pension. With all the decisions of study and future still before us, our choice of each other in Rome seemed destined to be short-lived, which made everything about that time more precious.

And more perilous, as I soon discovered. Rumor engages everyone, from those whose fears feed on it (my mother, of course) to those whose reason sees through it, but only after taking it all in. Malwida was one of the latter and she began to warn me of the whisperings about town, even our own literary circles.

"My dear Lou, I am sure much of it is nonsense but you must maintain some female restraint with Herr Ree. Given your passion and Paul's charm, it may be hard for you. But it's not about you. It is how you are perceived in society and where you will or will not be allowed to go if you transgress.

"A young woman must be careful about flouting sexual conventions. I'm sure, Lou, you've been careful and only seem not to be. . . . But come on, Lou, really, what can we think about a midnight swim in the Tiber? It's not only immoral, but unsanitary. Listen to me, girl. From now on, keep your feminine idealism intact."

Trina was setting the tea down before us in a late-afternoon private tête-à-tête in Malwida's parlor. "Malwida, I value your trust above everyone else's. I assure you that Paul and I would never baptize ourselves in such an unseemly manner." She smiled and let one of the tea cakes fall unceremoniously into her tea cup, momentarily surrendering.

I proceeded with my defense: "These past few weeks Paul and I have talked and walked through this ancient city with abandon, and our talk has led me to places I would never have gone in any university lecture hall. I have never felt more alive, Malwida. I love our wandering banter. I love not knowing what will spill off his tongue at any moment and being transfixed by where he takes me. Yes, he's warm and bold, and handsome in all his obvious ways, but he's also a natural teacher, who directs me to things beyond my reach and beyond ourselves."

So far, so good. She seemed placated.

I went on. "Most of all, he is teaching me to think creatively and to learn by doing in the circles of artists. The experiment is life! No book, no study program can do that for me. Others may read and write about life. But I must discover life for myself with all its risks. . . . So that's precisely what I am up to with the notorious Herr Doktor Paul Ree. Contrary to rumor he's a most gentle and obliging guide. And Malwida, you'll be happy to know that Paul does not take me anywhere I do not want to go."

Malwida, never tongue-tied, cleared her throat, as if banishing all lingering doubts. "I believe in your innate talents, Lou. You need freedom to develop them. But as you forge ahead in this experiment that you call life, you must remember that others don't question life, and its values and its behaviors are sacred to them and strictly prescribed."

"Sounds like a death sentence to me, Malwida."

"Deadly, to be sure, Lou, but not to those who accept social and spiritual convention. It's deadly only to those who openly transgress.

"Trust me," she went on. "I know about these things from not so long ago. The revolutionary banner we fought for and failed in '48 is now in the hands of disparate, freedom-seeking individuals—all artistes in their own right who share no common purpose. You too must find freedom, Lou, your language and voice, exchange it with other artists. But real freedom is something else. Some may say it's about setting every social edifice afire. But I can tell you only this. It's a common belief in an earthly hereafter."

I winced. The raw memory of my father's death and Gillot's perplexing phrase "the hereafter of the heart" echoed in Malwida's words. But her harmonious social vision hardly seemed plausible.

She continued, "My dear late Alexander crusaded for the anonymous downtrodden masses and today our Fritz with his progressive philosophy wants to liberate our passionate sensual soul. No, the wildfire of social change isn't likely to happen anytime soon. The least I can do is raise Alexander's girls and encourage individual artists like you.

"So I want to help you, Lou. But we have two things to contend with here: your mother's resistance to what she sees as your free-wheeling defiant lifestyle and also the perception of your sexual license. On the first I can help you. On the second I can only advise."

After her sermon Malwida undertook to introduce some other "teachers" into my unorthodox curriculum. She wrote to her friend Friedrich Nietzsche and invited him posthaste to Rome, where she promised he would find in me a kindred spirit and a sophisticated student worthy of his philosophy. She primed my mother on the benefits of an individualized course of study with Ree and Nietzsche and other artists of her choosing as my teachers in various cosmopolitan salons across Europe. She reminded her too of the incivility of living in Mother Russia, its social turmoil, and the prudence of staying away.

On the second question of sexual license, Malwida oddly counseled "virtue." "I detest false modesty and flirtatious frivolity in young women. It does them no good and only makes them appear priggish and dispensable. But I have come to see the value of virtue. There is nothing more distressing than a strong woman in the yoke of sexual surrender." She said a woman risked sacrificing her independence in submitting physically to a man, that even the most forward thinking of men couldn't resist it. "Dominance and submission pervade the animal and human kingdoms alike. Don't forget it, Lou." It was best to do nothing to compromise any of my hard-earned womanly freedom—except in marriage, where the man couldn't exploit the difference. Or so she said.

I remembered Aunt Jutta, her happy spinsterhood and her wild urges. I didn't know what to want: chastity, for which I'd surely be accused of being a "coy tease" (for I did like men . . .), or an unwitting husband whose premature death would release me to satisfy my wild urges. Whatever Malwida's advice was, I knew discretion would be key.

Mother had already played her trump card. I returned from Malwida's that afternoon to our Pension St. Anselmo to find a letter from St. Petersburg in the inimitable script of Hendrik. My heart quickened, recognizing something as familiar as the lines on the palm of my hand. But those vulnerable memories literally froze as I found Pastor Gillot castigating me for the folly of my ways—saying that I "must rein in" my "irrepressible urge to throw caution to the wind" and "to indulge" my "childish fantasies—at the hands of such older, world-wise men experienced in all manner of questionable human intercourse." He warned that my reputation was at stake, as my mother had clearly seen, and that if I persisted in this behavior, my studies would be forever compromised.

I was appalled at my mother's cheek. Who of all people would she enlist to talk some sense into me? Did she think Gillot would respond out of true concern for my virtue or out of jealousy? Did it matter to her? No, of course not, and she knew that. But respond he did.

So did I. Before so much as confronting my mother who was out visiting friends for the evening, I sat down and, my hand quivering, I wrote my beloved cleric that I was flabbergasted that he above all people should caution me about the designs of men. That I'd expected him to endorse my free-thinking way of life. That I wished no role models, least of all to be one myself. That if this "transitional state of confusion" between who I'd been and who I was to be meant to him sacrificing the freedom I felt now, then I'd gladly stay forever in this glorious netherworld. It made me happy. It pushed me intellectually. In short, it gave me the companionship I had never, never (underlined) before experienced.

Surely, Gillot, you of all people have known my trust—a union
I carry in my heart, my hands, and every limb of this body. Do me

the favor of granting me that same trust and if you are incapable of that, then leave me to my own devices. Mother will surely provide . . . !!!

Yours as ever, Lou

That evening I poured out my soul to Paul—citing Malwida's concerns, my mother's machinations and my past mentor's own admonishment. I feared I'd be returned to the homeland. Paul confessed that mother had visited him too, and only wanting to placate her and legitimize our continued relationship, he'd actually offered to marry me. But that was neither my mother's wish nor Paul's true intention.

You see, I knew this because Paul had joked early on that he would marry me only on the day I could crisply pronounce the word *Nichts* without so much as a trace of my native Russian accent. So imagine a marriage hinging on a bet to pronounce the word "nothing" perfectly. "Nothing" had become our substitute for "I do," I once told him, sending us reeling in laughter. (No, for whatever reasons, we would have "nothing" of marriage.)

Paul, ever the pragmatist, promised he would not leave me and that if all else failed, we could devise our own "tutorial study," our "raison de tête," he called it, for being together. With this, he planted the seed for a plan I soon hatched for a kind of roving commune of study that would move across the capitals of Europe expanding and contracting but always having at its core the "two of us." (It would just go on and on, though he didn't believe in forevers.)

I had not thought through the implications of our behavior on Paul himself. I saw him so much as my rock, the architect of our plan, and so I never understood his deep melancholy. I thought that Paul's rejection of marriage and his swearing off all forevers signaled a philosophical maturity. I did not see it as I do now, as a defense—

a sadder far more human surrender to impossibility and the transitory nature of all things (something Paul's "adapted" species and animals might not suffer, but he surely did as a man).

In the end, I could neither lead nor protect this great man who had taken me under his wing and watched over me in those early years. Now I can only remember him. And I prefer to remember him as the young man. The young man whom I called during the many years of our roving experiment by the apt pet name "Häusli," little house. He was the only family home I had. He smiled and would counter with the endearment "Schneckli"—the small snail wrapped in his protective shell. We had our pet names, our own language, like children really. We had made our home in each other against a judgmental world. And Paul made room for others. Even invited them in. He offered us up as a human experiment and throwing caution to the wind, he let the chips fall as they may. And so they did with us very early on.

Before long Nietzsche himself arrived, manuscript in hand, at Malwida's bidding, at Paul's beckoning and with me precariously positioned as the bait, the catch and potential mate and heir apparent all in one to the great philosopher. I could not make this up, if it were not true. Life is like that. It surprises you, with truths you would never have dreamed of. And asks you to believe them. Paul was one such truth in my life, that young as I was, I never quite believed. A truth I recognized too late, after that light in his eyes no longer spilled into mine and his steady hand had long since slipped from my grasp.

5

An Unholy Trinity:
Fritz, Paul and Me

"There are some things that should never be in a cathedral. And gargoyles are one." I said this on our afternoon walk to ward off some unwanted thought. I have never understood the grimace of those leafy, sometimes bestial stone faces peeking out from every corner, column, crevice, smirking down from on high. Were they there to frighten off evil spirits or invite them in? And what about that other strange gaping mouth stretched above the portals of those ancient Celtic churches I have read about—the splayed sexual organs of "Sheela-na-gog"—a woman on her haunches clearly in heat, crying her creativity through the centuries, waiting to be filled. What saving grace might that face impart to the faithful?

Entering churches has always made me more than a bit nervous and in Rome there was no avoiding it. What bothered me was that line we cross at the church door, between who we are and who we aspire to be, that threshold of body and soul. And doubting Thomas, I always felt like an impostor. I'd come to look and not to believe. So I looked for her—that squatting woman with the inaudible scream, amongst all the ghoulish and sweet faces, the eyes, the wings, curled lips and tongues up there above the portals of God's many

houses. I never did find her. That gatekeeper of our humble beginnings—pagan, peasant and female. Clearly not Roman.

In my own life I did not need to venture through any ancient portals. My mother occupied that all-too-real, menacing space between
who I was and who I wished to be. Mother's presence was ubiqui-
tous and her power too horrible to be pitied. But strangely enough
in those early days in Rome I and my loyal companion Paul were
finding refuge in its many cathedrals and chapels simply to elude
her watchful gaze.

Mother wasn't much interested in Rome's holy architecture. Its
divine images everywhere reminded her of the religious fervor over-
taking Mother Russia and the peasantry's indulgence in devotional
icons that warded off the rational (and to them pagan) spirits of the
state. But mother was a Protestant with her own God. And all these
images on the walls and ceilings, on the frescoes of the great masters, Michelangelo, Perugino, Botticelli and others, seemed like so
many false idols to her. Clearly to be avoided. She couldn't see beyond the sacred symbol to the human art. She was ever suspicious
of the church's hold on the people and here in Rome's splendor she
would not grant its artists any special dispensation. No, when in
Rome my mother did not do as the Romans do.

Paul, an ardent atheist, wanted to dispel any last shred of faith I
might still have in me, and he was a provocateur, if nothing else. So
he took me that afternoon to view Michelangelo's famous sculpture
of Moses at the Basilica of St. Peter in Chains (San Pietro in Vin-
coli), just off the Via del Polveriera, not far from Malwida's villa.

Paul never preached his brand of materialism to me. He simply
would show me or describe two things and wait for me to make the
connection. And so it was with Moses, an extraordinary creation of
Michelangelo's, commissioned by Pope Julius II in 1505. This sep-
ulcher was to eventually grace the pope's tomb in St. Peter's Basilica. But life intervened and Pope Julius died in 1513, leaving his

feuding family to think of their shrinking coffers and to defy his last wishes by having him interred in a far less expensive tomb. So the aptly named setting of St. Peter in Chains. For his part, the artist was left to shift his focus to the Sistine Chapel.

That day I raced up the eighty-five steps from the Piazza Cavour, stumbled into an open area and had an extraordinary vision: an out-sized marble sculpture of a seated Moses, distractedly gazing to the left, peering out above all the admiring onlookers, his right hand at his side gripping tablets in defeat and the other on his lap combing the ends of his serpentine beard—a beard that hid a silhouette of the artist himself in its curls. Most appalling of all were the horns, the two strange udders emanating from his head.

I fell back faint and found myself cradling my belly as if I were rocking a phantom child. I reached for Paul's sure arm and moved toward him standing at a distance by the door.

"What is it, Lou? Are you sick?"

"Paul, he's the saddest man I've ever seen—so human and no, otherworldly. His limbs so powerful, yet frozen. And that head is al-most bestial."

Taking my hand, Paul explained it was Moses at a moment of in-decision. He had come down from the mountain holding his tablets and had just caught sight of the idolaters.

"Paul," I said, "If you didn't already know the story, you couldn't guess what he would do. You would sooner suppose he would give up."

"Lou, I do know the 'story' (with emphasis on the story) but Michelangelo could sculpt only what really happened. A man with his own vision confronting idolaters with theirs and the only thing he knows for sure is his frustration and indecision. Mere mortal that he is, faced with a choice of salvation or perdition, anything more than what is. The human condition. That's the power of this sculpture."

"It's too lifelike, isn't it?" I whispered beneath my breath. He went on, "It's all there is. Life in all its uncertainty and nothing else. It's all we've got. In fact, the artist himself is rumored to have hurled his chisel at his creation, shouting '*Perchè non parli?*'—Why don't you speak to me?—So, dear Lou, what do you think, why don't you speak to me?"

"What could I say about this magnificent sculpture that hasn't been said? It has made me sick? If I believed those horns were rays of light, I would be enlightened now. But I am not. I'm wondering if Michelangelo, someone capable of replicating the body's every muscle in its minute detail, could have missed what that divine inspiration actually looks like."

Paul pulled my head to his shoulder, kissing my hair, and said in his perfunctory way, "He was an artist, Lou, so he played with illusion. Rays of light or marks of the Jew. It is a harmless form of idolatry itself—and what a legacy it has left us." "Yes," I sighed, "'God's creation' in all its ambiguity." And he chuckled, satisfied with my questions.

We walked in silence out onto the piazza, coming immediately upon a troupe of players, one of whom was bearded, draped in Roman garments with a crown of horns on his head. This jester was surrounded by laughing children with outstretched hands. I remembered my excursions with father to the circus and his admonition that we should never forget the itinerant children and always reward their play. And at that very same moment I remembered the slicing pain, the frantic abandonment of calling out as a child in the night to God to make himself visible to me and that he did not come. "So that's what it's about," I thought as if sleepwalking. "We're all children."

And I dropped a few coins into their small palms.

"Did you know that the artist called his Moses, this mighty sculpture, *The Tragedy of St. Peter's*?" Paul mused as if continuing our tour on the way back to my pension on the Aventine. And then as an aside, he added: "But tomorrow, Lou, I will show you something else, its intended home—the Basilica of St. Peter. And there I'll introduce you to someone who will satisfy your quest for ambiguities. And maybe even clarify some."

"What do you have in mind, Paul? A human gargoyle, no less?" And we erupted in laughter.

"Oh," he smiled with his nostrils slightly flaring, as if having caught scent of something special. "Fritz would truly love that."

THAT next afternoon was so ungodly hot and bright that Paul and I literally bounded through the huge doors of St. Peter's into the cool gray sanctuary of the vestibule, making our way to one of the small side chapels that line its interior like a rosary of stations of the cross. Paul sat in a pew, writing pad in hand, telling me he normally liked to steal away into a confessional—the appropriate place, he said, to write his blasphemous thoughts—but this time he wanted to keep an eye out for our guest who he warned was almost always late, and not because it was fashionable but because *he* was not. He had "his own rhythms, his own time."

Not wanting to stand on ceremony, I wandered up the side aisle breathing in the sweet incense, comforted by the smell of life and death, baptisms and funerals, and all of the intervening sanctified moments the church held like clipped wings—memories of lives come and gone—wondering which one this day suffused through the hollow memory of its body. I thought of father's funeral, my confirmation in Sandpoort, and made my way back to our chapel, the altar of St. Thomas, lighting a few votive candles to mark this, our own secular ceremony.

I have always loved ritual though never quite seen its core. And I feel its comfort in the single light of a candle—that flaming breath that dances at the slightest movement and yet catches itself upright.

I stepped into the interior of the altar to catch first sight of our visitor as he appeared in that refracted stalwart flame.

There was first a soft step slowly making his way with a distinct waddling walk. Then the outline of a figure that seemed to stop and go, not to look around but to simply collect himself and go on commanding his walking stick forward. Seeing him Paul stood up and motioned to the man, who nodded. I sat crouched on the altar step. And when he arrived, embracing Paul, he turned to me—this medium-build slightly paunchy unprepossessing man—with a penetrating gaze, and Paul announced my name. I stumbled forward to take his hand, but I froze as he seemed content to smile, not wanting to touch. He simply leaned on his cane for several awkward seconds, for what I do not know, as if to inspect me more closely as part of the tableau.

I was stunned. I could only speak his name: "Herr Doktor Professor Nietzsche, it's my pleasure."

And waving his cane up whimsically in a semicircle through the air, he seized on my gaze and said in his inimitable mellifluous tone: "Yes, yes, Fräulein Salomé, I know." Then uttering a chuckle that echoed out into the cathedral, he added with a hint of conspiracy: "From what stars have we fallen to this place, Fräulein Salomé? Tell me now really, do you know?"

I don't think I ever answered his question. But I never did forget it, or that face with the hugely overgrown mustached mouth, and eyes that I would learn were myopic but did not blink with that frittering inquisitive squint of the half-blind. They simply peered in a seemingly innocent wide-open gaze, commanding one's attention and registering insights that others of us never saw.

I felt momentarily disarmed, as if he had reached into my past and was exposing the transient souls of Gillot and Io, but of course knew he could not know that. Introductions made, Paul said in jocular fashion: "Fritz, shall we go off to Malwida's now. She's expecting us for tea." "Yes, Paul, let's. Especially since I have here for you my latest, *The Joyful Science,* announcing the 'death of God' in its very first lines." "Well, well then," Paul whispered, "I'd say this is hardly the place to get an impartial reading."

With one hand on Nietzsche's shoulder, directing him to a side entrance, Paul took my hand and, as we walked with this small strange enigmatic man shuffling his way through his thoughts past the visiting faithful, he stopped to retrieve the rosary that had fallen from the purse of an old lady who hobbled before us. Delivering the beads back to her, he wound them securely around her thickly veined hands folded in prayer, gave her a gentle pat and bid her farewell with a respectful smile.

I did not know then I would wrestle throughout my lifetime with this man and his elusive influence posed so playfully that day in his initial question to me. Its short-lived life drama would cast its shadow broadly over both our divergent paths. But it was a question others seemed all too eager to answer years later. Some ascribed my flirtation with Nietzsche to a blatant opportunism on my part; others to the primal craving for my father, a futile attempt to "reenter his bowel-womb and repossess his penis"; and still there were some who held an equally distorted but far more foreboding political view, seeing our friendship as a tainted Jewish alliance against the Aryan supremacy of Wagner.

And yes, Nietzsche was not without his own detractors too. But they were less likely to attack his person (as they seemed only too willing to do with me) than to chip away at his thought. It seemed a much more civilized fate to me.

No, Fritz's philosophy when you came right down to it was absolutely anarchic. It took down an entire architecture of Western thought, delivering it to its roots, wanting to take back the disembodied mind, spirit, state, nation, religion and place it squarely in the super-sensing individual in a kind of latter-day Dionysian bacchanal.

81

Now I ask you, was that not enough for them? No, no, Adam always had to have his Eve.

Life is like that. There is no way of predicting its assaults. And so there were numerous postmortems to our relationship, the most damning coming from Nietzsche's sister. I said nothing and refused to field insults about this deeply complex man, even when Sigmund begged me to defend myself. Instead I followed Rainer's wisdom for surviving life's daily perils by learning to live with life's enduring questions.

∽

"I can't tell you how much it pleases me to have all of you, these disparate parts of my family, at last together." Malwida greeted us that late afternoon as we all straggled in from our excursion to St. Peter's and took our seats in Malwida's elaborately flowered parlor.

"Oh, my dear Frau Meysenbug, you are always so kind. You're better than a mother to me, though I'm too good a son to let her ever hear that, isn't it true, isn't it true?" Fritz quipped in his characteristic way of enunciating his sentences. Winded from our walk our tired guest settled into an armchair. Trina scuttled back and forth from the kitchen that day, as Malwida had planned two courses for us—the first being afternoon tea and crumpets, then later a second serving of bread, cheeses, cold cuts and wine—designed to keep us talking or at least eating well into the evening.

Malwida had clearly planned this evening. She had had little time to converse with her primary guest, the great philosopher, for he had spent the first days of his visit closeted in one of her guestrooms in the throes of migraine, with shades tightly drawn to shield him from the pounding light. But then as soon as he recovered, he insisted on retiring to a pension around the corner. So there we sat, her prodigal son and errant children, her captive audience. Home at last.

Nietzsche regaled us a bit with the tale of his fitful journey from Messina and flight from the sirocco winds, and his current writing, mostly aphoristic, which seemed to be the way his insights unfolded of late. And then changing the subject, he lit on Paul and his psychological writings which he chuckled were ahead of their time, all too human.

"Paul, the critics may eviscerate me," he said, "but it's you they want—your own brand of 'Reealism,' isn't it true? It's really you they're after, you and your rational science, but you, my friend, will never deliver yourself to the public sacrifice. What was it you once wrote? 'One humbles oneself, because of the thought that one will be raised up'? Now that is real honesty, isn't it true. I wish I'd written it myself. It's you and ones like you to whom I am indebted."

Paul squeezed my hand sensing the dueling edge of Fritz's remarks and then, seizing the challenge, he said in a characteristically warmhearted way: "Yes, Fritz, but I'm no 'visionary' pathfinder, spouting a new morality 'beyond good and evil.' That's too bold and uncertain a fate for me. I'm flattered to be your occasional scout, but I'm more suited to the plodding service of science. We scientists are always testing our theories and waiting for life's proofs. It's not for the impatient or for poets to be sure, but for types like me. A perpetual student, a follower.

"Take as a case in point," he nodded to me, "our own experiment in communal living and study." As he unfolded our scheme, Malwida's face blanched, her eyes squinting with each disclosure—two bedrooms joined by a study filled with books and flowers. But that, just a start as others would surely join too, we'd adjust living arrangements as necessary. . . . Brightening up, Nietzsche's mouth seemed to curl from under its brush. The ice was broken. And the questions poured forth. What would we read? Flaubert?—Too bourgeois. Baudelaire?—Not bourgeois enough. Who would we invite? Perhaps Rodin.—"Why no, no commune would be large enough!"

Where would we take this roving theater? Rome, Vienna, Paris?—
"Well, shouldn't we just forget France altogether. After all, if we're
not inviting her countrymen, we may clearly be discriminating but
no need to be rude!"

From Malwida came the one discordant note: "Yes, yes, my dear
friends. But really you must think now, before you act. What will
they say?"

"Well, I can't presume to speak for *them,* I never have, isn't it
true?" Fritz opined. "But, let's not nip this flower too soon in its bud,
Frau Meysenbug. I think it's a splendid idea." And so right there in
the presence of our hostess—a most unwitting accomplice—our
trinity was sealed in embryo. We had in the great philosopher himself our first ardent follower.

Malwida was not satisfied. Before she would let us go, she would
have her say. She mentioned that the cousin of Cosima Wagner had
visited her the day before and said she sat opposite Herr Professor
Nietzsche on his recent journey and was asking after the famous
professor. Would he be coming back to Bayreuth that summer to
hear the debut performance of Wagner's *Parsifal*?

Nietzsche was suddenly uneasy, clearly pierced by the memory,
and said in a soft conciliatory voice: "Well, I really don't know. I
think I half expected to see him in Messina. But I didn't. You see, I
have my Greeks and he has his Teutons. And let's not forget his mad
and very rich King Ludwig too! And so the twain shall never meet.
But for us, well that's perhaps another story. And as to music, Frau
Meysenbug," he said, making his way to the door, "I've thought of
Fräulein Salomé's poems, the ones you gave me my first night here.
I've reread them. These are verses for song. We shall see."

We walked behind him and escaped our separate ways into the
darkness with me holding this strange man to his word. His
promise. Or was it just my wish? But I could feel my heart racing
with that private thrill of being discovered, for the first time.

Such was our first night and all three of us met that following week at a local café to chat and to refine the plan for our roving experiment. He and Paul traded aphorisms and edited new ones for his next book. But the laughter was always cut short. Constantly plagued by headaches, Nietzsche was sent scurrying off to his pension around the corner. Then not long after, he announced that he must seek his cure in a kinder climate. He would travel north to the lake country. Couldn't we meet him there? And wouldn't I have some aphorisms to share of my own?

It was a fortuitous plan, since mother wanted me out of Rome. It was too hot, literally and figuratively with the gossip she imagined. She wanted us to go north with the thought of eventually making our way home. Seeing an opportunity in her plan and not wanting to tell her about mine, I feigned a persistent lung infection and convinced her that a brief visit to Orta and its island jewel San Giulio northwest of Milan would be good for us all and just the place to recuperate. Satisfied for the moment that my plan was working, I refused to think beyond that.

Less than a week later Paul, my mother and I boarded a train north. Paul had his own reasons for wanting to move our troupe northward, thinking that at some point he'd bring us all to his ancestral home in Stibbe. But as we sat together on a train going in the same direction with different destinations in mind, I knew Paul was wrestling with something. When my mother got up to go to a dining car to fetch a cup of tea, Paul finally told me what was on his mind. He had received a written message from the great philosopher saying that I would be a suitable match for a marriage that he could not guarantee would extend beyond two years, but he would be ever so grateful to Paul if he would convey to me his most sincere proposal.

I was dumbfounded. "What? Paul, how utterly absurd! I don't even know the man. He must be mad. I could no sooner consent to such a man than I could, than I could to . . . "

"To me?" Paul said with a meek and telling smile.

"But you know, Paul, you understand, you know why that part of my life is closed. I'll have to tell him I want his friendship. To see how this trinity of ours, to use his phrase, unfolds. That's it for me. I could also tell him I simply can't risk forfeiting my father's pension or something like that. But you'll let him know, won't you, Paul, if he asks? I can't imagine facing him."

As I leaned into his shoulder and squeezed my penned list of aphorisms into a crumpled ball, he said: "Dearest, what can we expect of a visionary—remember Michelangelo and his horns? Fritz has so much to offer." Then he laughed: "You know, how he said I'm all too human. Well, he may be not human enough. . . . But the scientist in me warns you, Lou, never say 'never.'"

"Paul, you're the only one I'll ever need."

And folding both my hands into his, he whispered: "Yes, not to worry. Fritz may write with a knife, but he's a pussycat at heart. Anyway, dear, I assure you I'll ward off all fierce predators."

So the rest cure that lay ahead of us was suddenly fraught with anxiety. I kissed Paul's hand and closed my eyes and imagined a candle flame refracting the same cathedral light in which I'd first seen this strange man, now an awkward suitor. Dozing off, I woke to the natural paradise of Orta, and to the sudden panic of no panacea. Only the bitter medicine of telling him the truth.

❧

Orta was an extraordinary retreat, an island lost among the lakes just below the Alps like a rare pendant pearl—a verdant town of leafy forests of larch and chestnut, wisteria in the air, and splashes of red camellias and whole trees of holly berries linked by tall languorous palm trees standing like timeless sentries, the silent claim of the south on this northern town facing the snow-covered mountains. Everywhere were hilly promontories with fieldstone arbor ways on their paths and wooden benches inviting the weary hiker to perch and gaze. The lake country is for seekers of solitude. And given the tensions within our little group, we needed its seclusion.

PAUL, *I remember you there. Your spirits seemed brightened, even relieved. But how did you stay? You loved us both. I think we must have known that. So we counted on you in different ways. You to save me, and you to deliver me. Two contrary impulses. You somehow embraced us. Loyal to both, without ever betraying a moment's trace of your own inner conflict.*

You and I holed up with mother and Fritz for a week in close quarters, in a small pension overlooking the exquisite moody lake. And yes I recall the slam of the pension door each morning like clockwork at daybreak and spying you from my window with fishing rod in hand, escaping down to the water's edge to satisfy, as you later said, your daily quotient of gambling urges. "If Fritz is casting about for bites, I'm afraid I've got to create my own—the real kind."

Was it there, Paul, that it began to happen? Did I break from your line? Did you know what was coming? Each sunrise you trudged back up the path with a flapping catch for breakfast or none at all, still satisfied, and pronounced the day begun. That was what I loved about you. Life was always a question, and you lived its ambiguities as if its point was the question. Mother was even beginning to like you.

Do you remember those lines from The Joyful Science? *"Life is a means to knowledge. We want to become the subjects of our own experiments, our own guinea pigs!" Do you remember me wondering if you, if we in Orta, Paul, were the inspiration for those words? But, you would have none of it. You grinned: "Fritz is writing the future. I report the here and now. Nothing today, Lou, but we don't know*

87

about tomorrow," you'd say laying your rod at the door in your off-hand fashion.

NO, no I needn't intellectualize Fritz anymore now. I did then in order to get away from him, to escape that personal tension that would forever be unresolved with us, and because our failure, whatever failure it was, always sent a fleeting feeling of shame like an electrical current through my body. And though I'd spend the next decade poring through his works, much of it with Paul (still trying to extract myself from Fritz's hold), and later even publishing a critical memoir of his ideas, when I first confronted Nietzsche back then I knew nothing about the work, next to nothing about the man and everything about me—or so I thought.

I was just twenty-one and he was a rapidly aging sickly man in his late thirties. How he could have seen a match in us, I will never know. Except of course for the obvious reason, which completely eluded me at the time—the one which I was most ill-equipped to see or do anything about—namely, to take care of him. No, no—he would say it was my "clever mind," a rare gift indeed that drew him to me, ripe to become heir to his legacy. Yes, he said even that. If love is not always blind, it is most always desperate.

But age and one's own infirmities have a way of grounding one's perspective, and looking back I now accept "mortality" as a motivation for our all-too-human behavior. I was too headstrong and idealistic even to consider all this when Nietzsche and I made our famous ascent up Sacro Monte on Orta.

✒

For lapsed believers, we seemed always to make our way to sacred places. Sacro Monte was a trail of some twenty postmedieval chapels, from the sixteenth century, that wended their way up a gentle hillside incline. Each chapel way station was a scene not of Christ's life but of a man who had relinquished his material goods to serve the poor—St. Francis of Assisi. In contrast to the savior himself, Francis's example counseled asceticism, not redemption but absolute denial of worldly things. It must have rankled the souls of industrious believers and infidels alike.

This monument to this most humble of men is of course quite grand. Remarkable for its time and ours, its life-sized terra cotta statues against a pastel frescoed background tableau are strikingly theatrical. They pit magistrates, papal emissaries, Western and Islamic merchants, even the sultan of Egypt himself, against the penitent presence of this Christian missionary. And one views these dramatic encounters from a distance through iron and wooden grills as if the moments themselves are held captive and timeless to a changing audience of wayward onlookers.

Despite the deep religiosity of the hero marking his life in the footsteps of Christ, there in Chapel XIII in the midst of a frenzy of highbrow and lowborn followers, virtuous ladies and wanton women, and a minstrel show, sits a self-composed domesticated creature that looks like a gargoyle—a monkey no less—sitting on its hind legs with sexual organs for all to see.

"What's that doing there?"

"Well, well, Fräulein Salomé, they weren't all believers, now were they? That, my dear, is the artist's saving grace, his doubt."

"How so?" I said astounded, reminded of Moses' horns.

"If this, his creation, is all a brilliant fantasy, he will have one object in it, your gargoyle monkey right there, who sees it all. And if you notice, of the twenty-odd witnesses to this spectacle of Francis's public humiliation and procession to the gallows, it's only the monkey who looks directly at you, at us the audience. The truth of our origins, perhaps. Darwin would love this and so would Paul. We must tell him."

"But Herr Professor, this artist's alter ego, you say, is animal and if the truth be told, very nearly priapic. What could the artist be thinking? Surely not a symbol, like Luke the ox, John the eagle, Mark the lion . . . "

"No, just us, Fräulein Salomé, no need to blaspheme the sacred. If that's an apostle, then his name is Thomas," he quipped. "Dear Lou Salomé, you call things for what they are. You speak what you see. It's a great gift but bound to get you in trouble. You might just become the threat of your own pronouncements. The filthy little monkey who sees through the surrounding charade. Beware of too much truth, Lou." I was caught unawares at his use of the familiar "you." Whether it was a compliment or an insult, I did not know. But I was surprised at how he overestimated my valor and I answered: "I'll remember your warning, Professor, though I can't imagine what that truth might be."

I chose to say no more.

Strange, I thought as Nietzsche and I hobbled our way, peering through the gates at the dramatic moments in the life of a pious man, at first an infant, and soon a stripped naked pariah who would be visited by pope and magistrate alike, and finally let into the inner sanctum, and at death anointed a saint and his renegade tribe drawn into the fold.

Fritz looked on quizzically and said in a low tone: "Funny the extent one must go to get the church to submit, and once it takes its renegades into the throat-hold of its pantheon, who hears you then in the death-rattle, as life breathes out of you? Do you think he thought that, Fräulein Salomé? Did he know? Whatever doesn't kill us makes us stronger. I need to rest," he said motioning to me to sit beside him on a trailside bench. I thought then that he, this man I knew to have questioned all orthodox faith in his writings, was in his heart, his questions, if not religious, a deeply spiritual soul and I felt a kinship with him there.

"What do you have in that notebook of yours now, more poems no doubt? Paul tells me you've tried your hand at aphorisms. Do you think I could hear them?" Paul had stayed down below with my mother who was not up to the climb. My protector absent, I blanched and felt cornered but relieved not to have to confront him with anything personal and only my modest jottings. Summoning courage, I warned him I had written only two and they were terribly raw. Steadying my hand on the notebook I read him the first:

"The optimist finds joy in the very feeling of life. The pessimist finds a feeling of life only in joy."

He was quiet and threw his head back as if looking to the sky for a sign. He began pulling at his walrus mustache. And then he caught me staring at his profile, with his thick unkempt brown mane brushed over his head, curling around uncommonly small ears. "Yes, they are small, isn't it true, but they hear such outrageous things," he laughed. A magpie burst from the tree behind us, causing me nearly to jump out of my skin as I skipped on to the next one:

"Woman does not die of love, but wastes away for want of it."

"Well, Fräulein Salomé, I think of what you mean to say here. In the first, 'Some get a feeling for life only from joy; others get joy from a feeling for life,' and in the second, 'The greatest pain is self-hate,' isn't it true, isn't it true?"

I felt deflated, embarrassed, and collecting myself I came to my defense:

"Yes, Herr Professor, but your interpretations seem to ignore in the first instance man's nature—a certain disposition to be happy or sad—and in the second the female sex itself."

"So you disagree with me, Fräulein Salomé," he smiled, leaning forward and patting my knee. "Well, well. It appears we have something to talk about."

We walked on in silence.

We came to the summit, the last of the chapels, when we were suddenly caught in a shower and ran for cover to a bench in the chapel portico to wait out the rain. Sensing my frustration, he spoke softly saying he needed types like Paul and me, he valued our community not only for himself but for the ideas he would leave behind. I was clever, he said, and would not take his word unchallenged but test it against my own experience and make it my own . . . a new morality . . . a new kind of evolved godless man. An heir to embody his legacy . . . and me, "a woman no less!"

I had no idea what he was talking about but he spoke calmly as if reviewing travel plans already agreed upon.

"And then of course there is a way of doing this, Fräulein Salomé, which I presume Paul has already discussed with you. A tutorial arrangement of sorts—a marriage of perhaps only two years. Now what would you say to this?" I was aghast. Though I had been expecting it, I still thought he must be joking, that somehow he thought I should be flattered when I felt only insult. He was oblivious to his effect.

"Oh, Herr Professor, I could not. Who would I do this for? You have just now equated a woman's need of love with self-hate. Well, Professor, I tell you I love myself too much to do without it." And suddenly a faint smile came over his face and I felt cornered. My excuse of losing my father's pension had completely flown out of my head. I had given as grounds for my refusal—my own selfish womanly need for love. What could be more bourgeois than that!

"Your love-matches," he mused, "I've never believed in them. Those marriages, I once wrote, have error as a father and need as a mother. I know this because they both gave birth to the likes of me."

And then, not wanting to insinuate myself into his humor, my hands folded resolutely in my lap, I spoke with my head low deliberately avoiding his gaze: "Herr Professor, I'm sorry to disappoint you. But I know I don't want marriage now, though I do seek love.

And love does seem to me a condition of marriage, though marriage not a condition of love."

"So all is not lost here. There's a glimmer of hope then, Fräulein Salomé, for love if not marriage, isn't it true."

No, no, no, I thought, he's mistaken my meaning, as he leaned over and took my hand. It was then I noticed for the first time his delicate hands with long exquisite fingers meant to play an instrument producing music at their very touch. Then turning my hand over, he planted a kiss in the center of my palm, and folding my fingers into a grasp, like petals of a flower, holding in the light, closing out the night, he let go.

I think I've never experienced anything that was simultaneously so strange and oddly intimate—a gesture even sensuous in its awkwardness. It was getting late. Paul and mother would be worried, mother about my virtue and Paul about mother and yes, perhaps me, wondering what happened to us. I got up from the bench and raced ahead to the path.

That late afternoon in May 1882 we descended the mountain with Fritz's mood seemingly transformed and mystifyingly buoyant, for reasons only he knew. He gave that day a demarcating significance in his correspondence similar to A.D. He would write the date ". . . 188? after Orta." It was a beginning for him and he reveled in its potential. He would write to a mutual friend and professor from Basel of our time in Orta, confessing: "At last, I know now I want to be human again." And so the rumor of our ill-fated kiss on Sacro Monte was born with Fritz somehow descending that hillside an innocent and me, as I soon discovered, the forbidden fruit of his imminent fall.

6

Coming Off the Mountain:
After Orta

"By now you surely know, Paul, that Lou is a willful girl with sometimes uncontrolled impulses. Where are they all this time up there? . . . Can you believe that once as a child she called out to me in the lake to drown—I her mother. But no, she would never tell you that."

"LOU, you really do test the limits, insisting on that photograph with Fritz and me, poor dumb asses that we are (you know I hate such staged things) and you standing there like a circus master, you monkey you. Oh what a real calamity you sometimes are, my Lou."

"FRITZ, how could you now possibly think of sacrificing your reputation and all that we've accomplished together to cavort about the countryside with that bold girl? Yes, yes, I'll go with her. But mark my words, that one has designs."

"SHE'S Malwida's poet friend. A Russian of high birth—they call her the 'Empress' I'm told. Her father, a general to the tsar." "It appears our hermit philosopher has finally come out of his shell. And

I hear she's not content with just one, but has two." "Not bad for him, of course. But such a girl and noble no less." "Well, Russians, you know those Romanovs are going to the dogs."

THEY said this and even more.

SO no, I did not kiss the Great Philosopher up there on Sacro Monte, and though you know already from my earliest childhood in St. Petersburg I never learned to dance, I confess to being tone-deaf too and never especially disturbed by this fact. I think it was all of a piece. I simply did not hear the music. Still when I read years later that he had winced back then at what he termed the "rasp" of my voice, I was crestfallen. No matter now. Despite it all, dance we did with words that summer.

I had gone to Bayreuth in the company of Fritz's sister, Elisabeth. Before that, we, that is, Fritz and Paul and I, had already met briefly after Orta in Lucerne, where the subject of marriage once again reared its ugly head. He circled round and round the subject, its loyalty, its noble commitment. We reasoned that any such earnest laborious union would be foolish—would completely thwart the "free-spirited gaiety" of our project. The "unholy trinity," to use his term, that we were all so eager to try out for the next year. It was telling too that we never once spoke of attraction (or the lack thereof).

In our heightened enthusiasm to seal that youthful pact, we had ourselves photographed. Something we would not easily live down and I for one would live to regret. . . . *There we were. The three of us. My two mentors tethered as workhorses to a cart with me wielding a whip in one hand and sprig of lilacs in the other to add some levity to the moment. Yes, what a sadomasochistic threesome we made. No telling, the excruciating slice of whip on hindquarters, the yelps like fervent puppies to stop, to go, that preceded that photographic moment and the soft touch of flower, the scented relief, the yip for more, Paul clearly uncomfortable in the pose, and the crack again, my Fritz now smiling, game to the play. The pain. Up with those trou. Button that blouse. Stand strong now. Philosophers have feelings too, if somewhat perverse. Stop the giggling. You're shocked. Eyes on the camera. This is it for posterity. Whatever we do, this is how we'll be remembered. Two philosophers and their gentle female charge. Now that'll set the tongues a wagging. They'll never know, will they? Never know, it never happened. They'll always wonder . . .*

And they did. It may just as well have happened for all the righteous uproar that picture unleashed on us all, but principally on me. Apparently it was easier to believe something must have happened than nothing at all. The camera doesn't lie.

At the time though, it was just a spontaneous spoof on our grand plans for a Troika of pure and free study. It was silly and we all laughed about it and Paul departed for his home in Stibbe and Fritz to his in Naumburg. And I to Hamburg to a family wedding and then quickly to Berlin to see my mother off, called away to St. Petersburg to my father's sister's deathbed and to look in on Evgeny who was never well. I joined Paul there in Berlin and went on to Stibbe for a brief introduction to his family and his mother whom my mother had enlisted by written request to chaperone Paul and me in our various local excursions ("I'm sure, Frau Ree, you understand youth as I do, and will take the proper vigilance"). Then at long last I made my way alone to *Parsifal* in Bayreuth—an event to which Fritz's sister, Elisabeth, had wished to accompany me so she could introduce me to that circle.

Fritz would not be there for reasons of having fallen out with the great composer some years before, namely, for not being supplicant enough. He was beginning to be suspicious and indeed to hate the work.

"No, Lou, Wagner's deluded," he would say. "He's full of Schopenhauer's dreary submission, and that's benign enough. But he adds to it his own damned Christian and national sentiments. And that's dangerous. He's stuck, stuck in a resignation that surges so seductively and smashes us into mass renunciation. That American writer had him pegged all right. He's better than he sounds." Fritz was writing about the problem with Wagner at that very moment.

What was missing in Wagner, of course, was "the exuberant humor, light feet, fire and grace, bold logic, the dance of the stars, the tremor of southern light, the smooth sea—the perfection of *The Joyful Science.*" What was missing in Wagner was Nietzsche—a suitable heir to Wagner's Holy Grail. His toadies could not know that. But the Maestro knew all of it and, feeling betrayed, banished Fritz as a detractor. So Fritz was clearly not invited. And yet in the way that masters always view their servants, somehow they still expected him to show up.

Elisabeth, of course, was a staunch defender of her brother's reputation and work (it was after all her livelihood) but she was a social climber at heart. Wagner's influence in culture and the court was boundless, while Fritz's following was at best rarefied. She was getting on in years herself and didn't want to be left behind. And seeing an advantage for all in rapprochement of any kind, she pressed on in her machinations to insinuate herself and, by extension, her soon-to-be-great philosopher brother back into Wagner's circle. Acceptance into society was the least compensation Fritz might grant her for a lifetime of tireless devotion with its sacrifices of children and home.

"Fritz is such a minor composer for such a major mind," Wagner said, when I first met him. A man with imposing plumed hat like a Dutch painter floating about the crowd. "I do wish we could talk, but the music gets in the way. His insane reverence for Bizet! What can one say? A tragedy really. Cosima and I miss him dearly but he has clearly found another path, hasn't he now, and on its way you, Fräulein Salomé," he said, pushing his way dismissively, hat flopping forward, cushioning every adoring gaze to the audience awaiting him in the intimate soiree following that second performance of *Parsifal.*

98

"No," I said, "we found our way to him and actually revere his writings," as I craned my head back to Wagner.

Quickening her step, Cosima took my arm firmly to spirit me away from her husband. "You should know Fritz is an ill man for some time now, Fräulein Salomé, not suited for an upstanding girl like you or for any, for that matter. Dear girl, *his* is a private contagion. *Contagion,* do you hear me? You would live to regret it," she said in that perfunctory way of one who knows as she delivered me back into Elisabeth's hold and the countenance of Paul Zhukovsky, a Russian painter who had designed the set of *Parsifal,* and Herbert von Stein, the fiery tutor of the Wagner children.

Before she let go, I turned to her, saying: "I am grateful for your gracious invitation here, Frau Wagner, and I am sure you mean well by your words, but you are so wrong about Herr Professor Nietzsche. I know that, and Dr. Ree does as well. There's so much to learn from Fritz and we all intend to pursue this during the coming year in an intimate commune of study in Vienna or Paris."

Her eyes began to skirt my gaze and her brow crinkled as if she'd caught scent of a foul odor. She offered, "Well, I tell you, as it reads in scripture: Beware of false prophets, my dear," and then leaning over in a whisper outside of Elisabeth's range, she pinched my elbow and jabbed, "But we all make our own bed now, don't we."

My god, if anyone had, Cosima had. She had been mistress to Wagner for many years and born him five children before they sanctified that union in marriage. Strange how the highborn, she was Franz Liszt's daughter after all, see themselves oddly exempt from their own moral pronouncements.

I had just witnessed her husband's opera, set in the times of the medieval Knights Templar and the Holy Grail, hailing the triumph of virtue and compassion in the world. It's a tired old story set against a musical backdrop of extraordinary subtle emotional intensity. At its center were the eponymous hero and a beautiful young girl named

Kundry. Wagner's drama celebrated woman's chastity and suffered her sexuality and reconciled those two sentiments by killing this poor girl off once she was finally let into their inner sanctum and no longer needed to drive the action. And all the while the music drew us in, commanding our deepest sentiments. Well, as you can imagine, not a dry eye in the audience (sniffles, handkerchiefs out everywhere and spectacles clouded over). There we sat overcome by the music powerless to resist, to question its seductive message, and not to believe and feel its visceral redemptive truth—right there before us, compassion unleashed into the Christian world.

But what about that poor girl, I thought? What a price to pay? Who was she—this innocent Madonna, this seductive whore, first laughing at the dying Christ—a Sheela-na-gog in medieval garb— and then washing her master's feet—a doomed Magdalena? Forgiven for what? And this wandering girl is redeemed in death while he Parsifal is redeemed with a sword, the grail, his *life,* a brotherhood and an order that survives. No compassion I could see, and no justice either.

I sat there thinking about the letters flying back and forth, uncommonly intimate ones from Paul in Stibbe, confessing his love to me for the first time, and letters from Fritz in Naumburg wanting to meet alone after Bayreuth in the Tautenburg forest and conceding that Paul was a better friend to us both than he could ever hope to be. Wouldn't I come? Kundry, I thought of Wagner's poor heroine, what on earth have you done, girl, what have they done to you? And what will they do to *me?*

Opera, so popular in my time, with its outsized emotions, was never something I easily understood. Its symbols and its histrionics seemed to me to tear the inside outside, ripping into the soul and displaying for all a spectacle of unbridled feeling. There for us to emulate, to parrot, and people loved it. We could go there to feel our joy and see our common pain sung, our remorse, our redemption, outside, and then return to the raspy voices of real life, life's inner messy complaints, absolved of our own sinful slip-ups and missed connections. Not unlike Cosima warning me.

There was something religiously confessional, humanly pragmatic in it all. Something that perhaps quieted our troubled souls for a moment in this grand musical communion. (Something irresistible really, though confusing and still false to me. But then I was tone-deaf.) Needless to say, I did not comment on *Parsifal* that evening and stayed in my small circle of Zhukovsky, von Stein and Elisabeth.

"Tell us about Fritz. We miss him. What's this we hear that you and Dr. Ree are planning with him?"

"Well, we are actually going to live and study together next year. Just where, we're not yet sure."

Elisabeth looked aghast, while the men were interested, and then I said, "No, no, I have a picture of all of us together. Let me get it." While I went to pull a small photograph from my purse, Elisabeth turned on her heel to make her way to another circle.

"Well, that's a pose for posterity, I'd say."

"Curious to see what he'll write next. But then I suppose you and Dr. Ree will be the first to know." There was patter and laughter and a bit of butting play, as Zhukovsky took me away to a parlor to talk into early in the morning about our homeland and the tumultuous goings-on in our native St. Petersburg.

The next day was a catastrophe. It was late morning and I was sleeping off the festivities of the evening before in a pension I shared with Elisabeth. There was a loud clapping at the door and despite the pillow I pulled over my head, the latch suddenly lifted and in burst Elisabeth furious.

"Fräulein Salomé," she cried, no longer the familiar "Lou" of the previous evening, as she pulled back my down comforter to strip me of any possible hiding place. "Get up, girl. Surprised to find you alone. Was it that you were bored by so many admirers or did they tire of you? . . . What you do on your own time is your own affair. But you and your antics shall not subject my brother and his reputation to such ridicule."

My eyes opened to words spitting venom from pursed lips. Her hands securing a pin in her thick dark hair. I noticed the pulsing vein by her right temple and the streak of chalk gray above her forehead announcing age arriving too soon. "You with your feigned interest in my brother's work. You may be his guest in the country in the coming weeks in Tautenburg but don't think for a moment that I don't see through your pretext." I arose and reached for a dressing gown and motioned Elisabeth to a chair. "You obviously have no regard for my privacy but at least consider the other guests and lower your voice."

"Let me explain something to you, Elisabeth. Despite your reproaches of my so-called sauntering behavior and my supposed claims on your brother, there is one critical element missing. Namely, attraction. Whatever you may think, Elisabeth, we women can and do have a choice in such matters. My sole interest in Fritz shared by Paul Ree himself is for his philosophy, his friendship and the considerable knowledge he can impart, of his own doing, I might add, to us both."

"Fräulein Salomé, with your mad tales you have paraded my brother like a circus act before the society of Bayreuth and I cannot condone that." She was trembling.

"Elisabeth, it may please you that if there exists any confusion about our relationship at all, it comes from your brother and his absurd proposal. And it would do you well to know before you take his defense, that it is he who has entertained wild notions of a marriage of convenience—with its multiple roles of mistress, nurse and amanuensis. He whose morals must be questioned—though let it be noted that you, and not I, have raised the question."

Her eyes squinted as if closing out the light. "I assure you I have tried to disabuse him of any such fancy," I said, "and I swear I could stay the night with him in the same room and never be aroused. I simply lack the desire for more." Slamming shut the open book on the night table (of all things, Paul's copy of Fritz's *The Birth of Tragedy*), Elisabeth stood up, and announcing she would tolerate my visit in the coming days but not welcome it, she stormed out the door with a parting shot. "So Fritz isn't good enough for you, you say. Well no, surely not for one who reserves her affections for a married Russian cleric."

I left for Tautenburg a few days later dreading a confrontation with Fritz who surely by then would have had an earful of Elisabeth's invective and dreading most that I could no more defend myself against her false charges than I could explain my own all-too-blunt and truthful retort. I could not satisfy her suspicions. I was either the brazen hussy with sexual designs or a cruel tease with none at all. There was no middle ground, no way out for me in her scenario.

I recalled the monkey staring through me on Sacro Monte and Nietzsche's warning of the damning consequences of speaking bold truths. Now reformers like Luther himself might counsel to "sin boldly" (*pecca fortitis*) and the enlightenment men after him might "dare to be wise" (*sapere aude*), but I ask you, what woman could do that and survive? Not I. No, not I as I spiraled into a feverish freefall alone in my modest rented room in the vicarage on the edge of the Tautenburg forest.

THE smell of wet cedar wafting through balloons of diaphanous veils waving in crowds and crowds of animals, street urchins, and more and more diminutive people all pushing in closer, wanting to see. My back exposed naked, a searing burning and a tightening around my waist, no my neck. Rope, dragging, pulled, tied and I growing larger and larger with each tug. And a man with walrus mustache, mane wrapped in a bandanna and tiny hairy ears in woman's dress with hands quizzically folded in the lap of his skirt and face, frowning to a bystander: "Don't know. Who is she?" Empty chariot above with a floating golden fishing rod. Back there a man is falling off his horse. And I growing larger and larger, bursting, the hold tighter and tighter. My feet, my bony toes throbbing, a slime of slipping. The man is falling off his horse. I try to reach but cannot. The kind face of a sultan in black floppy hat and blinding cross hovering over me, smiling, saying: "What have we here? Your hair, your hair." And the man in the dress handing over his shears. "No," I cried. "I cannot." And an ungodly small rodent-like animal sniffing through the tresses as they dropped. With my eyes. No, no, the eyes of my mother. And the horse and the helmet now rolling and the man and the man . . .

"Papa, Papa," I screamed. I wailed. And suddenly calm. I woke to tears streaming down my face, to the breath of wind whistling through pines and a slanting light beyond the window. And words that lingered in the fresh mist, as if just spoken: "I thought I saw an eagle and what I found was a delicate fragile bird." Though I couldn't tell who spoke them.

Before me was the face of a young woman, the vicar's house-keeper. "Fräulein Salomé, we've all been so worried about you. It's over now. Don't fret, dear child. The doctor's been here and Herr Professor Nietzsche every day. He just left, when your fever broke, while you were asleep. You need to gather your strength, dear. Here have some water. I've left you some soup. I'll go now. I'm just next door. The professor will be back tomorrow."

Coming to my wits, I wondered what I had said, remembering fitful dreams, and I sobbed into my pillow. Church bells clamoring me into a sleep with nothing, nothing but their punctuating stops. I didn't know what to hope for.

While I had feared the professor's peculiar notions of my ministering to him in sickness (and in health), he ended up nursing me back during that damp month of August 1882. A little more than a week into my stay I was able to get out of bed and Fritz came to my pension. I could hear his footsteps approaching on the path, sometimes accompanied by Elisabeth, who seeing me spying her from the window turned her head, deliberately shunning my gaze as she returned to the cottage she was sharing with her brother. Fritz came in and sat. When I felt better I would read to him. His eyes were so bad it was a labor for him to read alone. He reported on what the various critics from Bayreuth were saying about Wagner ("Well, Lou, he may have won the crowd, but he surely corrupted taste!"). He uttered new aphorisms that made us bicker: *When you go to women, take the whip.* And we wrote an occasional letter to Paul.

For days we conspicuously avoided all talk of Elisabeth and what she must have told him and managed to engage in animated abstracted philosophical banter on what he was writing, with no personal bearing on us at all. But it was pretense, hiding a festering truth. Til one day when we ventured out on an afternoon walk in the forest, he caught me off guard and told me something that seemed absolutely out of character, even for this man who was perpetually out of character.

Fritz said he had followed me after Lucerne to Berlin where I was meeting Paul and seeing mother off to St. Petersburg. That he'd never let us know he was coming, didn't know where we were staying, and yet he roamed around the city skirting the patronage of small cafés on the Kurfürstendamm, spotting a likeness here, a memory there: "A certain curl to the hair, a slanted smile, a mauve wrap, but none of the jewel, the Lou, the you I was looking for." And then he boarded a train back to Naumburg the next day, without ever having contacted any of us, content, he whispered, to have given himself over wholly to a passion. Had I ever truly given myself over to a passion, he asked, as if inquiring about tomorrow's weather.

"No, no, dear young Fräulein Salomé, surely not, it is but a sport for you. And for me an impossibility, as the lovely Cosima undoubtedly has told you.

"I don't know who I hate most," he said, "you for knowing, me for my foolish desires, Cosima for her sadistic affections or my sister for telling me of the goings-on in Bayreuth—exaggerated as they may be. You know sometimes I can hardly stand to hear her voice."

We had come to a swampy field in the forest that was wholly devastated with warped leafless trees, many of them broken. Realizing my puzzlement he explained that this was just part of a natural process of succession, life giving way to new growth. I remember thinking of that putrefying field when I read from the work, *Zarathustra,* he would next publish: "Behold, I am that which must always conquer itself . . . and truly where there is decline and the falling of leaves, behold life is sacrificing itself for power."

At that moment alone with him in that ghostly barren patch of forest I only felt something imminent—abandonment, an impulse to find my way back, when he said: "But now, now you must see, I cannot go on with this anymore, with these winter plans, with you and Paul. I must go on alone, my passion for you an illusion I can never act on. You now see through the charade of it all."

I could not. I only saw a created rumor born of the jealousies of two women, Elisabeth and Cosima. No truth, nothing more than the insistent wanton truth of their lying. And they more powerful in their need than I. "Two friends are most often separated by a third," he had written.

I couldn't see through my tears, protesting my innocence ("I never mocked your proposal, never"), admitting complicity ("That was just social banter in Bayreuth, nothing, nothing at all"), and pleading that he not desert us. But he did, in a rueful, accepting and no longer accusatory way. I was disconsolate and did not catch his meaning then, any more than I do today. Just that his mask had dropped and he had retreated to his home in Naumburg, to Elisabeth and his mother and his peripatetic way of life climbing for heights that in his writings sounded alternately brilliant and wildly delusional.

The great philosopher was approaching the summit of his greatest work beyond which he would witness the abyss alone. In my flight to Paul in Berlin, I would miss him, miss this man dearly whom I would never truly know. From afar and from everywhere and anywhere, words of the "eternal shame" I had become for him faded at last into silence. I carried with me all of it, the parting stab of his pain, helpless guilt of the falsely accused, my indignant anger at being fantasy's cast-off—and in the end, with no more desire to inflict blame, just the wound of a person I could never forget.

Months later, he wrote tersely to my attempt at reconciliation: "I want to live alone now, dear Lou. I am too unhappy for having made you unhappy. We'll bear it together."

Love's loss is like that. It holds on for dear life, as it did for us both.

A friend of Nietzsche's once said that he was like a man who came from a country where no one else lived. And there he returned. In subsequent years Paul and I tried to retrace our tracks to that faraway place, to find our way back by reading Nietzsche's published works. That map led us not to the man himself but his amazing creation—Zarathustra—portrayed in the work *Thus Spake Zarathustra*—opening with a personal epigraph reading like a signpost that only the initiated could recognize: *"after Orta."*

We struggled to understand this alter ego—this anti-Christ of his with his foreboding words that signaled a dangerous rupture from all human community:

"Of all that has been written, I love only what men have written with their blood. Write with blood and you will find that blood is spirit. . . . Once spirit was god, then it became man and eventually a mob." While some would at the time interpret this hero as a Jewish conspiracy and then quite conversely others would later see him as the prophecy of a very real Aryan monster devoid of all human spirit, we thought then this hero was nothing more, nothing less than Fritz's valiantly battling his own mortality, his increasingly broken mind and body, and brilliantly evoking a spirit that would triumph and survive him.

Some people are born posthumously, he once said, and with Zarathustra he had created his own heir to his philosophy. A true fantasy that could not disappoint him, whose spirit, fused with his blood, would soar and remain a star in the afterlife of his work. "He who writes in proverbs and in blood wants not to be read but to be learnt by heart." So he summoned not the mind but the heart as his final resting place and that I knew was most certainly true.

That work he wrote in a teeming frenzy over a mere ten days not six months after Orta and in the next half dozen years or so, he would complete several other books—*The Wagner Case, Twilight of the Idols, The Anti-Christ* and *Ecce Homo*—all mixing extraordinary insights into human values with megalomaniacal excesses signaling an advancing disintegration. In these years he wandered constantly, seeking his solace in a search for an unthreatening and nurturing surrounding. He would constantly find himself coming back to Italy—decrying the xenophobia of the French, the anti-Semitism of the Germans, his very own intolerance, and finally lighting on the natural grace of the Italians, who always loved him. He most wished to die in their embrace. . . .

Solitude had become for him not only a state of mind but a requirement of self-revelation which he brashly sounded with bravado in his books. But I was not convinced as I recalled his words from an earlier work (*Beyond Good and Evil*): "Every philosophy conceals another philosophy; every opinion is also a hiding place; every word a mask."

I LOOKED for him behind his words, in words from a letter to Malwida in which he bemoaned his extreme loneliness which had made him a wild wounded animal, he said—separate from all community and unable to let a single word penetrate his self-imposed exile. "The wound is not hearing any answer, and having to bear, most terribly, on one's own shoulders, alone, the burden which one would have liked to share, to shed (why else should one write?). One could die of being 'immortal'!"

Italy and his beloved city of Turin would witness the final mortal act of this wounded animal. He had found his way there, I am told, from Nice after having in his half-blind state misread the signs and boarded the wrong train to Genoa and then in a fitful embarrassed state of confusion he finally made a connection back to Turin, to a room in a boardinghouse on the Via Carlo Alberto that would be his last truly safe haven.

There he celebrated in letters his food, which was for once plentiful, his accommodations (always most Spartan) and a public that he felt revered him, and he wrote with a fury—his loneliness shedding defenses and issuing a lyrical power at last authentic, an integrated lone voice—in one of his *Dionysus Dithyrambs* of that time:

> *Solitude is*
> *not pain but ripening—*
> *For which the sun must be your friend.*

A few months later, on one of his compulsive daily walks through the city, he came upon a horse being beaten by a livery man in the Via Po. Dropping his cane he ran toward that wounded animal, shouting "No, no enough, enough," and wrapping his arms around the coarse hair of its neck, his face against its warm throbbing body, he collapsed. He was collected by his devoted landlord, Davide Fino, and brought back to his room where he wailed for days and days and danced naked in fits of laughter and crying and when he could not be consoled, he was finally entrusted to the care of a Dr. Wille in a clinic in Basel.

Fritz would have loved the names, the irony of it all. He would have had something to say at once outrageously true and dissembling, but he was beyond all that—the spoken word. Now the work written in blood would speak for him.

"I would believe only in a God who could dance . . . I have learnt how to walk: now I can run. I have learnt how to fly: now I am light, I am flying. I see myself under me. Now a God is dancing through me. Thus spake Zarathustra." I think of those words every day of my life. No, Fritz, it is not a god I see, reluctant learner, heretic (you would be pleased) that I always was. No, I see only an unparalleled man, all too human, you who dance through me:

Distance
like the pain
that's localized
isn't wisdom
but it does clarify

what it means
to be apart
on an earthly plane
that has touched
one horizon.

Absence
leaves us
in between
in the crystalline
cold that burns
a breath—

the light
we never can hold
within us.

Distance
is the absence
of a heart,
halved and dark,
plotting its own
reunion.

—Thus spake Lou.

I learned of his death in August 1900 while reading the notices in a newspaper on a train traversing the Russian steppes with Rainer. He had spent the last years after the clinic at home in Naumburg with his mother and then, on her death, with his sister, who had married a known anti-Semite in Jena.

I looked out to the infinite landscape unfolding before me, our lives skirting its surfaces, and closed my eyes, imagining his arms outstretched to that quivering animal, the momentary commotion, the gathering, the going away and the glimmering cobblestones of that Italian square now empty. And nothing to fill the silence but the faithful blazing "friendly" sun that always returned to light his absence.

How much of us does the earth hold? No more, I think, than those words inscribed in the blood of memory. Years later, no doubt as the author of a book on Nietzsche's work, I was approached by one of Nietzsche's biographers. He opened our interview with a letter from Nietzsche to his sister written in 1883, a year after our parting, with the disarming admission: "Of all the acquaintances I have made, the most valuable and full of consequence was with Fräulein Salomé. Only since knowing *her* was I ripe for Zarathustra." And though he kept asking me all manner of personal inquiry into the man to which I would not respond, I recalled instead the work, the words, the creations, my theory of his many masks, til he came to the subject of Orta.

"But what of that intimate walk there together, now so famous for its mystery?" And suddenly I felt my own mask dropping. My heart quickened and I said: "If I kissed the Great Philosopher on Sacro Monte, I no longer remember."

Why did I lie, why did I say that at all? Was it false pride or simply memory's desire to reward his affection? Or was it just to satisfy his query once and for all. I felt a certain sweatiness in my hand. And remembering the dewy kiss he had folded into my palm that day, I opened my hand in a grand circular gesture of letting go, feeling a lightness, his awkward kiss set free, not unlike that moment back in the cathedral, and startling my guest, as Fritz had me back then, I said: "Do you know, the very first words he spoke to me? It was a question, 'From what stars have we fallen to this place?' It's what I choose to hold of him, dreaming only our beginnings not endings. But I like to think Fritz now must know the answer. I'll have to ask him."

INTERLUDE

Why wait any longer for the world to begin . . .
Why wait any longer for the one you love
When he's standing in front of you . . .

Ain't that the truth, sing it. I turned up the volume. Only talk I have up here in the cabin. Bob and me.

No, we don't see what's before our eyes, do we? I think I get that. Too young, life bounding forward. And you, Lou, no different. A crazy triangle. Famous philosopher—weird and impossible, wants a muse, needs a nurse, probably syphilitic, a mother you want to shake, and a loyal man who is standing watch, right there by you. Too close maybe. Safe perhaps, one who couldn't? Or just too reliable. And so you pass. Yeah, I think I know what that is. You couldn't believe it, right? You knew it but you couldn't believe it was true. Or maybe it was just too soon. Twenty-one. Well, I've done that. A long time ago in your Germany, no less. What we give up in the throes of youth. Funny how life and stories intersect . . .

The wind is beginning to rage out there. The bears are gone, their deep claws etched into the trees. Bear runes. Leaves swirling. Have to get out and rake them up. Stretch these limbs. Thanksgiving, a trek to the mountain man / lumberman's camp or maybe someone will come up before the fall of winter. We'll see . . .

113

She's moving on. A lot of chutzpah or just faith or something boldly original in that girl. Still moving toward what? . . . Gather some wood now. It's wild out there. Clear your head . . . "Stay lady, stay, stay while the night is still ahead." She doesn't let up now, does she? Inhabits my dreams. Or I hers. She'll be back soon enough.

7

Finding a Soul Mate

Put out my eyes, and I can see you still;
render me deaf, and I can hear you yet;
and without feet I can go to you;
and absent speech, I'll conjure you at will . . .

And if you set this brain of mine afire,
Then in my blood, I still will carry you.

Death has a way of commanding desire for life in all of us who are left behind. A whole life is telescoped into one precipitous moment leaving us with that one unfathomable certainty—the all of who we are, the nothing of who we will all become. Perhaps that is why news of death seizes us with a fierce defiance to halt the natural progression toward our own demise, to live beyond it, to even imagine and to fashion our own resurrection on earth. I think that that may be the hold of all faith.

So like children clasping to a blanket in the dark we create a hereafter now. I gradually began to understand the wisdom of Gillot's "hereafter of the heart," though I did not hold it sacred in the grand tenets of belief but in the smallest personal comforts of someone's story, someone's fantasy, someone's memory, someone's poem.

These lines from Rainer's *Book of Hours* were a quieting solace to me then and actually were in my hands, and not yet published, when I first learned of Fritz's death. They comforted me in a way that only poetry can do—holding desire in the moment, containing the pain of letting go and warding off the silences in words, in words that we write to survive. Inscribing our time—our particular time—with the magic of an inner necessity. This is where we hold the dead, where they truly reside.

But those silences do prevail in life. And they catapulted me back to that time we spent together "after Orta," when we thought, wherever we were, we would never part.

After the fiasco with Nietzsche, Paul and I moved into an apartment in the Charlottenburg section of Berlin. While Paul worked on a new book, I audited classes in the Philosophical Seminar at the university and began to write a rather emotionally taut autobiographical novel about a young girl's religious and sexual awakening, called *Struggling for God*. Not wanting to engage the gossip of a roman à clef and not wishing to invoke my mother's wrath from afar, which my brother reported to us was seething in St. Petersburg at my questionable living arrangements, I decided to write under a nom de plume—Henri Lou. It was an amalgam of Gillot and my Christian names. Since it was the secret of our lives, only the two of us could ever recognize the truth of my story.

Little did I think then that this slight book would become a bestseller and be translated and read by more people than all the books I would later write combined. I did not have much feeling for this bastard child I'd let out into the world, but its annual royalty was a welcome relief for our rather stretched circumstances. It supplemented both my father's pension and Paul's income, giving me a degree of financial security independent of St. Petersburg's purse strings and insuring that the German bureaucracy would look favorably on my rather permanent visiting status. And yes, it allowed for those glorious summers in the Engadine.

Up there on the Engadine later that summer I remember Paul, ever the protector, shielding me from Nietzsche's barbs and entreaties alike, penned in letters that Paul intercepted and I never saw. I would hear about them much later from friends and in biographies. But one sun-drenched afternoon while rowing together in a small dinghy on a serene lake, Paul did read one of those letters aloud to me.

Fritz was writing some terribly distorted damning dream into his *Zarathustra,* whose source, he wrote, was Orta (just so that we knew). In it Zarathustra, Nietzsche's prophet of the *superman,* is looking up to the clouds for inspiration and sees a circling eagle with a female friend, a serpent (*eine Schlange,* unmistakably feminine in German), coiled about his neck, and Z declares: "Those are *my* animals, he the proudest animal under the sun, and she the cleverest animal under the sun. . . . Would that I could be clever like my serpent. But in one day cleverness abandons me. Ah, how it loves to fly away."

Paul stood up and suddenly rocked the boat, creating a threatening wake, as I shrieked for him to stop. He shouted into the echo: "The god of the *superman* has spoken, Lou, and he doesn't like our blasphemy." Then ripping up the letter, he tossed it dismissively into the wake saying, "Food for the fish. Fritz must have had pea soup that day, Lou. What a mind. What an imagination!" And sitting down again, he caught my stunned gaze, my hands shaking, gripping the sides of the boat, and he smiled slyly: "If only the Great Philosopher could see his fretful little serpent now!" I leaned over the side and scooping up a fistful of water splashed it unceremoniously into Paul's face. "You, Dr. Ree and your antic philosophy, are all wet," I said and we dissolved into laughter. "Thus spake Lou."

Paul had written asking me to come back from Tautenburg. He said that the most essential use he could be for me was always as my *Häusli,* that I would always have a home in him, someone I could rely on, and that beyond his book, this was his sole task in life. So we set up a life there in Berlin of soirees, mostly of men friends who assembled to discuss a new determinist philosophy that preoccupied Paul. He had published earlier his *Origins of Moral Feelings,* in which he laid out his positivist rationalist philosophy. It met with a tepid response, especially in light of Nietzsche's much more acclaimed focus on old heroes, the "twilight of the gods," that was gaining greater favor among the literati. It was safer than the more immediate notions we carried within us in our mortal and modern souls.

But in those few years I could see that with each essay or the novel I published and with Paul's own growing dismay with philosophy and his failed attempts to earn a position at the university, he became increasingly depressed with the *soeur inséparable,* in Nietzsche's words, the inseparable sister that I had become for him.

Before long Paul decided to pursue a medical degree in a program in Munich, which seemed completely consistent with the scientific philosopher he had become. Without ever a hint of any finality, he left me in our home in Berlin, and continued to write and come home during his semester breaks. Though he'd said he did not know if he could ever live without philosophy, he seemed relieved to have finally found a grounding in medicine for his scientific pursuits.

Our landlady, Frau Becker, who had looked at me with suspicion when we first appeared at her door, announcing she rented rooms and not beds, now seemed to take me under her pitying wings in Paul's absence. Funny how some women overcome all hindrances to answer another woman's perceived distress. Imagining me an abandoned wayward girl, she took pains to look in on me and to invite me to tea that she served from time to time for her boarders in the late afternoon. "Fräulein Salomé, a young woman like you should not languish alone. You need some company, conversation to lift your spirits. Do come now, girl." I gave in to satisfy her pain and it was there, at one of her afternoon gatherings, that I would meet my future husband. But it wasn't quite that simple.

The truth is that during those months of separation, I was enveloped by loneliness and doubts that tormented my sleep and plagued my days: Why had he left? Why? Had I, resisting his loyal desire all those years, driven him away for good? But he knew about Gillot, he always had known, why I could not. He accepted my limits. Had he finally acknowledged his own? "Why" became such a tired weak refrain to that unremitting "yes" of silence.

With Paul gone, our philosopher friends all retreated to their own gatherings, occasionally sending me an invitation to a dinner with their wives or to a ball. As Paul's intellectual companion, I had been accorded a special access, but without him to mediate our unusual relation, I found myself suddenly an outsider, a young woman estranged from her family, her foreign home, a woman maybe even deserted and as gossip had it, a woman scorned by the wayward Great Philosopher himself. Guilt by disassociation, I would think in morose moments. So Frau Becker's invitation to me that afternoon was a hand extended that proud as I was, I was glad to accept.

Fred Charles Andreas was a man in his mid-forties, the son of a Malaysian German mother and an Armenian father (a princely line), who was born in Jakarta and had grown up in Germany and spent his lifetime negotiating two starkly differing worlds, living with an Eastern intensity in an alien moment and with a Western rigor independently studying the lineage of a lost Persian heritage.

Impossible to inhabit both, he suffered its schism.

But I didn't know that then. When I met him that autumn afternoon, he was a reserved distinguished-looking soul, the German tutor to two Turkish students who were staying in Frau Becker's rooms. And his face was remarkable. I will never forget it.

119

What I could see of it, framed in a thick wilderness of salt-and-pepper beard and a shock of white streaked hair standing on end crowning his head. His black eyes peered outward with the pleading intensity of an alarmed animal. And yet there was such a mannerly calm about him—almost a gentle ferocity.

I sat across from him at Frau Becker's elaborately appointed rosewood table and with those eyes settling on me, he said: "Fräulein Salomé, what is it that you do?"

"I am a writer, a 'Schriftstellerin,'" the first time I had actually ever said that. "But my writing is all very new. And you, Herr Andreas?"

"Oh, Fräulein Salomé, *you* set down the new texts." (I knew he must be a philologist, parsing out the German word for writer as "putting down script," strange, I thought.) "Well, I, I just decipher the very old, the oldest in fact. I am working on the scripture of the *Avesta*, the writings of the ancient prophet Zarathustra. Those ancient texts are still very new to us, uncovered in just the last century. So unraveling its meanings is what I do. And so I'm doing something very new about the very old. The original, in fact." And he laughed.

I was startled by the rumors, by Fritz's threats of a forthcoming *Zarathustra*, and here I had the man who knew the source, who knew the original word. I had to know this man. Where could I find out more? Were there university lectures? He was not with the university but only with its program in diplomacy, and didn't know about lectures, but if I wanted to know more, perhaps we could meet for dinner. That is how it began. My quest to know more and soon a married life.

☙

"In the beginning was the word. And the word was made flesh . . . "

These first words of the *New Testament Book of John* were obviously not the whole story. Those words came on the heels of the proclamations of so many prophets scattered all over the world:

Zarathustra, Moses, Buddha, Confucius, Mahavira (founder of Jainism), with their own scriptures of the *Avesta*, the *Rig Veda*, the *Bhagavad Gita*, all who lived within a span of fourteen hundred years before the birth of yet another, Jesus Christ. And his very own flesh would precede his written word by another seventy to a hundred years. What could those scribes have been thinking? Prophecy, of course, a savior, a sign, a man who gave the word meaning. And that was not the end, no, no it went on with Muhammad six hundred years later, his scripture the *Quran*, the birth of Islam and the crushing persecution of Zoroastrianism by Arab Muslims just fifty years later, and their expulsion to India. And last but not least, Luther and his contrastingly tepid cerebral rebellion with his ninety-five theses nailed to the Wittenberg Cathedral door.

And the instinct to revise, to inhabit the word festering still. It never ends. Out there beyond our Christian reach, a man in India named Mohandas Gandhi now preaching a powerful spiritual sword of nonviolence, and further north in a mountain village in the climbs of Tibet a boy child born not long ago, the fourteenth Dalai Lama they say, anointed to speak the hopes, the fears, and the disparate dreams of human community.

"So in the beginning, in the beginning then, . . . " I said, sitting across from Andreas, as he laid this all out for me in the quaint Waldsee (Floriangarten) restaurant, a local haunt, and lifted a glass of "Rotwein" to my lips, waiting for our Jäger Schnitzel.

"In the beginning, Fräulein Salomé, there was a host of men whose words were set down in texts, how many we do not know, whose words are lost. But we are left with some. And those words punctuate moments in our history, in what we have become . . .

"You see, I think there are no real beginnings. How many beginnings lost? There is only this moment. And theirs and ours is only an enduring word captured, translated and understood perhaps, far removed from the speaker. That is all."

I thought he was the oddest man alive. But speak we did to each other. I, a fledgling writer, and he, as I would come to know, a consummate translator and unassuming man who gave words meaning. We met regularly twice a week on evenings following his tutoring sessions.

So began our strangely formal courtship and my practical education in world religions, something I had only studied in general terms with Gillot. But Andreas was an archeologist of those religions and he gave me a far more concrete understanding of what the delivered wisdom of "struggling for God" was, that strange title I'd given my novel, and what that actually meant for an ancient lost culture whose spirit he sought to retrieve in their most primitive words.

"Oh maker of the material world, thou holy one. What is the first place where the earth feels most happy?" he read to me from his notebook, seated on a bench shaded by linden trees in the Schlosspark. It was first and foremost God and light of the hearth, and after that, home and family, and then cattle and then planting and finally, the fifth place where the earth was most happy was "the place where flocks and herds yield most dung." These words were from the *Vendidad* (the law against the demons), the oldest extant Zoroastrian text, the beginning that seemed to me fixated on contamination and admonitions throughout against touching dead corpses of dogs and men—which "made the earth feel its sorest grief." I saw nothing spiritual in all this and yet I found myself at once laughing and then suddenly in tears, sitting with Andreas at dusk in the park as he closed his book.

"Fred, I don't understand any of it," I said embarrassed at my display reaching for my handkerchief in my purse.

"Lou, they were just human. Death was their demon. Theirs was a prescription to survive circumstances we can't even imagine, and it's not any different today. Then it was a dung heap, today it's a tithe to a church, a faith. Whatever nourishes community. But death is still the hold, the demon of life. I don't question it, Lou, their humanity. But you do, don't you?"

"No, not their humanity, but the spirit, I just don't get it," I protested.

"But I tell you, they are inextricably linked. Well, you want more today in this more cultivated society of body and soul. But you, Lou, wouldn't have touched those dead dogs. Survivor that you are. As much as you may resist the spell of these words, I think you are seeking, as they were back then, questioning and wanting to believe. But for now though, I think the earth would be most happy if we went to eat!"

And he took my hand gently to go. Yes, he was a formal man but kind at heart and not without humor.

I spent those autumn months seeing this unusual man who collected words that he patiently pieced together like shards of broken pottery, assembling an emerging form from these verbal remains of a culture's elusive spirit. Fred was always waiting for those words to speak to him and so his work was never finished. In the same way that he was open to the spirit of the words he studied, never prescriptive, he accepted me and my writing, my stories and essays, with their intellectual roots in Western thought, for who I was, as my own emerging spirit. I was not to be shaped but carefully observed. And he did that, watching me, with a gentle intensity.

It was a curious closeness that developed between us, a friendship of two starkly differing people on parallel courses that did not intersect but whose presence, even that separateness, we grew to depend on. We were two foreigners each staking a claim on alien soil—he the pioneering scholar/translator of Persian culture and I a self-appointed critic of Western letters and culture. His claim seemed true to life and mine, well, somewhat made-up. So distance, that sense of never quite belonging, had always been core to our distinct experiences of this homeland we'd come to and it would later become fundamental to the home we would build together.

There was a strange comfort in that for me. Andreas was avuncular, never invasive, simply there, my father's kiss before he died. Before long on one of those walks through the Schlosspark, he asked for my hand in marriage.

Though it would take some considered time to deliver the news to St. Petersburg, it traveled through our rooming house with telepathic speed. Frau Becker, its source, was bemused, proud of her matchmaking and at the same time alarmed. Paul would be coming back for the holidays and semester break. What was to be done?

"Fräulein Salomé, don't be obstinate now. There are choices to be made in life," she yelled while wildly flapping the bed's feather coverlet and slapping it down to air out on the windowsill.

"No, no, Frau Becker. I know what you're saying but Paul, Paul will always be a part of my life."

Frau Becker began to toss the pillows with a vengeance, wanting to shake some sense into me. She warned, "Fräulein Salomé, we all have our time. And yours, young lady, has come. Now be sensible."

I suddenly remembered Aunt Jutta and Malwida and my mother and missed them all. What would they have said? I was always too stubborn to ask. "For such a smart girl, Lou (now using my first name to make her point), I wonder about you. Time waits for no one. Trust me in this." And she slammed the door behind her, shutting out any further comment on the subject.

On his return Paul caught on immediately and though he had already left to pursue his own path, he was shaken. Fred came regularly to dinner twice a week like clockwork, listening intently to my nervous banter, taking my hands into his at the door and stiffly kissing me, not on my cheek but my forehead as he left. Despite the confusion, Paul did take to my unlikely suitor. He was impressed by his soft-spoken, learned demeanor, his devotion to the science of words.

But the months of our separation hadn't prepared him for being let go. This resolution, this closure to our relationship, we hadn't expected. "I can't pretend to understand, Lou. Marriage, who would have thought it? My Lou?" He stroked a stray strand of hair aside from my brow, his hand squeezed my shoulder and then dropped. He said with wistful resignation, "Our promise is *Nichts* . . . " (*our* word).

He was never openly angry. He was too much of a Mensch for that, but he was firm. "You don't mean it," was his answer when I said he would always have a place in our home.

"I'm not up to another Troika. Life isn't a rehearsal, Lou." His look was faraway. "We can never repeat it, as much as we might like to."

"Paul, this man, Andreas, his presence is a deep comfort to me. He is wise and patient. He will never hurt me and he will not leave."

"Look, Lou, Andreas seems to me a good enough sort. He'll look after you and that's what you need. But never let on to him that you know him too well, or he may be left waiting forever.

"I . . . Lou, I must go now. There's a card game at the Solnitz's across town. They need another player. It'll be good to connect with them again. Don't wait up."

Paul came back that evening soon after I'd retired and I heard him restlessly moving about in the kitchen. Outside was teeming rain with sporadic thunder. Sometime in the middle of the night I heard him go out again and then, looking down at the street corner, I saw him pause under the gaslight and draw something from his wallet. The door opened again and I thought he'd thought better of his night plans, of braving the storm. The thunder receding into the distance, I finally drifted off to sleep.

The next morning I found a note on the kitchen table with the words, "Be merciful, Lou. Do not follow me." Beside that hastily scrawled last missive was a photo he had carried about with him of a bright-faced child with long blond curls standing before a gazebo in the glare of snow. Me as even I could not remember. I collapsed in tears and neatly folded his note and placed it in my purse, thinking there will surely be a time to discard this, but not now, when he comes back, when we have outlived this. But there was not. Not ever.

&

Death is much larger than us and it catches the living unawares, as it did me once again just a year after Fritz's passing when I was informed of Paul's tragic end. And words from that same collection of Rainer's came to console me:

> *What will you do, God, when I die?*
> *When I, your vessel, broken lie?*

You see, Rainer knew, he knew the full range of our creative impulse to defy mortality, and yet to succumb to the utter fragility of life. He bravely spoke its beginning and end. It was a salvation to be with him.

A MAN sets out on a mountain walk. It is late afternoon. He has seen his last patient. A pregnant peasant woman with husband and three howling children in tow. They have lost the last, they can't be too careful. He examines her and tells her there is still time. She should go home. Frau Nagel, his midwife nurse, is here and she will come by in the evening and call for him at the Hotel Messina. They want to pay him. "No, surely not, not to worry," he says. He hugs the small boy who leaps like an eager dog into his arms. "Nature must take its course," he says, "and we must wait for her now. It is she who decides our time and we who serve her." He walks along the gorge enjoying the height and the grandeur of the peaks, the phalanx of tall pines he loves as friends, that earthy musk in the wind, and the tumbling noise of water blotting out all memory commanding the fall of life now, life that cannot be stopped. A rain sets in. He has forgotten his walking stick. How foolish, he thinks. He will go back. They'll need him sometime around mid-

*night. He turns and his heel yields to a rock giving way to the wet
ground and he slips with nothing to hold him into oblivion.*

On October 28, 1901, Paul's corpse was found in the River Inn beneath the Chanagura gorge just outside of the village of Celerina in the
Upper Engadine of Switzerland, a village we had visited during our
summers together and a place he had made his home, staying in the
same room in the same hotel and ministering as a doctor to the poor of
this mountain enclave after his estate was sold in Prussia in 1900. The
day of his death a child was born and they named him Paul.

Much has been said in the ensuing years about him, that cold rationalist that he was, he chose his time. Or had time chosen him?
The gambler. No matter.

Years later when asked about Paul Ree's meaning for me in my life,
I recalled his profound words about life not being a rehearsal, and nodding my assent, I could only utter two words, *irretrievable loss.* Mine.

୶

Marriage was never a ritual I had prepared for in my solitary imaginary life. Not at all. I had spent so much of my youth resisting it.
But I had consented to marry Fred and I do believe that it was his
very formal distance and our considerable age difference that allowed me to enter into this pact in the first place.

The formality of the arrangement obviously did mean something
to him as the vow to our future of living together, but the particulars
of how it was done were left up to me to create. And I found myself
secretly thrilled with the prospect, sending out announcements to a
select few immediately. There was immense comfort in this ideal-
ized togetherness and immunity from solitude. Though I didn't tell
my satisfaction to anyone. I just rejoiced in it silently for a time.

Marriage in the spring. We would move to his place in Tempelhof
and then to a larger space of our choosing. My life choices would

finally be settled. I would be looked after. The public sexual issue about me no longer an open question. But that wasn't quite right. I began to feel a creeping trepidation on two fronts—the marriage ceremony itself and how we would do it, and not incidentally, what the intimacy of this bond would entail. I could be creative with the first but with the second I knew I could not. And he must know and I must tell him.

But how I would do that, I didn't know, so I turned to Aunt Jutta. The one who had saved my mother, her brother and herself from the hands of my demented grandfather and a sure final resting place in the silt of the Neva River—and the one who had saved me too back then from the throat-hold of my pietist past. Yes, with all the best intentions and with the determined instinct of a tracker, Jutta had forged a way out of that family wilderness for me, a path that led to Gillot. She saw me safely off to my European studies, wishing me safe passage in my travels, and returned to the armor of her own privacy, quietly living out her free-spirited spinsterhood ostensibly alone on the outskirts of Berlin.

We had not seen each other to talk at any length in almost a decade, except for two or three times when I had seen her in passing at a family wedding or funeral. But she kept in touch—occasionally sending a note, and I sent to her an inscribed advance copy of my novel (letting her in on the secret of my authorship).

Jutta was tickled by conspiracy. She was the family patron saint of difficult cases of which I had already proven myself one from the beginning. So despite the long silence, I thought that turning to Jutta was like asking advice from a trusted family doctor who knows the deep family history, your medical secrets and just what to prescribe to fix things. Jutta had seen me through my confirmation and now perhaps she might help me through the next milestone. I had doubts and fears about marriage, and she with her experience would be able to put it all in perspective. She would know what to do.

I sent her an announcement right away along with a note saying I wanted to see her alone to discuss my plans and needed her advice on how to break the news to my family. Jutta was quick to respond, sensing a plot and some intrigue:

My dear Lou, I am so happy for you, my sweet girl. Please do come for tea next Thursday at three. And have no fear, your secret is safe with me. But marriage, my dear, is a public declaration meant to be bellowed from the mountaintops to all and sundry. St. Petersburg included. Louli, trust me, we will climb this one together and we will find a way. Next Thursday then—

—Yours ever, Jutta

I arrived by local train in Jutta's leafy village of Koepenick on the other side, the southeast edge, of Berlin not far from the Muggelsee, and then I went via coach through spitting rain down a long tree-lined road with farmland on either side to a modest stucco bungalow on the village outskirts. The bungalow was tucked back in a meadow of tall grass and wildflowers. As the coachman opened the door to help me down, I pressed some coins into his hand and he tipped his hat and was gone.

The door suddenly opened and there stood a tall broad-shouldered woman in her middle years with gray peering eyes, tanned outdoors face, streaked white blonde hair swept up and swirled in a wild nest atop her head, waving her hands and smiling with such glee. Jutta emerged dressed in jodhpurs, boots and riding jacket running down the brick path with arms outstretched to greet me.

"Lou, my Louli, you are so grown up. Let me look at you," she said, her hands firmly placed on my shoulders. "It's a bit of a trek across the city and out here, isn't it? We would have picked you up in our buggy, had we known which train you were on. Bettina should be back momentarily from her marketing. She especially wanted to stop by the bake shop to get us some sweets. She'd better be quick, though, it's a threatening gloom out there. The birds have already taken for cover." She motioned to the clouds. "Come in now and make yourself comfortable."

Hanging my wrap beside her riding crop at the door, she tugged her boots off and led me in stocking feet into a small room lined with mahogany bookshelves and appointed with leather sofa, an oval table and two plump overstuffed chairs on either side of the hearth. As I took a seat on the sofa, she stoked the fire, fetched the whistling kettle from the stove in the adjacent kitchen and poured the steaming water into a pot on the table, securing it in a tea cozy.

"We'll let it settle now. Forgive my dress, dear. You can see, I've just returned from riding. But truly, we never keep up appearances here, no reason really to do so out on the farm. There's only young Karl who tends the land with a few farmhands, and Bettina, of course.

"Anyway, my Louli, it's wonderful to see you again, my godchild. But I feel that somehow we've *spoken* more than we've actually *seen* each other in all these years of your life. The distances, no doubt— St. Petersburg, Switzerland, Italy. But here you are now in Berlin, for some time I'm told."

Grasping my hand, she leaned forward with a hesitant smile and looked me sympathetically in the eye: "Well, Louli . . . tell me really, sweet, to what does your Aunt Jutta owe this rare visit? Here have some tea now," she said, pouring the tea and jumping up to deliver a platter of cucumber and tomato sandwiches to the table.

She was right of course. In all those years, Jutta had been my confidante from afar—even back when she had directed me to Gillot. I began my story there and went on for over an hour, telling her as I had never told anyone before the full story of my time with Gillot—my girlish transport, my shock, disillusionment and eventu-

130

ally my flight. My exploits with the Great Philosopher and my dear companion Paul Ree, mother's eventual tiring of me, her stubborn and unruly daughter, and her return to St. Petersburg. And now, Fred Andreas, the wonderfully wise older man with faraway intellectual interests in the East who thrilled me and whose hand I had accepted. He would be there for me, that I knew, but I feared that in marriage I would disappoint him. I cannot. I simply cannot.

Jutta sat there, with folded hands under her chin, seeming to weigh what I was telling her. Her eyes sometimes drifting outside the window. A door suddenly opened in the kitchen. And through the portal came a woman with a plate of assorted tea cakes—a deeply handsome woman some ten or fifteen years older than myself, with dark eyes, bushy eyebrows and a tail of chestnut hair trailing down her back.

Standing there, Jutta placed her hand on Bettina's back, massaging it in a few circular strokes: "Lou, meet Bettina. Bettina, this is Lou, my godchild. Do sit down, Bett. Were you caught in the rain? Have some tea to warm you up and some of these delectable condiments you've brought us."

"Delighted to meet you," she said shyly, with the inflection of the south, offering me her hand and sitting down tentatively beside me. "We have read your novel and your pieces in the *Gartenlaube*."

Bettina proceeded to drink a cup of tea and scarfed down a couple of sandwiches as we chatted about those publications. But then sensing a conversation interrupted, she did not want to stay. Making her excuses and saying she needed to look in on Karl and make sure he had secured the horses, she collected her skirt, wrapping it up into her waist, and made her way swiftly out into the storm.

"Lou, from what you've said, this man, Fred Carl Andreas, cares deeply for you and you must decide how deeply you care for him in sickness and in health, as the vows say. But all that lies between is for you two to determine. No vows can dictate feelings. There are many ways of a relationship, Lou. But the most important thing is that you are absolutely honest with each other. Honesty, nothing more, nothing less, is what makes love last. Whatever you decide, I am there for you, marriage or not. Just send word, my Louli."

"I think I truly do want him, Jutta, but I must talk to him to be sure he wants me. I will need you, Jutta, whatever we decide. And if there is a marriage, you will help, won't you? I mean, I don't know how to do it."

"Of course, my sweet, we will be there with bells on. We'll plan it all, including a special carrier pigeon to St. Petersburg. Not to worry."

The rain had let up and a few rays of light were poking through the clouds on the far horizon. It was getting late and Jutta asked Karl to take me in their buggy into town to the evening train. While Karl fetched the horses from the stall to hitch them up to the buggy, Jutta and I walked through the garden drenched in fresh rain, suffused with the scent of honeysuckle. She sensed something still lingering in the air and she said: "Louli, what else do you need to say?"

"It's something I've always wondered, Jutta, and mother would never tell me. Your father, my grandfather, did he ever hurt my mother?" "Hmm . . . " she sighed suddenly stopping. "That *is* hard to talk about, my Louli. Our father, your Opa, was a deeply disturbed man and in the end, a madman. But no, no, your mother was spared all that. Though she knew . . . " Somehow it became clear to me, Jutta was not.

And then planting a kiss on my forehead, she said, "We can talk more about this some other time. Oh, dear . . . do you know what a burden you lift from me, my sweet child?" squeezing my shoulder. "You were always so perceptive. May it never get you into trouble. May it light your way. Your father would be proud."

And coaxing me forward she laughed. "We'll expect word now in the next week—for better or for worse. We might even meet him!

Don't worry, Lou, I am here. Safe journey now," she said, giving the horse a slap and waving Karl on.

I watched as she walked back up the brick path and met Bettina at the door, both blowing a kiss to me. I was no more certain of my future, but on my trip back to Charlottenburg I did feel safe. In an angel's embrace, though she would have roared at that. No, just an ordinary woman of independent spirit who forged her own path, amazing really—a woman for whom giving was natural, its own reward. Jutta who had watched over so many and now me. There was much for me to learn in that.

And she would remain there to counsel me in life's give and take, its small crises and its celebrations that loomed so large ahead.

 ✑

Only a few years ago I was reminded of that day so long ago—with my mother and Aunt Jutta and Bettina all now deceased. I received a note from the sister of Karl Meierhof, the young man who managed Jutta's farm. The same young lad who had taken me to the station that day. Somehow she had managed to find me in Göttingen.

I remember pressing some coins into Karl's hand that evening as I hurriedly stepped down from Jutta's buggy and I was struck by his refusal (his surprising use of my aunt's first name): "Jutta wouldn't approve, Fräulein Salomé." But I insisted, and giving in, he said, "Then if I must, I'll give it to someone who can use it."

His sister was writing to report that Karl, who had inherited the land upon Jutta's death in 1919 (ostensibly from natural causes but no doubt of a broken heart, her Bettina having died of flu in 1918), was now dead too—a victim of the infamous Koepenicker Blut-woche. It was one of the first massacres of the Führer's maniacal SA. Not six months after Hitler's ascent to power, his thugs visited the seat of the workers' movement in Berlin, and lighting on

Koepenick on June 21 of 1933, they rousted a now aged Karl from Jutta's farm, and hauling him into one of their interrogation facilities, subjected him to all manner of torture, stripping him naked, hosing him down, beating him in the Wassersportheim and then leaving Karl, too old to run away, with dozens of others—all social democrats, Christians, Communists and other suspected enemies of the state—dead, in a heap by the side of the Wendenschloßtraße. It was a warning, a threat to all the citizenry, even those who came to collect the bodies, of the cost of defiance or even the rumor of association.

Karl's sister was writing me to say that Jutta's will had stipulated that her land was to go to the one who had tended it all those years and in the event of his death (Karl never having married), it was to go to me. She further explained that while the Nazis had now seized the farm and any lands of worth belonging to those who had died, Karl would have wanted me to know. Simply to honor Jutta's wishes.

Those monsters. They could extract life but not confiscate the soul nor the spirit—that vision of a hereafter now that the Juttas and the Karls of this world lived and died for, passing it along like a torch to those who followed to light another time. History will only tell if we are up to it—if we who knew them can find our way.

I remember her words, her tone, her voice from that visit as if it were today: "It's a threatening gloom out there," she said. "Even the birds have already taken cover." Strange, how these times can rob even our most natural words of innocence.

8

⁓

A Marriage of Strange Convenience

"Fred, my dearest . . . " *No, too coy, suspect. Bad start. That won't do.*

"Fred, I do love you. You know that . . . " *Pathetic defense.*

"Fred, there is something I've been meaning to discuss with you. It's about our impending nuptials." *No, no, that's not it at all. "Nuptials," what a noose of a word, if ever there was one! Don't lower the boom. It's not about the "nuptials." It's about living together.*

You look too grim. Smile now. Be tender. Assure him of your feelings for him. Besides, those are not in question. You want his sympathy now. You want him to help you figure this out. Declare your loyalty . . . tell him. Let him know what's troubling you. Ask him to decide. Do something with your hair! It looks like a nest no bird would flock to. . . . Oh, God, this isn't me!

I stood there before the long oval gold-leafed dressing mirror in my bedroom, trying to rehearse my words. Standing there slouching, on one hip, then the other, til I felt I would drop. Failing abysmally. My mouth in its lopsided, hopelessly sad slant, slanting to the truth. Nothing to do.

I had been fretting about this ever since I returned from my visit to Jutta some two weeks before. I knew she was right. I must be honest with him. If our marriage was to work at all, I knew what I had to do. "Honesty is all," she had said. "A relationship can be many things. No vows can dictate that." I knew I must tell him. I hoped she was right.

I saw him twice a week like clockwork for our dinners during those two weeks and though I was looking more and more a wreck torn by what I knew I must tell him, we'd been talking about a small wedding to take place in two months' time, about where we would live and what I would take with me and when we could finally relax into the safe haven of our work—he in his translation and I in an essay I'd been working on. But I had to get on with planning the event itself. A few people who would be present and some witnesses. And St. Petersburg must be notified. The ceremony most probably Lutheran, the readings of our choosing, perhaps even here with a willing pastor in the intimate setting of the place where we had met. It was all up to me to arrange. Frau Becker stood at the ready. But I was not.

I have always had trouble speaking my fears. But speak them I would, I'd decided, that evening after dinner. And since the words seemed to escape me, I tried to make myself presentable and prepared a light meal of salad, soup and vegetables with some wurst for me. He preferred a more vegetarian diet. There was a knock at the door. My heart stopped.

There stood Fred with a young Iranian student he'd been tutoring. "Lou, this is Farid, one of my tutees. I thought to invite him to our evening meal." I caught my breath. A reprieve. "Yes, Fred, of course, there's always room at our table for another guest. It's a light spread, I'm afraid. Do come in."

I led them into my small kitchen and looked to the open window and a willow that was swaying in the wind and felt its lumbering weight and I became immeasurably sad. They stood at my modest table as I pulled up another chair and laid down a table setting. As I reached for the platter of cold cuts and vegetables and placed the bowls of cold carrot soup, Fred uncorked a red wine, set out the goblets and filled a carafe with water. I thought to light some candles and thought again. No, too intimate. I scooped them up and lit a small oil lamp instead.

"Farid has just returned from his sister's wedding in Iran, Lou. He and Halil from Turkey should be here in the spring for ours. Perhaps here in Frau Becker's more expansive parlor setting, if that is how we choose to do it."

"I don't know, dear. Frau Becker is certainly willing and that would be lovely now, wouldn't it. I have yet to make those arrangements, to settle on all the details. Jutta will help me though, I'm sure, and I plan to be in touch with her in the coming week." I'd just about finished an essay I'd been writing for the *Gartenlaube* but now there were no excuses. No more excuses for what he must know.

Farid, hesitant before sitting down and fingering a package at his side, said, "Fräulein Salomé, I didn't mean to intrude on your dinner but I have here something for you, a gift for Professor Andreas and you from my family. It's a gift for your wedding and a tribute to Professor Andreas's work with me for which he accepts so little."

As we sat down, he handed to me a brown paper package that I opened to discover a beautiful long wide ivory silk scarf embroidered in gold with amazing markings I did not recognize. He explained that it was the gift of an aunt who had received it from her mother and who had not married but now wished to give it to him in gratitude to the man soon to be wed who had trained her nephew so well. He explained that this shawl, like others made for the Persian ceremony, had in it seven strands of colored thread and a needle meant to sew up the mother-in-law's lips to prevent them from ever speaking an unkind word to the bride. I thought we all have our guardian aunts, don't we, and, Fred's mother long dead, maybe this scarf coming from his Persian side would silence my mother instead.

I delighted in that, folding it gently, not wishing to get stuck by the needle. Confident that it was there. I would look later.

He sat there telling us of his sister's wedding, the ceremony and symbols, the pomegranates, the apples, the honey, the sugar cones, the light to the east, the bowl of water, representing enlightenment and purification, kicked over at the entryway of the bride and groom's new home. And I thought, listening to it all—the foreignness of it all, that it was suddenly possible. Though my pietistic faith would allow only so much joyous display, there was much to do here, a certain decorum and rituals to be observed. I must get on with it. As we finished our fruit dessert, Farid stood up making his excuses of an early morning class at the university and Fred saw him to the door, where our guest disappeared scaling two steps at a time up into the attic quarters Frau Becker let to students.

Fred joined me in my small sitting room, where I set down a bottle of port with two glasses before the gas hearth. We were alone in a huge silence made audible by the relentless tick of the clock, marking my time, steadying my racing heart. No escape now. We would talk.

"How lovely, Lou. Not our usual after-dinner stroll but it looks like an impending downpour out there. . . . Can I pour you some port?"

"Why yes, Fred, it's good now that we have a few quiet moments to talk. I've been meaning to for some time. . . . It's about our marriage. I've wanted to proceed with the arrangements. But something has been stopping me."

"What is it, Lou. What's troubling you?" he said, his piercing gaze trying to find my darting eyes and his hand stretching out to me. I stood up, my eyes welling, as I sipped the port and withdrew a few steps. Then turning I said, "Fred, I know I have accepted your hand. I know it is you I do want and I honestly wish to be your wife. But I fear I'll disappoint you. What I mean is, I cannot be a proper wife and for reasons that you cannot know, I barely understand myself, I fear I can't submit to a sexual union. Nor do I think I'll ever be able to. You must know this and I do not expect you to accept this condition . . . Fred."

He rose from his chair and pulled me gently to his chest and said, stroking my hair, "Lou, you are truly an extraordinary woman but these are just common jitters." I pulled away. "No, no Fred, you don't understand. You must let me go."

He was incredulous. He seemed to wander out of my orbit, his eyes lighting on every object but me, as I sank into a chair. He said in a whisper escalating to a full voice, "Lou, I do want you as my wife, my beloved for all time. . . . I have cherished your deep interest in my work, our walks, our talks, your face all these months and I have come to depend on you as surely as the first and last light of the day. I have never had that. . . . I don't pretend to understand your reasons."

"And I too, Fred, truly, . . . but I know this part of myself. It's not you; it is me, my limitation. I am sorry." I fought back the tears. And then pacing with a quizzical menaced look of a trapped animal he said: "I know you have lived here with another man and I have never questioned those relations. I've trusted you. I trust you now but no, now . . . this, I do not accept what you say . . . and I'd rather not go on at all, Lou, than be cast aside. It is an end for me."

And lurching to the hutch, he grabbed the penknife beside his pipe and opening the blade, he thrust it into his chest. I screamed in disbelief, rushing to hold him. Nothing connected. Slow floating images. The knife dropping like a forgotten implement, skittering on the floor. Blood oozing, first a spurt and then a blur of red into seaweed rust soaking into his shirt. Clutching one hand to his chest and my hand with the other, faint but still conscious, he sank into the chair. I ran to get a towel, pressing it against the wound, to stop, to stop . . .

I screamed "Fred, Fred, no my darling, never this" over and over again. And wailing for help. Frau Becker burst through the door shouting "My God, what have you done here?"

"No, no," Fred tried weakly, "Not her . . . leave her, leave her alone." And then ripping a sheet from the linens to wrap around his chest, she took command telling me to summon the doctor four doors down, number 17, Dr. Stengel.

I ran out into the street yelling, crying all the way, and knocking furiously at the door. A face sweet smiling, the maid, and then the grave doctor collecting his case, me explaining the accident, how serious, I could not say, "It's bad, we must be quick. He's injured himself with a knife to his chest, he's bleeding," I screamed, as I ran down the steps, with him in tow, racing back to Frau Becker's.

The doctor emerged from my bedroom that night and reported that it was a surface wound, that it could have been much worse, so close to the heart. Fred was resting now, he'd given him a sedative, but he must stay here and have strict bed rest for a day or two; he would return tomorrow to check the dressing to insure against infection. And then looking at me with a searching gaze, he said he must write up such incidents.

I stood there in a stupor not knowing what he was saying. But Frau Becker, overhearing the conversation, slipped out of the bedroom and inserted: "Herr Doctor Stengel, it was the professor who did this to himself. I know it. I was here and he told me so." "Well then," he said, closing his case, looking at me askance, "It shall be so." And she led him to the door.

No, no, I thought, I had not done this. It was he who wielded the knife. But my words had punctured his heart. They were the force. Frau Becker with an arm on my shoulder assured me he would be well and taking her leave said, "Lou, he's a good man. You must take care of one who would not live without you. Such men are few and far between." Did I need anything? No, I would be fine here by the fire. She'd look in on him in the morning. It was the first night we spent together—a violent act of self-assertion that launched our marriage even before any vows were spoken, lasting for decades through the calm and occasional storms of our natural lives. Fred had spoken, his heart not to be denied, and I heard him. . . .

Life in the days and weeks that followed became forgiving. I forgave him his insane foolishness and he forgave me my sexual fears. But in the way that violent things left unspoken often lie dormant on the tip of one's tongue, ready to be triggered by any random event, Fred's suicidal act that night was never really forgotten. It became in our heart of hearts something like Damocles' sword, a threat looming overhead, lest we tempt fate again. But in our everyday life, that night became almost instantly an "accident"—something not intended, something we survived long ago, best left behind. And something our marriage would prevent from ever happening again.

The wedding such as it was took place some two months later. Jutta had taken command of all the arrangements. When I wrote her about Fred's "accident," Jutta took it upon herself to drive her buggy alone across town a week later to visit me for a long chat over afternoon tea, and then stayed for our evening meal to meet Fred. Jutta advised me to stop harping on my fixation with abstinence, and if in hearing me, as he surely had, Fred still wished us wed, then that was his choice. We could make of our marriage what we wanted. But it would be best if we wed quickly (less time to have second thoughts or invite third parties to speak theirs on the matter).

Of course, mother had to be invited, though with Evgeny once again ill it was not at all clear that she or anybody else from my immediate family would be able to come. My older brothers were themselves away in military service. So in that event, it would probably be prudent, if not too odious for me, to invite Gillot, the pastor who had confirmed me, to perform the ceremony, if only to give my mother some peace of mind in having the St. Petersburg side of the family represented. Jutta would, of course, be my witness.

It was to be a small ceremony in Frau Becker's parlor, attended by just a few of Fred's students and colleagues from the university's department of diplomacy and two or three other friends I had managed to hold onto from my friendship with Paul—the Danish literary critic Georg Brandes, the philosopher Ludwig Haller and the experimental psychologist Hermann Ebbinghaus. Since Fred's parents had long since died, and an older brother had emigrated to America, only a couple of remaining cousins from Hamburg might come. All in all, with spouses included, the wedding party and guests were not likely to exceed thirty people.

Frau Becker would orchestrate the catering arrangements, the selection of wines and a fine champagne, the hiring of a harpist and flautist to provide some musical levity to the celebration, and Jutta would manage the very delicate communications with my mother and Gillot in St. Petersburg. She invited both, discouraging the one and then turning to the pastor as the only possible substitute for the bride's first of kin. As for me, I merely selected some readings—as Jutta gladly deferred that literary task to the "writer in the family."

And so as Jutta had predicted, it all went without a hitch and on one Saturday afternoon in early April of 1888, I stood with Fred facing Gillot under the canopy of Farid's white silk scarf, held on either side by Jutta and Bettina. We spoke our vows not to each other but to our reflection in a mirror that had been placed next to Gillot, whom we faced.

Looking back, this little concession to Eastern ritual was oddly symbolic of the marriage itself, for we did not lean on each other in the traditional sense, expecting a to and fro, a merging of opinion in our exchanges. Rather, we stood beside one another, close but always apart, pursuing separate paths in a common direction. Our shared life would advance in tandem, but our separate ways, though parallel, would at no point intersect. There was comfort in that for me and eventually for Fred too, I believe, though I'd never actually grasp the nature of that comfort. I merely accepted it.

Gillot would never know of this, our most unusual unspoken vow of wedded union, and I would be the last to give him the satisfaction of imagining the least advantage over Fred. Though as we spoke our vows that April afternoon, dipping our ring fingers into a bowl of honey (a little creative flourish of Jutta's from her reading of Eastern wedding rites), Fred surprised Gillot and me by using the Germanic "Friedrich Carl" which he would continue to use as his legal name thereafter. As I completed my vow in response, we turned to each other and I tasted the sweet fruit of his smile against my quivering lips, feeling then the quickened pulses of both our hearts in our first public kiss to the applause of our guests. We had done it. I was truly buoyant and happy at that moment. Despite it all, we were one.

Later at the reception, Gillot quipped, "Well, Lou, I see you are ever 'Lou,' but Fred has taken the name you no doubt have chosen for him. This too is a confirmation of sorts," harkening back to my own confirmation in Sandpoort and the name he had given me. But resisting his claim on me, I mused: "Yes, Hendrik, but in this instance Fred has imposed nothing on me. Only on himself. What a lovely gift, don't you think, and a sign of trust for a husband to give his heart not only in spirit but in his very name to his wife in return for her taking his surname? Mother would be pleased. I trust you as her emissary will tell her."

Raising his glass to me, he nodded an assenting touché, saying, "Frau Andreas, if I may, you are as quick as ever and right of course. That is the least I can do. May you both prosper and especially you,

Lou, in your marriage." He took my hand and kissed the ring finger, and he turned making his farewells. I would never see him again.

Looking back it is so disturbing, painful really, to think that in invit-ing Gillot to officiate at my wedding and even in confronting him there I somehow still needed his blessing.

Our wedding bands we returned to Jutta at the end of the cere-mony that evening (they were hers and her long deceased hus-band's), we having yielded to tradition for just so long—the length of the ceremony.

Such was our bond without bands. We moved to quarters at Fred's flat in Tempelhof and then, wanting a larger apartment with a study and outdoor space, we eventually moved to a garden apart-ment with its own orchard on the perimeter of the city in Schmar-gendorf. Our life during those first years was carefree and somewhat bohemian, our company more frequently artists than academics. We joined a theater group championing the bold naturalist movement, the "Freie Bühne." We ate natural foods. We dressed simply. Fred donned the peasant shirts of my native Russia and I obliged by walk-ing barefoot in our garden. We read up on utopian communities and breathed the air of naturalism. We celebrated the unbridled explo-ration of every aspect of our human nature—with the exception of its sexual component. I avoided the subject, reconciling my fears by thinking that marriage, our marriage, had triumphed over our baser instincts, and likewise I refused to see why anyone involved in a sex-ual relationship would see marriage as a next or necessary step. Or vice versa. That was *our* choice. Or so I told myself.

I have never been able to accurately portray what my husband meant to me during those first years. That he lived with my refusal suggests a man of superhuman interests, but he was my security and so much more. What in fact he opened up for me was a more visceral sense of the world, of the not quite human—the world of animals.

We would certainly, given the circumstances, not have children, but dogs we acquired with abundance over the years. The first was the most rambunctious and memorable of all for the strengths and weaknesses it brought out in both of us. He was a puppy when we got him—a beagle we named "Dar," short for Darwin. Just as Darwin's theory was at the time unleashing a wildfire throughout the world order, Dar the "Unter-Hund" (Under-Dog), as we called him, was spreading havoc in our small household.

Darwin won his nickname for his inimitable fondness for those apples that fall not too far from the horse. Prowling the streets of our small village he would return with his finds firmly clenched in his teeth and deliver them onto our doorstep, one after the other. Fred, in discovering his bounty, declared, "Well, dear Lou, we have all heard of the 'Superman,' but what we have here is a true revelation— 'Darwin, the Under-Dog,' returning to us the stuff of creation. We are what we eat." And we erupted in laughter as Darwin yelped with his squeaking puppy howl. Fred added, "Your Fritz would love to see this now, wouldn't he, Lou? A challenge to his Z!" "Yes, dear, I think he probably would have something outrageous to say to this," I smiled. "But I somehow think this little mutt's namesake would approve."

I was largely immersed in writing religious essays in those early years—one on the real Christianity, another on "Jesus the Jew," and after studying the spiritual life of my husband's Eastern focus, an essay on "the Problem of Islam." Darwin wasn't much impressed. He would eat them and I would return from marketing or from the university to find them strewn in shreds on the floor. And I would have to begin again. I had always been a one-off sloppy writer. But Darwin required me to rewrite and rethink, and so these essays were probably my most refined. If I could not restrain him, I could at least restrain myself. Or so I told myself.

I was grappling with my own life choices at the time and with the spirituality that had obsessed me since my youth and that had driven me somehow to seek refuge in a curious detachment from human relationships and real life. Maybe this abstinence I now observed with my husband was all of a piece. I began to see this spiritual feeling as false and yet completely central to the person I thought myself to be.

Though I no longer believed in a God out there, I still professed a deeply religious sentiment. I set out to explore on paper the origins of this schism between my own godless thinking and my faithful personal feeling, and I looked to the history of religions for some answers. I couldn't be the only one feeling this way. These religious essays began shedding light on all my personal relationships, with Gillot, Paul, Fritz and now Fred. As new insights into the nature of spirituality spilled onto the page, I gradually began to define a faith I could finally embrace as my own.

I was staking a claim on faith—a hope of renewal. And my conclusions about religion didn't take me into the institutions of faith but into the very heart of human feeling—my own. I found myself taking exception to Fritz's notion of an anti-Christ. While I had admired Fritz's courage for critiquing orthodox religion, he had renounced not only a Godhead, but all religious sentiment as well. That cut too close to the heart. There may not be a god out there to believe in but there was definitely a human heart primed to believe. How did this happen? How had we, how had I been so forsaken?

God was to me what we made of him, I wrote, and was born of our desire to reconcile two contrary human impulses, *Demut* and *Hochmut*, humility and hubris, our need to serve and be saved, and our need to control and master. Faith was a tightrope, but not Fritz's superman's tightrope over inferior man. Faith was a tightrope bridging a chasm traversing two points: one, our reality of "I am nothing"; the other, our desire of "I am all."

You see, God was manmade. Proof of our human imagination. God could better do without us than we could without him. The

Fritzes and Pauls, the intellectuals and scientists of the world, may have outgrown him and others institutionalized him like a museum piece, an artifact of times gone by. But to hordes out there whose lot was miserable, God in his almighty invisible presence was their only hope for a future and his church scions were there to exploit that need.

So despite our enlightened world, as I saw it, faith's hold was overpowering not just to those who blindly believed but to those moderns who professed by habit. And even those who had lost their faith could be left with a profound gaping feeling. The hole of a need, which they were powerless to fill. It was an entirely emotional need couched in spiritual garb.

I came to see this religious sentiment without a god as a moving force in my life, the questing voice of poetry, my reach for the noble wisdom of philosophy. The natural instinct to be more than human, more than who we are.

I began to see my relationships with men—my early pursuit of the man who of course could not take God's place—in a more critical light. Though I had not intentionally misled my suitors and my husband, I began to see myself as completely deluded and even manipulated as to my own intentions.

In one essay I showed how this religious sentiment played a role in the entire evolution of religions. Man needed a god against nature's threats, thus created a god and his laws, believed and relied on him for social cohesion, and then, advancing in our knowledge, outgrew this created god. Though my knowledge of the workings of the world could release me from reliance on God's objective interventions, my need to know that I would not die in vain, that I was one with the universe, was still there. My research on Islam also revealed that the great character of that originating culture would be subverted by its institutions. I predicted that the great religions of the world would eventually expend their usefulness, but religious sentiment and its social conventions would live on in a multitude of gods designed to suit our individual yearning.

The last Christian essay, "Jesus the Jew," went out into the world and eventually brought an unforgettable young poet into my life. In it I made the outrageous claim that Jesus himself had known his own limits of faith, limits any one of us could know of this world, the certainty of despair, when he cried out at the end of his life to a father who had not saved him, "Father, why have you forsaken me?"

But his brothers, his followers, would not let him go. Faith was the tether—their hold on his death, and on their life. Jesus was that first courageous unbeliever, a poet speaking his disbelief. And years later that other young poet would echo that same plea at the end of his life in the first line of his greatest cycle, the *Duino Elegies:* "Who if I cried would hear me in the angelic orders?"

Fred read them all and actually wept, saying, "Lou, these will not be accepted or published soon. You know that. Perhaps not even in our lifetime. But they will find their time, Lou, and their audience." I clutched him and kissed him, he stroking my hair, and I loved him all the more for his faith in me. We sat as we now did many an evening in our garden under the full bloom of a magnolia tree with apple trees lining its perimeter. The cicadas were buzzing their chorus and Darwin was chewing away at the poor lilac bushes, delivering to me sprigs for which he howled insistently for a reward.

Fred had not changed and was ever there in our chaste intimacy. He challenged our vow only once during an afternoon nap, and reacting as violently to his passion as he had that night to my refusal, I awakened to my hands around my husband's neck. Kissing me, my lips, my head, my breast, he retreated, saying: "No, Lou, my dear, you mustn't fear me. Never me. Never again. Because I love you."

And now I'd come to understand through these writings the false guard of my own religious sentiment. No, our married life would not be any different. We had squelched all sexual attraction from the very beginning. But I began to feel the pain of loves I had forsaken in my life. And writing my way into my own need, I heard my own heartbeat and became aware of desire I had denied.

Yes, I would write more, a novel perhaps and something about Fritz's work and Ibsen who was all the rage—all the wild ducks—his women who interested me. But that was intellectual work—more of the same. More to the point I would have to love and live differently.

I would be tempted. Frieda von Bülow, an adventurer, an artist and patron of the arts who had spent a great deal of her life in Africa, came into my life and it was at one of her soirees in Berlin that I met him.

Georg Lebedour, a journalist, who standing there in the milling crowd at Frieda's evening party, approached me and blurted: "What no ring, what's this?" To which I said: "We actually forgot them at the wedding and decided that must be a sign, they were best left forgotten." He let go a hearty laugh and patted my shoulder.

He reminded me of Paul when I first met him that night in Rome, the same kind of swaggering *je ne sais quoi* attitude, and I wanted to know him all the more. Frieda was introducing the star of the evening, the dramatist Gerhardt Hauptmann, but Georg's dark eyes were tracking me and mine skirting his glance.

He was a French socialist journalist sporting a blue work shirt and shoulder-length wily black hair pulled back under a black beret with worker's insignia and he took our abandonment of rings to be a signal of openness in our relationship that he couldn't know was quite the opposite, but was all too eager to exploit. And so he would not make a hasty farewell that evening, or on others for that matter.

He was ferocious in his pursuit, like a dog. He was open, show-ing up on our doorstep, having read a piece I'd written on women's psychology and another on Ibsen's women published in the *Freie Bühne*. We talked for some time. He baited me for parallels to a do-mestic life that must have reflected absences in my own. He was tall and gangly, smart, sensual, a bit wild and absolutely political—a man of radical action—not Paul at all. And yes, I did want him. I confided my attraction that evening to my girlfriends, Frieda von Bülow and Johanna von Niemann, the desire he unleashed in me and my resistance, no longer religious but human, the bond that I had sealed with Fred—a bond that my senses nonetheless moved to break.

But Georg was a man of no restraints. No proofs required, just action. And before long, he wanted to insinuate himself into our home. At first, Fred was welcoming, but soon he became restless, realizing something unhinged in this suitor's intentions.

I wrestled with Fred: "No, it's his socialist bent. It knows no bounds. He wants me to write for the *Forward*." I wrestled with Georg's insistence, his insights into the sexual hypocrisy of my marriage, but soon came to resent him for intruding.

Georg, intuiting my attraction and undaunted by my refusal, regarded it all as a "political moment," as he would say, whose time had not yet come. He was shortly thereafter thrown into prison for his political activities, and though I visited him once in prison to acknowledge what we knew to be the truth but what would never be, his confinement spared me my marriage. He sent me a note declaring his own inner and outer revolution, but ceding to my "no," saying, "Don't worry Lou. You will find your moment but from where I sit, dear Lou, know your kind of 'normal' is nice." It was a bittersweet call to arms, a call to rise up from my complacency, that I resisted.

Fred for his part was sad and wandering. He knew I had changed, that though we were ever together, I would find a separate way. He said, "You miss him, Lou, don't you, though I am relieved. But you must do what makes you happy." I would assure him, "No, it's you, old man, who makes me happy."

As my heart raced and I was quick to pacify him, I knew full well he'd understood this flirtation. And calmly tousling my hair and kissing the crown of my head, just as he did with Darwin, he let me go, saying, "Yes, Lou, you are my girl, my dear girl."

WHAT madness then in those days of the nineties. The world was festering, priming for change. Charlotte was confined to the rest cure of her room: I closed that fine book, Charlotte Gilman's *The Yellow Wallpaper,* and it opened a world that resonated to me and all the women around me.

My women friends were crying out to me for some statement of allegiance and I had only myself and my nose in Ibsen and all his women, all those wild ducks, Nora and Hedda and all their anonymous sisters confined in extreme circumstances to their homes in the attic. And as I would later find out, another Emma, it may just as well have been cousin Emma of my youth, an Emma Eckstein, was treated for her depression upon her father's death by my dear Professor Freud, who together with Wilhelm Fleiss, a neurologist, proceeded to operate on her nose, unwittingly disfiguring her, leaving her forever in pain but still a faithful servant of analysis. And yet another, Anna O., for her part, resisted her treatment for hysteria in mocking consternation, calling it "the talking cure—the experience unleashing in her a determination to champion a burgeoning movement to tend to poor women through social work. And there were untamed others that I would later read about, hordes of maverick prairie women across the sea who traded their attics for the wanton bonds of roving prostitution—one Etta Place, who, roaming with Butch and Sundance in their outlawed escape to the southern Americas, would eventually abandon the siege, returning home sick and alone.

Charlotte, Nora, Emma, Anna O., Etta and all the nameless others suffering their rebellion and their confinement and I in my own, knowing its limits but limits I had accepted as a vow. Yes, I believed women must be free and equal but I also knew we were different.

For myself, I may have let go of my pursuit of the man-God but not of my womanly soul.

I was the oddest duck of all those wild ducks in the attic. I loved my space, closeted in my nest with Fred and Dar, and though I recognized my instinct to be free, a freedom I'd openly declared, I internally fought it. I waited now for the breath, the breath I knew would come, that sounding in a flutter would finally take hold and lift me out, out there into the wilderness. No, it would not be a husband driving me out, or a doctor's promise of cure or a bandit's lure of adventure. As it happened, it would be a song—a song I could not resist.

INTERLUDE

So many promises we can't keep
So many promises we still seem to need.
So many marriages just not to speak
So many promises . . . broken . . .

A fragment of a poem I never finished. Yeah, I think I know what she did. Married on the rebound. For the safety. And I guess old Fred held her hostage for the promise she couldn't keep . . . and she him in an odd way for that secret love that did not break her resolve but lodged like a stone in her heart. He held her hostage with a life. No, not a child. No chance of that. Sexless marriage. Held her hostage with his own life. Must have known she couldn't go. How bizarre. How ordinary. Insane marriage of convenience. A holding pattern. A home. They must have needed that. What an odd duck she was but a wild strong one. He must have known she would fly. She must have known he would keep her. Strange, perfect, meant for each other.

I look at that unfinished poem from a marriage now long split up and I fold it neatly into my desk drawer as a keepsake. Of what, I don't know. My hard-won independence? Funny, how it all changes. Can't feel the fire or pain of those words anymore. I remember the public wars back then but not the private hurts. Where did they go?

Computer's down. No e-mail. Set pen to paper. Snail mail. Have to send off a note to that son of mine. Haven't heard in a while, but he's young, out filming, dating, I hope. And that other "geriatric" wayward one. What's his excuse? Saving the planet. Does he really have to go so far, to the ends of the earth to make his point? Well, I'll be brief in my note . . .

I look around this study of mine—yesterday's coffee cup, crumbs here and there, open books strewn all over the place, Post-its with scribbled notes on the walls, a month's laundry in the corner and there on top of it all that old rag-doll of mine, now limbless. That puppy'll eat anything. And I can hear my mother saying "Anna, your room is a reflection of your mind." And I smile. It will all keep til tomorrow. Still got some time left here. Get back to Lou.

"Meant for each other." Well, for her maybe. But for me? There seem to be so many ways. How does one ever know?

9

❧

Rainer and a
Morning Star

. . . I often stop and wonder
Why I appeal to men
How many times I blunder
In love and out again . . .
Falling in love again
Never wanted to
What am I to do
I can't help it.

"Falling in Love Again," The Blue Angel

A song resonates from the new radio box into the stillness of my living room in Göttingen—lingering like an echo announcing the ghost of a long forgotten visitor. This disembodied voice, her falling notes—a relief from the constant rant of that one weasel's staccato claims for space *über alles.*

Not here. Never.

Fred and Dar, they have departed this world. Here now with just a low somber female voice moaning her need for love—renouncing

155

the hold of man, I am alone. How many men lost in the war, how many hopes lost in the fall of Weimar. How many now to follow a tyrant? And this young woman with her long throaty lugubrious song. What had she lost? Though her body has strayed into the blank recesses of memory, that voice of hers rings as clear as the bells tolling the hour and the certainty of our most uncertain tomorrows.

I met her in 1923 or '24 when she was just a damsel in her twenties, at a soiree given by Alma Mahler Gropius in Weimar attended by architects, analysts and artists. Alma brought the young aspiring actress over to meet the "muse of her favorite poet, Rilke," she said. I blanched and then looking into those soulful blue eyes I pushed her away, wincing at a stabbing pain of the girl I had lost so long ago, never had known, saying, "No, no, my dear, Rainer was always his own inspiration. If anything, I was merely his ear."

Tossing my head back I laughed with an absurd trill. She looked perplexed, hurt, retreating, those wide pleading eyes so wanting to become someone she was not and mine looking into hers and suddenly wanting to cry, when her gaze lit on my shoulders and she said in a startling baritone, "Frau Salomé, those boas are magnificent. I must try that."

And so she did, I am told, "fox boas and a monocle"—her trademark. I would never see her again but the world would in celluloid. Her world-weary voice now floating out famously into the cave of my old age. Her Lola in *The Blue Angel*—a stylized female, the invention of a child who truncated her given servile Christian name Magdalena into Marlene—becoming the modern Madonna-whore who was all the rage and they loved her, ever tantalizing, leaving before she was left. Who had cast her off so early, I wondered? This girl who now survived in the rapture of an immortal lament, falling over and over again in and out. Her song.

Not mine. No, true, falling in love was not something I ever expected but once I had, that love was everlasting. Let me tell you about it. It happened for me before the turn of the century and it was wondrous.

⁓

He was her poet, and now the world's, but to me back then and ever since he was simply my first true love, a love awakening my pleasure and beginning his song.

Desire!

> *How shall I hold my soul, so that it*
> *Does not touch on yours? How should I*
> *lift it beyond you, to other things?*
> *Oh, I would gladly shelter it amidst*
> *lost shadows of some forgotten spot where*
> *it might not swing when your depths stir.*
> *But all that touches us, yes everything*
> *brings us together like the bow-string*
> *which pulls from two strings a single chord.*
> *Over what instrument are we so tightly drawn?*
> *By the hand of which violinist are we thus born?*
> *Oh sweet song.*

—"Love-Song," Rainer Maria Rilke

It was a tumultuous time, those years at the turn of the century—change was fomenting, workers' movements organizing. The impressionist painters who left their studios to look outdoors to a new naturalistic vision of the common man began to look inward, to turn the mirror to the eye of the singular beholder. All hell was preparing to break loose. A Norwegian artist Edvard Munch had painted his vision *The Scream,* opening the psychic floodgates into the wilderness of our human angst. I was just part of that flock really, more than ready to fly—wild duck that I'd been in my chosen attic. Though it would not be an artist's image but a poet's gaze that would give me wings.

René Maria Rilke was just twenty-one or twenty-two, a fledgling poet from Prague when I met him and I, well, I was in my late thirties. I had become known not just for my fiction appealing to the popular sentiments of women but for two critical scholarly books—one on Nietzsche's writings, the first in fact, and the other on Ibsen. The critics who til then had loved to hate my fiction now hated loving my criticism, combing through every insight, debating the why and the wherefore of those books. How dare she psychoanalyze the Great Philosopher? How dare *she—a woman*—critique the playwright's portraits of women? So my presence was a must at soirees throughout Germany and Austria. It was at just such a gathering at the novelist Jakob Wasserman's apartment in Munich in May of 1897 that I would meet him.

Rilke was a lithesome unprepossessing young man with large luminous blue eyes, hair slicked back, a wispy blond goatee and a pad stuck in the vest pocket of his loden jacket. He had actually approached me while I was in the middle of an argument with an older quite apoplectic balding gentleman with flushed cheeks and jowls that rippled, as he accused me loudly of heresy: "How could you name Jesus himself an unbeliever? How un-Christian. You, madam," he offered, "disgrace us with nothing more than the pseudo-intellectual fantasies of an effete infidel. There's a hell for your kind."

I stood aghast, thinking, "and I the one to defend religious sentiment?"

Suddenly a young man intervened, saying, "I've been within earshot of your rant, sir. And I must say it is most intolerant and offensive. It's foolish that you don't see the depth of this woman's investigations into the very human quest of a great spiritual leader." In the meantime, Jakob had come over to rescue me from this assault.

"Lou, I see you've met René. I have someone I want to introduce you to, that most remarkable comedic playwright, Carl Sternheim."

Rainer quietly taking his cue ushered my critic away in animated conversation to a corner, turning to me to say, "I'm honored, Frau Salomé. Another time, perhaps. Soon, I hope." I remember being struck by that luminous gaze emitting an aura of eternal youth through doleful eyes always looking up.

Who was he? I thought then and still ask myself today. Though our lives would intertwine—body and soul—I would only come to know him truly in his words. They were his life, his true passion, though he didn't know that yet.

I was a decade into marriage then and Fred and I had learned how to give each other plenty of leeway. We traveled, often separately, meeting up here and there, with Fred returning home to attend to his classes and his research in Berlin, while I, vagabond that I was and mobile with my writing, would travel sometimes for weeks and months on end, spending six weeks here and six weeks there with welcoming friends.

That spring of 1897 I was visiting my dear friend Frieda von Bülow in Munich. It was there at the Pension Quistorp where we were both staying in the heart of the student district of Schwabing, the day after my brief encounter with the young poet from Prague, that I received a single red rose and a most effusive note opening with the line, "Yesterday was not the first twilight hour that I was graced with your presence." And then going on to say that my essay "Jesus the Jew" had been the inspiration for his poem cycle *Visions of Christ* (which I had never read, much less heard of), he continued: "It was cause for jubilation when I discovered—what my dream epics render in visions was expressed here so masterfully with the gigantic force of holy conviction. . . . Through this unshakable parsimony, through the relentless force of your words, my work became consecrated and was sanctioned in my feeling."

I was dumbfounded by his words, feeling less worthy with each new phrase: "holy conviction," "unshakable parsimony," "consecrated work." I was made almost giddy by this breathless overture from this clearly intimate but anonymous admirer, closing his note with the seal of his solicitude: "When someone thanks another for something truly valuable, that gratitude should remain a secret between the two parties." And then, the coy punctuating note, his pièce de résistance: "My thanks are but long overdue and their expression is but a sign."

"A sign," I shrieked, "a sign of what?" What secret? In any event, it was a secret I could not keep, running immediately to Frieda with note in one hand and rose in the other, plunking myself into an overstuffed chair in the sitting room and reciting as tears rolled down my cheek the high drama of this suitor's plea.

Was this to be believed? Who could he be? Frieda smiled and looking me squarely in the eyes holding me down with hands on both my shoulders as if I should know: "Well, my dear, all I can say is I haven't seen you this lively in years." My heart *was* palpitating wildly. But who do you think, who, I wondered out loud. "Why—your defender of yesterday evening, of course. The young poet, Rilke from Prague. Quite a passionate fellow it would seem. I think they call him René. . . . That name's rather sensitive though, but he's not at all shy, now is he, and you certainly had an effect on him."

That was Rainer. He was from the beginning not to be believed. He was by nature exuberant and his words were always and forever stretching to catch up to him, to contain that feeling. We met the following evening after a theater performance in the Gartnerstrasse and then he simply showed up the next day with his *Visions of Christ* and my Nietzsche book in one hand and a fistful of roses in the other.

Reason or passion, business or pleasure. He was determined to make his case in whatever way he could. Rainer was young and his vision was unclouded and I seemed to occupy the heart of his gaze. I was established and recognized for my work at that point but

Rainer offered something that seemed pure: a deep and necessary affection that I for once did not deny or control.

There is no explaining love—not ours or anybody else's—so there was never any rationale for our behavior. From that earliest of times in May 1897, we became constant companions, and our friendship, though discreet, knew no shame or blame. My marriage didn't stop us. The age difference didn't matter to us (though I was sometimes mistaken for his sister and then once, to my annoyance, his mother!). Fame, desirable as it was, seemed arbitrary then. But the moment, the urgency of our banter, was all we lived for and we had that insane heightened sense that only lovers do that at any moment we could lose it all.

I was charmed by Rainer, overwhelmed by his naïve devotion and enticed by his sense of high drama. Not three weeks after we had found each other that moment of peril had arrived, when Rainer received a draft notice requiring him to report to the military office in Prague within a week's time. We escaped to a country inn on Lake Starnberg outside Munich for a couple of days and there under threat of parting we consummated our union to a chorus of cicadas and toasted our good fortune with a 3 A.M. breakfast under the lakeside canopy of cypress trees.

When it comes right down to it, there are no words to describe the feeling, that feeling of terror and delight, flying out of your self, inhabiting his body and him possessing yours. The thrill of soaring surrender. That unsurpassed moment of joy that makes the whole world seem trivial and silly by comparison. No there are no words for it. What Rainer gave me, what I felt there for the first time.

As we lay on our backs under a full moon I remember pointing out to Rainer that the moonlight was just a reflection of the sun and that its light had traveled untold distances to peek through the sentries of cypresses and spy this moment. And shooting an impish glance my way Rainer said: "Now Lou, you may think the moon is spying on us but I'd say, she's 'consecrating' this moment." And I kicked up my legs and we burst into howling laughter like a couple of baying coyotes. Then he turned to me and stroking the side of my face said: "See that bright one, that planet out there, our morning star. She's there night and day, whether we see her or not. Never mind, let them all conspire—the sun and the moon and the stars. Tonight, my darling, you alone are real to me."

And in the days that followed, he proceeded to celebrate his conquest in verse: "You my June night with a thousand paths / On which before me no initiate walked." The threat of parting turned out to be premature as only a week later I received a postcard from Prague announcing he was "free," that he had received a deferral for unspecified health reasons (his temperament all too obviously not up to soldiering was my guess) and that he would be returning on the next train to Munich.

With that reprieve, reality would begin to set in for us and we were forced to craft a mode of working together and a communal life with other artists that would justify our tryst. We needed some cover. We took a house with Frieda and others that summer in Wolfratshausen outside Munich (we called it "Loufried," replete with a homemade banner across the door) and with the arrival of visitors our barely six-week idyll was over.

The Russian critic Volynsky came and the painter August Endell and Frieda's endless stream of would-be adventurers out for a weekend in the country of being regaled by Frieda's stories of her colonial exploits in Africa. And finally Fred came too for a week or so, making no bones about his own discomfort with the communal experience, describing Rainer as an "earnest young man" and urging me to come home before too long, "with him, if you must, just not all the rest of them."

And when I asked him if he wanted a full accounting of my life away from him, he let go an abrupt laughing "no," saying, "Now Lou,

I think we have survived living this way long enough to spare each other any unnecessary details." It was his first and last admission of a trust that would withstand our separate intimacies. Less than a decade later our maid Maria would bear Fred a daughter whom he would never acknowledge legally as his own but whose mother I would see through her confinement and whom we would look after throughout our lifetimes in our home.

Rainer was no more enamored of communal living than Fred. And so he would occasionally escape into Munich to meet with his father on a weekend to shield him from seeing his living arrangement and cutting off his monthly stipend. But Rainer's distress with our artists' commune had nothing to do with propriety and everything to do with a lover's single-minded possession. And I had til then never allowed myself to be possessed.

During this period he wrote a sequence of poems, *In Celebration of You,* that were perfectly awful in their romantic appeal to me as the noble lady to his medieval knight: his "heart burning before her mercy, like a lamp before the image of Mary" (his letter to me, June 9, 1897). Mind you, I loved Rainer's sentiment but refused to be immortalized as his muse. His execution too raw spilling into unbridled feeling. No, no. Rainer yielding to my every wish, as if he could do nothing else, promised me not that he would stop writing these poems but that they would never be published in my lifetime.

Instead I urged him to produce a companion sequence *In Celebration of Me,* which did not come naturally to him but was published immediately and seemed to strike a narcissistic nerve with the general public. Even early on, not three weeks into our love affair, he was sounding the notes of an unrequited medieval singer: "I am yours just as the last tiny star belongs to the night that hardly knows it and does not recognize its light" (June 8, 1897).

He was besotted and I was too. His love seemed boundless and he was fearless to defend it. I remember once during those first few weeks while hiking a forest trail, we came upon a wild boar with her two sows. She instantly let out a squeal, began to gnarl and stamp her front hooves. Rainer jumped in front of me as I stepped backward, tumbling into the bushes, screaming "Rainer!"—causing the boar to seize up—and then dropping to his knees, he crouched in utter stillness and without even a blink stared down the critter. With Rainer in his stony pose completely lost in looking, the poor confounded animal soon lost interest, turned and trundled into the woods.

There was something about that early scene that captured Rainer's power for me—his utter command as he retreated into the silence—fearless to defend me against outside threats—whether it be critics' cries of heresy, a wild boar in the forest, a commune member's claims on my time, the imagined wrath of my husband. But as I would learn, his true fears, the lethal ones, were never of this world but born of his implacable worrying, hopelessly imagined, giving rise to physical complaints and the real almost palpable terror of falling into a bottomless chasm of despair.

I would soon discover he was powerless to defend himself against his own need. His love may have been boundless but his own need was even greater. He needed someone, something to intercede for him against the gravity of his own insecurities. He told me of a recurring nightmare from earliest memory of losing his footing and falling along with a loosened gravestone, inscribed with his name, into a pit—with no trace left of the man or the name for any passerby to notice.

When I think back to Rainer then as a young poet who had yet to come into his own, I am struck by how huge his aspirations were, yet how humble his expectations. Though he would rely on me early on to pull him out of periodic funks, and I would of course, because I loved him, it would be in the end his words that would provide the ballast of his life, his words and not me that would ultimately save him.

At the end of our summer idyll Rainer followed me to Berlin, renting a room in the Pension Waldheim on the Hundkehlestraße just around the corner from our home in Schmargendorf (an easy destination for our circumspect afternoon and occasional nocturnal encounters). There we resolved to read and study together as I continued my magazine work, a larger critical piece on Russian literature, and Rainer tried to establish inroads into the literary scene in Berlin.

At that time, René Rilke was considered a minor yokel from Bohemia, known if he were known at all for somewhat histrionic/mystical plays performed on minor stages, and yes, then as the months progressed in Berlin as my "curious companion, far too young" for me. Whatever people thought of our affair, they seemed far more critical of our age difference, and I'm afraid Rainer's true intentions were almost always suspect. Never by me.

In our home though, Rainer was a constant dinner guest and Fred enjoyed his conversation, his earnest inquiry into Fred's research. So Rainer was part of our home life and he would frequently let himself into our garden and the kitchen entrance in the late afternoon and prepare a salad, cold cuts and cheese for the evening meal that we would all share together in the open air of our garden.

Fred was pressing him to pursue his interests at the university and ease his struggle within the literary world by acquiring some useful academic credentials. But Rainer eschewed all formal routes—fearful that his creative instinct would be stifled in criticism.

"Lou, you know me, darling, I always embarrass myself when I try to go a prescribed path."

People, friends, that is, were asking me, "Who is he Lou, what is it with you two, now really?" And I responded, "Rainer is a fine poet,"—biting my tongue, and though I knew he was not yet, I did know too that the passion, the single-minded intensity, the poet was indeed there. He just needed the discipline and the fierce force of his words would come.

So much for my promotion of my lover's earlier career. Strange, as it would turn out, in the same way that I spent this last decade faithful to his memory, I spent those first years of the nearly thirty we would know each other faithful to his dream. I was always faithful to words, to dreams and to memory; people were another matter. In between, the man would slip away, my fidelity, ours, would falter.

That fall, Rainer, who had changed his name from René to the stronger masculine Germanic "Rainer" at my urging, was rebuffed in his efforts to crack Berlin's pantheon of lyric poets, presided over by that Teutonic incarnation of the Greek gods—the inimitable insufferable Stefan George. A poet of pure forms, Stefan embodied his work and wrapped himself in it like an austere monument to antiquity, invoking awe, radiating distance. He was the prodigious writer of admittedly perfect verse the human heart could not inhabit.

We were invited to a reading that November in Berlin given by and in honor of the eminence himself and afterward Rainer had ingratiated himself with no short order of sycophantic posturing, only to have George cast him aside as a "dilettante" and deny him even a subscription to their literary journal. (I was suddenly thrust back into the shaming memory of Wagner and his acolytes in Bayreuth.) The whole affair was made all the more humiliating by the fact that I had praised George for his exquisite formal eloquence and singular contribution to German lyric in an article I had just published.

Rainer was crestfallen but resurfaced, joining of all things "The Club of German Dilettantes" under whose auspices he arranged a series of prominent lectures on German letters, and he reserved an important one for himself on lyric poetry in the spring in his hometown of Prague.

BOTH Rainer and I began to feel the strain of too much togetherness, the grating reminders of our professional imbalance, and instead of my being his unqualified advocate, I had somehow become the measure of his failure: "My struggles are your long-won victories and for this reason I stand so small before you. But my new victories belong to you, and these are what I am permitted to give you . . . "

His appeals to me became confessional. His hypersensitivity now seemed to overwhelm him. He once compared this complete openness to all sensation to the misguided blossoming of a flower: "I am like a little anemone I once saw in my garden in Rome. . . . It had opened up so wide during the day that it could not close during the night! It was terrible to see it in the dark meadow, wide-open still inhaling everything through its wide open throat—with the much too imposing night above that would not be consumed."

He would announce himself strong and up to the challenge: "I question myself so often these days, as always in a time of great change. I am in the first dawn of a new epoch—I am expelled from the garden in which I have tarried and grown weary so long." And then he would sink back into a plea for simple communion with me and the wish for the modest disclosure—"confession," he said: "Til that time when I will speak to you quite simply and you will simply understand."

I was powerless to help him, my presence becoming almost an impediment to him helping himself. We needed to separate. Rainer would take a two-month holiday studying the art of Florence at the beginning of the year and then go on to Prague to deliver his lecture, and I, well I, I just didn't know.

Jutta came to us one afternoon in December, sending a messenger the day before telling me that she had to deliver some urgent news. She arrived that afternoon with Bettina and I ushered them into our den where Rainer and I had been working on a piece he had written for the popular magazine the *Gartenlaube*.

Fred was not yet home from the university. We made pleas-
antries and Rainer, addressing Jutta, said: "It's so lovely to finally
meet Lou's angel aunt." And Jutta blushed as I'd never seen her do
and she firmly grasped his hand in both of hers and said, "Yes, yes,
you are Lou's poet, I know, I've heard so much about you. You must
give us both now something to take home with us to read." Rainer
nodded saying, "Why yes, of course," and retreated with Bettina to
the kitchen to simmer a pot of soup they had brought with them,
and then went out for a brief walk with her to allow Jutta and me
some time.

I stoked the coal fire and Jutta pulling me to a chair said: "Louli,
I have word from St. Petersburg and your dear brother Evgeny is
very ill, his consumption, my sweet, and they fear he will not make
it long into the New Year. But my child, you yourself do not look
well. Are you not eating again? What is it?"

"Oh Jutta, this is *quite natural,* I am told, but it will pass. Honestly, though, I don't know what I shall do. I cannot do this. I just
can't, Jutta. Not here. Not to Fred. But there is no choice now."

Jutta looked woefully into my eyes and she stroked my face,
pulled me to her breast and then letting both hands slide down the
silhouette of my body she said with a reassuring pat: "Now Louli,
does your young man know?" And as I nodded my "no, not yet," she
asked: "When will it be?" "Late spring, Jutta, an anniversary," and I
smiled through tears.

"My sweet, you must now make your own decision and it is only
yours to make. I am here. Let me think now."

"But, Jutta, I must go to Evgeny first. He's all that remains. The
only thing left of my childhood. I must see him."

"Yes, my sweet, and from there perhaps to Johanna in Zoppot. Let
me contact her. It's far enough away from St. Petersburg and close
enough to Berlin, but you must not tarry there at home too long,
love. For your own peace of mind. You know your mother."

"Dear Louli, whatever you decide, I am here and I will be there for you as well. And Johanna can perhaps look after you and help with the proper arrangement. I will explain the situation to her. But you must tell him."

"I think I must let him go first." I said crying and wiping my tears. "Trust me. I know my Rainer's anxiety and he could not help me in this."

Rainer and Bettina came in through the door followed by Fred, and Rainer looked with a telling stare into Jutta's gaze and I think he knew then though I had not told him. We sat down to a table of banter and laughter that seemed like some hazy far-off echo and I in my confused cocoon felt helpless and dumb yet somehow blessed in the watchful presence of Jutta, this remarkable woman who had saved so many and now stood ready to shelter me and the life I bore. She did not ask for explanations; she simply did it. Rainer was right. She was my angel who had always looked after me and simply responded to my cry with no need of gratitude.

And Rainer taking leave that evening wanted to calm me, to quiet all those unspeakable fears of separation I'd kept from him: of death (my brother), of life (my child) and love (our own) that seemed to loom on my doorstep. He said, "My darling, don't worry now. You know where I will be and I will write each day to you, as we have planned. And we will hold together in our words. You must let me know where you will be after St. Petersburg and I will of course come to you."

We all celebrated a muted but intimate Christmas holiday early in December together with Fred and Darwin in Schmargendorf as I prepared for an early departure to St. Petersburg. Fred ceded to my wishes to do this alone but stood ready to come when I called for him. And Rainer, well he prepared for a brief visit with his mother in Prague and then his travel south for an extended stay amidst the abundant treasures of Firenze.

Yes, Rainer and I were both now expelled from our garden of pure potential. From then on out, we would only reconstruct its lost possibilities in the words we would speak and write to each other and to that vast unknowable world looming before us.

Rainer would exquisitely capture that resolve of embrace in separation just a few years later, after we had truly parted, when he wrote: "Isn't it true Lou, it has to be so. We should be like a stream and not wander into canals and carry water into the pastures? Isn't it true, we should hold ourselves firmly together and roar? Perhaps when we are old we will be permitted to spread ourselves out and empty into a delta . . . dear Lou!"

∽

I arrived in Moscow. Evgeny's eyes looked up in the glazed heat of a dying fever and he smiled as if awakening from a dream: "Louli, my sweet sister, I was in our gazebo today and the dolls they were all falling from their pillows and I was trying to catch them and there was that one whose hair you had cropped in a Dutch cut and her arm, her arm was falling, falling off into a river of blood and I tried, I tried Louli, I found it. I sewed it up and placed her on the pillow but I can't find her anymore. Louli, you must go back. You must check on her . . . the snowman, the snowman, remember him Louli, his clothes. They will keep her warm." I held his hand and pressed a wet compress to his lips as he slipped back into fever.

"Evgeny," I said, "I promise you I will go there and she will be safe."

Evgeny died that evening.

The house in Moscow was darkened yet brimming with the commotion of visitors. Mother was disconsolate, sequestered in her room. Jutta came and then my older brothers from their military posts and countless medical colleagues (Evgeny had managed despite his illness to become a doctor) but I did not stay. I could not bear to see him interred in the earth. He would always be up there in my dreams—the only real companion of my childhood.

I packed my bags and went instead out to our summer house in Peterhof and walked in silence around the blanketed gazebo, and entering it I lifted the sheets and found my Dutch-cut doll Cosima whose long braids I'd lopped off as a girl, a bit worn for her wear but intact—that rouge hue still lighting fat porcelain cheeks, just where we had left her twenty-five years before, and I bundled her into my cloth bag and took her with me.

Looking through a crystal on the window, no sign in the brilliant glare of snow of our snowman, no he too had gone with Evgeny. I was startled by a grown woman's face, my own sorry reflection, peering out into the beyond, back into my pitiful self. There in the distance stood a moose with full rack and a grandeur about him surveying the property as his own and I thought of my father and he was instantly gone into the wilderness.

I left that playhouse that had secured all my girlhood dreams exactly as I had come, stepping away into my own footprints. No exit from this place. I knew I could never willingly leave that space and its imagined world, except on that day I had a sense that he, my brother, now followed me.

I made my way to Zoppot and Johanna and lapsed there in her care into the gray static of a numbing depression too painful to remember and I waited. My dear Rainer sent me letters celebrating the spring and the singular female purpose of motherhood: "The way of women always leads to a child."

He surely meant well. But I could not respond. I was too despondent. I had lost all that I knew of childhood—my brother—my one real companion—and I didn't have the courage to bring yet another life into that loss. Life with its tether love had become a stranger to me.

Even love
can become
a stranger to itself—
The word
that hovers
too close
to nothing—

Hushed stroke
alone and gone
undeniably heard—
the birdsong.

ᴄ⌀

I heard her cry. I named her Cosima and I gave her up. The pain of giving and letting go of life too similar, indistinguishable. And though I would eventually emerge from that darkness and never see her, that cry of first life would haunt me forever.

Johanna gave her over for those first years of life to a wet nurse living in a small cottage just down the lane from her house and would later take her into her home as her own. Jutta came almost immediately and I sobbed to her that I had failed in all relationships: in marriage, in the bond of eros and now in motherhood. I had never fully realized any of them.

"Louli, no, no, you mustn't think this. Go home now, to your life there, to your husband. This child after all is not his, and you know, Lou, you are not a suckling mother. This little one you have borne into the world will thrive here. We will see to that. This is the world she will know and you must go now to Fred and continue your writing. Rainer must eventually have his life too."

"Yes, head children, the imagined ones, that is all I am capable of, Jutta, all I'm left with."

Jutta would go back to Berlin and though I did not see my child, once I gained my strength I would walk down the lane and furtively like the stranger that I'd become to all love, I would stand there at the gate with the chickens pecking nervously before the door and stopping in their frantic tracks to crane their heads around to their intruder. Behind a grove of oak trees I waited to hear her cry and then, when she was quieted, sometimes hearing a laugh of recognition and a cooing, I imagined her secure in the plump arms of a real suckling mother and I turned back to Johanna's.

I did that twice a day for a good month, never actually seeing her but knowing that voice, and that last time I leaned my head against the oak and looking up through its filigree of leaves into a brilliant sun, I breathed a prayer: "Evgeny, watch over her now—Cosima." And then I finally let go.

FRED embraced me in those summer months trying to comfort me from the loss of my brother—though he did not let on to know about the other. And Rainer came back to the Pension Waldheim and we pretended to pick up where we had left off. He was overflowing with impressions from the art and ambiance of Florence that he wanted to spew to me, anything to fill, to fill the loss he saw in my eyes, to reinstate the hold, the safety of the garden we'd once inhabited. I began writing with a fury about Russian literature, setting my sights on a return to Russia to rediscover my homeland.

Through that summer and fall I would make "Russia" a welcoming homeland for our lost spirits and through those following years together would cultivate with Rainer a singular passion for all things Russian, sending him to study the language and actually translate before he barely had the words to speak. And yes, in throwing myself and Rainer into its mystical religion with a quiet desperation, I wanted only to recover my loss, to be redeemed.

Russia became for Rainer and me the symbol of a natural sympathetic forgiving God, suffused in the humble spirit of the folk. We would share that people's misfortune, their dreams, their hopes, and overcoming my fears I would finally renew my faith in life again on Evgeny's final resting place—life not as individual and dying but as communal and ongoing—life not as the real suffering I'd experienced but as the saving communal belief I imagined.

Russia, Russia, the homeland of spirit, the folk. We would arrive as the faithful and invoke the wisdom of Russia's own scribe of the human soul and author of *Resurrection*—Tolstoy—and he would speak to us in his own imposing style, and, well, that would be a rude awakening—as unexpected as it was unforgettable.

10

_co_

Unforgiving
Mother Russia

"Who sent for them?" he said.

There is a saying that "character exists in the darkness." And I remember hearing the startling force of that question emanating from
the crack of the barely opened panel of huge mahogany doors to his
apartment in Moscow, and imagining the bearded sage who spoke
those words, wanting only to shrink into the shadows in hopes, in
hopes that he had not meant us or thought us too unworthy.

But that was not it at all. Count Lev Tolstoy had had too many
uninvited visitors from the authorities that spring of 1899 who
wanted to censor his public defense of the workers' movement, his
charges of police brutality, his support of conscientious objectors,
and to silence his critique of the Orthodox Church as well. But this
old man's hold on the Russian people was much deeper than any
temporary restraints on his person or his actions might attempt to
control. He wrote the people's suffering and gave legitimacy to the
undeniable humanity of their world. He was their witness, their
voice, the Russian people's first real historian of their heart. At that
time, this man of seventy, Tolstoy, who was still galloping in from the
countryside, dismounting to make love to his wife, not old at all,

found himself also fighting the internal censors of his own publishing house, the Orthodox believers within who began to consider the grand man of letters perhaps a little past his prime, a liability as he put the finishing touches on what would be his last great novel and his last valiant attack on Orthodox dogma—a novel with the curious title *Resurrection*.

And so his frame of mind was definitely not one to suffer fools lightly when Fred, Rainer and I arrived on his doorstep on Good Friday in late April of 1899. We had been in Moscow barely a week, immersing ourselves in the festivities of Easter week, when Rainer solicited the painter Leonid Pasternak, Boris's father, to arrange an introduction with the great scribe Tolstoy. Pasternak had been commissioned by Tolstoy to illustrate his new novel *Resurrection* and so Leonid was only too willing to oblige us with a hastily arranged introduction.

The maid led us to a small parlor in the back of the apartment where she set down a tray of tea cups and small plates for tea. As we walked down the corridor lined with religious art and sketches of peasants in the countryside, a robust man with tired probing eyes peering out through a lined, almost engraved face and full white beard appeared from the front parlor, ushering us in, saying, "Yes, yes, Leonid has told me of your coming."

We passed a tiny dimly lit study where a small squat woman with dyed black hair pulled back in a bun and a halo of small spit curls framing her round face sat at a desk. And as Tolstoy stopped to invite her to join us, she made a sour face, motioning to the heap of manuscript before her, his no doubt, that she was copying, and with an abrupt "I cannot be disturbed now nor can you for that matter," she let her annoyance with our visit be known. "You must excuse Sonya," he said, adding, "She will not be joining us. She has a deadline," and let go a chuckle.

We sat down and made our nervous introductions. He had read a couple of my stories, he said, "with pleasure," but he did not elaborate. He was aware too of my *Nietzsche,* and commenting on Fritz he said: "He was abnormal. He was a real madman, but what talent! . . . Great God, what savagery! It's terrible to drag down Christianity so."

It was a real conversation stopper to which I could offer a meek response: "The man I knew was certainly courageously searching and where that quest brought him that may have gone too far. But that passion, it was a direction, no? He gave us all that." I could see Fred seemed uncomfortable and Tolstoy shot a glance at me that was piercing and a gentle nod that seemed to say, "Well, yes, another time."

And then, as if by diversion, turning to Rainer, he asked what it was that he did. "Well," Rainer blushed, his eyes downcast: "I write some things and I am right now translating Chekhov's *The Seagull.*" "I'm afraid I don't know your work. But Chekhov, that's ambitious," he said.

Tolstoy pulled a cord to ring for their maid Tatiana who emerged with a pot of tea and some freshly baked tea cakes. And then Tolstoy lapsed into an animated discussion with Fred about his research into the Babid sect in Persia, which clearly interested him no end, asking that he please send him his writings on the subject.

Both Rainer and I, feeling ourselves somewhat out of our element in their conversation, tried to engage this great holy man in our intended plan to participate in the Easter festivities, the bells of Moscow almost medieval, the incense, the remarkable spirit of the folk coming to life to celebrate their savior. Tolstoy suddenly became very stern and said, not mincing words, in an angry tone: "You must stop this and be smarter than all that and not honor the superstitions of the folk. That Eucharistic hogwash. It's what precisely oppresses them." We were properly silenced.

I asked him about his novel *Resurrection*. He didn't say much only that it was about a resurrection of human community, here and now, us in this room, nothing more and nothing less. And then returning to our Easter plans he warned: "You go out there looking. I am not in the least bit interested. Believe me, Jesus was an extraordinary man, just a man, and he has been dead two millennia. His resurrection is simply the example of his life, lived and died with grace and dignity. You will not find him in any delusion of bread and wine transformed into body and blood, only in the eyes of the next human encounter, be it husband, wife, friend or nameless stranger on the street. That is the real Christianity—the miracle of our own poor humanity."

It was time for him to go back to his work he said and both chastised and entranced by his larger-than-life presence, we found our way out and back to our hotel. And though we would not heed his words and went out straightaway amid a huge chorus of church bells to celebrate the ancient rite of Jesus' resurrection amid the folk and took in all the religious art and sought out all the peasant poets, and embraced their mysticism to inhabit the real Russia, I would not forget that grand sage's warning. If only to grant that he had lived and loved and suffered his people too long not to possess a kernel of their truth.

We departed from Moscow to St. Petersburg where Fred and I stayed in the family apartment and Rainer was consigned to a pension. Rainer and I would meet in the late morning and make our way off to the galleries and then I would leave Rainer with his nose in a book at the library.

During that week I stole away alone to Evgeny's grave and stood disturbed that the grass had not yet taken root on his resting place and in a frenzy I wandered the yard's periphery plucking up all the wildflowers, daffodils, black-eyed susans, daisies and my favorite, blue gentian flowers, and sprinkled them on that site in a wild array of all that was in bloom, that survived him, if only for the spring.

Rainer feeling abandoned and surely tired in our threesome of being introduced as a "distant cousin" took up his relationship with a young Russian woman he had met and courted in Florence. He was not mine, never was, never could be. I knew that though I chafed at his absences from our evening soirees (and my mother did not), the reality was that life, his life, was leading him elsewhere and surely must.

All three of us soon returned to Berlin stopping for a night in Danzig to visit Johanna who assured me in private that Cosima was well and thriving, now walking, still living with her wet-nurse in Zoppot, and I pulled from my bag my old cloth and porcelain doll. "She is still young yet, Lou," Johanna laughed and promised, "but of course I will see that she has it."

"But, Johanna, this is fine with you, right, it's so much." "Yes, Lou, Katya is so good with her. This girl of ours will be fine. And one day I will teach her. She'll be in one of my classes."

Fred and I set off the next dawn for home with Rainer staying behind for a couple of days wanting to explore the Oliva wood, and with that cry of our child so present with my every awakening, I did not see her.

Tolstoy's *Resurrection,* I would discover months later when it was published and I stole away to read it uninterrupted in my study in Schmargendorf. It was the story of the deep guilt of a noble prince who during his youthful exploits had abandoned a peasant girl along with their child, only to find himself years later sitting on a jury in judgment of the girl/now prostitute for murder. The girl condemned to hard labor, the prince spends his days trying to expiate his guilt, and following her to an interment camp in outermost Siberia he finally is able to get her sentence commuted.

A story of guilt, expiation of one's sin, and making things right in this world. And no other hope, no other resurrection for us but the earthly human one of making amends for one's lapses, one's severe wrongdoings to another simple human being, which Tolstoy in his deep religiosity, his brand of Christian communion, made us feel were sins against humanity.

I could do nothing else but cry then in recognition, safe within the thick stone walls of my study. No one could hear me. No one had to know my secret. But with every sobbing impulse of my being I knew what I did not *want* to know—that Tolstoy was right.

The shame, the guilt of forsaking my own child. I couldn't bear it. I wanted to be forgiven by some larger personal being in some other lifetime and so I penned him a note which said: "Thank you for this gift of your novel which my mind accepts fully but my body's spirit feels still too forlorn to follow. Forgive me." *Resurrection* was a confession Tolstoy could make but I could not.

He did not answer and life beyond that walled-off secret of my heart beat steadily on filled with all the riches that we had accumulated and brought back with us from Russia. Rainer began writing with a power I had not seen before—haunting poems—the deeply internal prayers of a monk to his elusive God, a voice he had no doubt found amidst Russia's mysticism and through his immersion in studying Russian medieval art in St. Petersburg's library. He was invoking the images, the icons he had seen, and folding them into his works as his own creation.

> So the hour bows down to me, touches me
> With a clear metallic stroke.
> My senses tremble. I feel my own power—
> The plastic day I now hold.

They would introduce his first extraordinary lyric cycle, the *Book of Hours*—and we saw each other daily as he penned them in a fury and read them to me that fall and it was an epiphany. His words embraced me fully. They were visceral and tactile. For once he saw his feelings, startlingly visual, and we were never closer.

He was finally the poet I had suspected him of always being. He was discovering a natural refuge from his angst in the saving grace of his poems. He could live and find his temporary peace in those words, his glimmer of eternity in the here and now.

"Michelangelo, who is in the stone?" he would have God asking in one story he wrote at the time, and in a poem from this lyric cycle he would plead an answer: *"What will you do, God, when I die? / When I your vessel broken lie?"* Rainer knew. He knew he held the hand of the creator in his own.

The hold of his happiness began shifting from me to his poems. And from then on, though I would be his confidante from near and far throughout his lifetime, the making of his poems would be his only salvation from devastating episodes of self-doubt. It would be the focus of all our correspondence back and forth to each other, in all his emotional upheavals and appeals to me for comfort then and for years to come. His crafting of poems would be the single essential way out of his inner darkness.

We went back only once to Russia, together, that spring and it promised to be a wonderful time. There was a certain desperate expectation that it had to be. We went alone in May of 1900 and yes, we were ebullient and foolish lovers out in the open. This trip to Russia turned out to be our last real idyll with its zenith and its inevitable nadir. But at its beginning we lived those days with abandon as if they would last forever.

We stayed as kin (Rainer posing as my distant cousin from Prague) in adjacent rooms at a pension in Moscow and went out each day drinking in the art. Rainer could not get enough of the visual art in the churches and museums and was cultivating not only his art criticism but his poet's eye.

We sought out the art critic and translator Fyodor Fiedler. And he, well, I would much later learn through an account he wrote of meeting me and the great Rilke—that he was less than kind to me, and he'd had the audacity to publish it in St. Petersburg's newspaper for all to see:

> I saw her that summer of 1900 and I must say, she looked rather fat and dowdy, sporting peasant dress, unseemly with ankles show-ing, and hair all wild and not even pinned back. From what I'd heard of her, what I'd expected, she surely was a wilted rose. . . . Sad, really . . .
>
> And that poor "cousin" of hers would turn out to be one of the great seraphic geniuses of our time. Back then though he gave off no hint of future greatness. He was an unassuming sort, genial enough, and earnest in his hunger to know everything about Russ-ian art. I liked him for that. I thought it a bit ambitious that with so little Russian he was translating our masters. . . .
>
> Yes, yes, those two. They were an unlikely pair but they seemed devoted to each other. Of course, they said they were cousins and I remember we all thought it was odd. One rarely sees such affec-tion in a family.

We visited my friend, the writer and political organizer Sofya Shil, who gave special night classes to the workers and peasants and wrote under the pseudonym "Sergei Orlovsky." We enlisted her con-nections and made our way to Moscow's darkest districts seeking out the common man, eating, drinking and agitating with them in their canteens. Now Sofya who herself championed the workers' movement counseled caution in our excursions out into the coun-tryside to live amongst the folk, absorb their folklore and breathe in their wisdom.

"My Lord, Lou, what *are* you and your young man Rainer looking for out there with the folk? Don't encourage them in their backward ways. Don't cater to their superstitions. Without knowledge and learning and technical know-how, Lou, they will only trade one oppressor, the tsarist regime, for another—the old warlords of Mother Russia. . . .

"But Lou, no, Lou, you seem so happy now. You know, dear, we cannot turn back the clock. You will have to go back to Berlin soon enough and this folk that you both so idolize will have to be educated if they are to survive and thrive—for their own good and the good of us all. But go on now, you two. Enjoy the time you have together."

There were few supporters of our bohemian experiment during that second stay in Russia, and one day early on in chancing upon Leonid Pasternak and his family with ten-year-old Boris in tow in the Moscow train station on their way for a summer holiday in the Urals, we asked about Count Tolstoy and were told he was at his estate in Yasnaya Polyana.

Thinking back to those times and knowing what we do now, it's hard not to blush in embarrassment at our naïveté—our single-minded foolishness in seeking Tolstoy out a second time.

The truth is, that second time we barely saw him. We arrived on the doorstep of his estate and there his son greeted us, more precisely me, while nearly slamming the door in Rainer's face. Showing us into a library he left us to wait for a good hour and a half poring over the books, while a shrieking verbal battle raged endlessly beyond the walls. At last Count Tolstoy appeared and looking at us wearily he said: "Well, which is it? You can have lunch with them or you can go for a walk with me."

Choosing the latter we walked mostly in silence through the garden. Bending down picking at the weeds and burying his nose in every flower the count gathered a bouquet, no doubt to make peace with his wife Sonya.

He asked where we were going, as if suggesting our imminent departure, and we told him we would be seeking out a meeting with the people's poet Spiridon Drozhzhin out in the countryside. "Well, good luck to you on your spiritual journey. He's a good enough sort. But let me tell you something. You will not be enlightened by their mystical nonsense and they are not helped by your devotion. . . .

"So I hope you can find yourself out now. As for me, I must leave you to return to my long-suffering wife, Frau Tolstoy. I'm sure she will have something to say about my absence."

We left him at the garden gate, an old man resting on his walking stick, breathing the flowers' perfumes one more time, waving the bouquet in farewell and then turning back once again to face the differences of his most unhappy family. Rainer and I noted that visit in our journals with conspicuous brevity: "Day with the Count at Yasnaya Polyana." "Visited that holy scribe of the Russian people—Tolstoy. What a library!" We were properly mortified.

Tolstoy's advice again was lost on us as we arranged to spend some days visiting Drozhzhin in his village of Nizovka and staying in an *izba* (a primitive wooden hut), replete with straw mattresses, bedbugs and a steady diet of porridge that was so horrid that for one paranoid moment I thought it must have been a conspiracy prearranged by the count himself to cure us of our mystical delusions.

Drozhzhin was an unprepossessing man in a large tunic-like peasant shirt with a rope sash who greeted our enthusiasm for the Russian peasants with good cheer but he was genuinely perplexed when we insisted on going barefoot in our hikes through the woodlands. "If you had grown up without shoes, with only animal skins tied with rags around your feet in winter—you would not part with them now. As for me, I think I'll stay with these high boots."

It was a bit of practical advice our people's poet was gently imparting to us. But no, we insisted on soaking up the peasant experience through total immersion.

Rainer was the budding anthropologist collecting their words, gravestone rubbings, making rough sketches of the images within their churches and writing a scrupulous record of their songs. And I, well, I tried to harvest the physical side of their lives—going out picking berries each morning to sweeten the horrible pasty gruel that seemed to be a staple of their poor diet. I gnawed with some effort to smile and swallow the cured dried beef of their midday meal and poked around, never asking not wanting to know what floated in the questionable aroma of their stew. Rainer just laughed at me and gobbled it up, none the worse for his cheer.

At night we took the extra blankets they had showered on us and I slipped one under the straw mattress to keep out the cold and another on top to keep out the bedbugs and another two I would cloak over us to keep out the gnats. And I tossed and turned and Rainer would tickle and laugh at my silly efforts to settle in. And when I jumped up with a start at God knows what, the cry of a wolf or a coyote or a dog, he would nip at me and tease saying, "My dear, you may want to hide, but they've found you out." And then with a kiss and a pat on my hip he would turn over into a comforting snore. Rainer delighted in all the discomfort, shrugging it all off, and I, well I was a less ardent believer.

"They were kindly city people," Drozhzhin would later write:

German I think, though her Russian was better than good, just not colloquial. They just wanted to participate, to sing and learn our songs and to dance. Oh, they were quite a sight, those two, and I don't believe she had an ear for the music. They were funny really, tripping over their feet, not knowing our steps, but they seemed in love, in love with each other and the dream of our life here.

We don't see much of the city folk here that we like. They were different. They wrote down our words on their notepads as if we would never say them again. And so we all laughed together. Though we didn't really understand what they wanted, they were still likable and humble in their own way.

As we began to look a bit worn in our primitive surroundings, I came down with an excruciating case of poison ivy with blisters that caked my feet and oozed between my toes and climbed all the way up my legs to my thighs. For the rest of our stay Drozhzhin arranged for us more comfortable accommodations in the neighboring estate of Nikolai Tolstoy (a distant cousin of the count) until I was mobile again, this time with shoes.

Though our sage friends, the count and Sofya Shil and Fiedler and Drozhzhin himself, were perplexed by our wanderings, Rainer took from that time a number of memorable encounters with the peasant folk as some meager vindication of our quest. Once out in the country when a peasant woman took him into her arms and said, "You too are just *narod*," by which she meant "folk like us." And another time back in the gallery in St. Petersburg, where two farmers stood before a painting of cows grazing in a pasture and one pronounced firmly, "We see that every day," to which the other responded, "Yes, but when they paint them, that means we must love them." And they both raised their eyes bewildered and Rainer roared as he recounted this scene for me.

On the way back to Moscow by coach we came upon a dead workhorse on the side of the road with a blanket thrown over its large bloated body and the peasants keeping a safe distance, blessing themselves, casting their eyes away. And Rainer, wanting to see the virtue in it, said, "Oh, Lou, it's just their way of holding all beings holy."

Back from the countryside I told Sofya about the dead horse and how it left me with a sick feeling in the pit of my stomach. And she nodded her head in recognition: "You see it's a superstition that goes back to a tale about the Dun horse. The peasants will not touch it for three days in hopes that the spirit of the horse will rise again in one of those poor sods and make him tsar. . . . You see, Lou, their superstitions are not always so innocent. They reinforce what holds them back. Haven't you heard about the white troikas of princesses that trundle down Moscow's avenues on the way to the theater and race right through a crowd of peasants flinging them into the dirt on either side? . . . And do you know what these simple people will do, Lou? They will take a few grains of dirt or a handful of snow from the tracks, left by the royal entourage, and they will bless themselves with it. When they would be better off making a fist."

"I have not seen that but Rainer and I have both seen something much more internal and powerful to celebrate in this people." "Oh yes, I know," Sofya conceded, "the spirit of the plough. You take with you their spirit but they will ever be left with the plough, until they awaken some fine day to the fact that they must change that."

She laughed saying I looked weary and suddenly serious again, bending her head close to me, asked how it was going with Rainer. "I don't know," I said. "I thought he was so transformed by the strength of his writing this past year but he falls, he still falls back, Sofya, so precipitously into a darkness I can't seem to fathom. This, what we have, is never enough, only intermittent, and we must always go back to *my* life. And I know it's not enough for him, nor should it be. I know he is ready to fly. And I hate myself for wishing the peace I had before it all began, four years ago. Yes, I know I must be very tired now, tired of it all, tired of a helpless sorrow I can't seem to change, but there is still such special affection between us. . . . "

"Then maybe it is time, maybe you must let him go, Lou. That feeling will survive it, wherever he goes."

"Yes, I know that. I've been meaning to suggest that he spend the winter in Moscow and not come back with me. We need the break and he needs to find his equilibrium apart from me. He'll never find it with this back and forth, our furtive escapes together only to return to the reality of my life in Berlin, a reality that excludes him. My dear old Rainer, I know him, whatever happens, wherever we are, our spirits will always be bound. You see, we're not much different from those peasants out there, now are we, left with a dream and the plough of our writing."

"Yes, well dear, in matters of love, none of us ever knows better, do we?"

I decided to visit my mother and my brother Robert's family at their vacation home in Rongas, Finland, and one afternoon in a café just around the corner from the Moscow library where I sat sipping tea with honey and Rainer nursed a beer, I told him I needed to go there to get some perspective. I couldn't help him in his depression. I said nothing of Moscow or a longer separation. I was afraid for him and for myself. The truth is Rainer did not want the on again off again tryst of our love life together, and I felt that the approach of our every journey's end only set him off in a downward spiral.

He pushed his mug aside and said we must go back. He was angry and silent, but he gripped my hand firmly as we walked with only the echo of our steps on the cobblestones following us. Once we'd returned to our pension rooms, he sat picking at the threads of the armchair and staring out the window, as a sheer curtain waved like a contorted spirit that could not get out. Tilting his head to the side as if slowly turning over his thought, he told me he would set off in a fortnight to visit Johanna in Danzig.

I became agitated and impatient blurting to him, "Let go of that relationship. It was a mistake."

And looking directly at me, through me really with tearful blue eyes, he said, "A mistake that is now barely walking and talking."

I threw down the clothes I'd been packing and fell onto the bed pounding the pillow and sobbing. "Rainer, I did what I had to do. I could do nothing else. She couldn't be ours. We both know that. We could not give her a life together. I may have expected recriminations from my mother and deserved them from Fred, but from you?"

Taking in my words, he very calmly rose, a shadow of wincing pain causing him to bite his lip, drawing blood, and coming to me he pulled me to my feet and tried to steady my fists—stroking and stroking my hair back from my wet face. Giving into his hold, I sank to the bed, and clutching my head tightly against his beating heart, he whispered: "No, No Lou. I know. I know that. You were absolutely right and I was never even there to help you. You wanted to spare everyone, and you did—everyone but yourself. I'm so sorry. *I have no excuses. I should have words for this, but I do not. . . .*

"I will never say farewell to you. There will always be a *Wiedersehen* for us [a seeing each other again], but do you know there's a primitive Indian phrase for goodbye that says it better. Fred told me about it. 'I go, you come.' That'll be our parting promise, Lou. It's the way our farewells have always been and ever will be. I have to believe that."

I groped for my handkerchief and lifted it to wipe the blood from his lips and he said, "No, no, my sweet, I should be the one comforting you. I should have been there." We held each other just rocking, trying to rock away the sadness.

"Yes, my dear Rainer, there will always be a place for you with us, with me in your darkest hour. Promise me you will know that."

"No, I won't forget, Lou. After Danzig I'll probably go off to an artists' colony in Worpswede near Flanders. I've been thinking of that lately. They are mostly visual artists but that world speaks to me so viscerally now and, well, I think that community might be good, but I'll write to you always, telling you where I am, and I will ever wait for your word, for a sign."

"Rainer, you have my promise."

We sat there rocking each other into a weary slumber and the next morning I awoke alone. Rainer had left with a penned note on the back of a theater program:

Dorogoya moya ["My darling" in Russian], I have settled our accounts with the Hausfrau. You go now and look after yourself, and remember always "I go, you come."

—Ever yours, Rainer.

INTERLUDE

It's been snowing for days out there. I'm in for the duration. Gorgeous to watch its relentless squall and so amazingly soothing—its calm sleep in moonlight. It's Christmas. I've made all the phone calls, sent all the presents. I wonder about my friend in the Arctic, now that'll be really roughing it for the holidays. Sent him some Glen Morangie, some woolen socks and some long johns. Not very original but not a lot of choices between McDonough's general store and the gift shop at the Buffalo farm. My son, maybe he'll be up for New Year's. Do some cross-country skiing. Or maybe not, he's got his own life now. Got to learn to let go.

My gift to myself, a huge luxurious Eucalyptus bubble bath, now bubbling over. Dar licking up the soap bubbles. Cabin fever. I worry about this dog. I pour myself a glass of champagne and sink into the bubbles, close my eyes and let my mind wander . . . Christmas—a child is born . . .

Was that the cry Lou carried all those years? No, it wasn't her father at all or the loss of her innocence or her faith in Gillot but very simply the loss of her child. Something she could never bring herself to speak? And all those critics and biographers saying she'd surely been pregnant, aborted Rilke's child. She must have. What else? No trace of a child. And they said this with only the evidence of their own prejudice—their need to see her as an ambitious unnatural woman unsuited to motherhood.

So she neither confirmed nor denied. She didn't defend herself. She merely registered the hurt and harm of such a rumor to so many. Oh yes, at the very end of her life, she said she astonished someone by saying she "hadn't hazarded the risk of a child," by way of explaining her primary contract with God and her first love of Gillot, and then went on to say she had failed in every aspect of love: marriage, motherhood and eros. Was this truth or some final evasion of all of it, who would ever know? Years later though after her death when it could no longer hurt her, one critic, a biographer of Rilke and a woman no less, saw through it all, saying Lou most probably bore Rainer's child and she just let it rest. What with her marriage and the fragile, hardly dependable state of her young poet lover, Lou did what so many with no other options did in her day; she quietly gave the child up and went on with her life.

Later she would excise from their correspondence her own letters to Rainer at the time, leaving only his, the only hints to her secret in words extolling the virtue of motherhood. And the child, well the child, like so many other nameless children in Germany, Poland and Eastern Europe, lost in the tumult of those war-ravaged decades.

11

❧

The Human Hand of Creation

The hand. That huge plump lined hand caked in white plaster with blackened fingernails. Rainer loved its physical hold and he envied the art that could caress, could touch on its fingertips the immutable intricate form of conception. He knew he could not have it and he loved it all the more for the spirit that suffused through surfaces. He wrote:

> *If he forms a hand, it is there alone in space and it is nothing more than a hand. And God made only one hand in six days and poured water around it and arched a sky above it. When all was complete, he was at peace with it and it was a miracle of a hand.*

And so he married a sculptor, Clara Westhoff, a student of Rodin's whom he had met at Worpswede, the artists' community he soon tired of after Moscow because of its simplistic leavening ways: *I cannot work here, Lou. They have only today and no tomorrows. Not the space or the vision to truly imagine.* Clara soon bore him a child, a little girl nonetheless—Ruth—and though they took refuge to a country cottage in Westerwede, it was a home he could not hold on to. And all the grounding he had yearned for, he discovered he could not comfortably inhabit:

> *I used to think it would be better, if I would one day have a house, a wife and a child, things that were real and undeniable. I thought that I would become more visible, more palpable, more real. But see, Westerwede was real. I really did build my own house and everything that was in it. But it was an external reality and I did not live and expand within it . . . but it does not give me the feeling of reality, that sense of equal worth, that I so sorely need: to be a real person among real things . . .*
>
> *My house was nothing more than a strange woman for whom I was supposed to work and the people close to me are nothing more than visitors who do not want to leave. . . . Oh how I lose myself each time I want to be something for them. How I leave myself and cannot come to them and I am en route between them and me. It's as if I were traveling to an unknown destination and I do not know where I am or how much of me is really there and within reach.*

Clara his dark enigmatic sculptor, for her part, confided her own doubts to her closest friend, the other artist "woman in white," the remarkable painter Paula Becker-Modersohn, whom Rainer had met at Worpswede. He'd had a brief flirtation with her but she was spoken for at the time. Clara wrote to Paula that she could no longer bear the burden of a house that they built and built and were ever servants to and somehow could not peacefully settle into. She longed so to pack her things, her chisel, her utensils, her pads and pencils and cycle away beyond the horizon where she could finally work again. What kind of a wife, mother, was she, she cried. "I don't recognize the haggard woman I've become."

No, unlike Rainer, the mother in her was shamed, but the artist's voice was insistent and, well, that's the only freedom she knew. Surely

Paula would understand that. Paula did commiserate but she did not know at the time that this minor drama would presage a much direr one that would take her own life just a few years later at the height of her own career as a painter, when she died in childbirth.

Rainer and Clara's experiment in domesticity had failed and they left their child with Clara's parents and made their escape to Rodin's studios outside Paris in the village of Meudon where Rainer took up a position as the great master's secretary, ostensibly to organize the artist's life, but it would be the artist in Rilke that would soon get the better of him.

Rainer was never an organizer but ever a correspondent he was, even in a French for which he said "there surely must be a purgatory." But rather than communicate details that did not interest him in the least, he corresponded quite with abandon and at length on his own with bankers, artists, buyers and sellers and all soon ran amok. It was a disaster.

"Get out, get out, I can't have you, monsieur. How dare you speak for me? No, I can't have you here anymore. *Il faut travailler*," Rodin shouted enraged, tearing down the sign over the portal and showing Rainer to the door, pointing with a fat index finger to the vast space outside his compound. "*Il faut travailler*" (It's necessary to work)—a phrase Rainer had prized, had only wanted to replicate, but at that moment consigned Rainer's work to serve with all the others in quarters beneath the stairs the creation of the one true artist who worked above them.

And the master whom he adored, whose hands and snout would peer up all too closely and lecherously on his models' contortions while he worked and whose frequent afternoon retreats would be noted with a scribbled sign on his studio door "In the cathedral," was beyond this meek secretary's reproach. Rodin's wife, Rosa, would shoot through the bushes at one of Rodin's mistresses, the remarkable sculptor Camille Claudel, and still, and still. . . . Rainer saw it all but never questioned, never said a word. His eye was simply captivated by the wonder of Rodin's creation. By the extraordinary surfaces that played with light and seized an eternal moment of human movement in the painstaking crevices and contours of his stone bodies.

Rainer undaunted would deliver lectures on Rodin that year in Germany calling out to full houses: "Is anyone listening?" and later publish an exquisite monument of a book to the Great Master, though he himself had fallen like a cracked mold onto Rodin's studio floor. Fred and I were in the audience in Berlin with Clara and later alone with Rainer. Fighting back my own foolish feelings of first claim to his affections, I put in a good word for Clara and some normality in his life and he looked at me with raised eyebrow and said quietly, "Lou, my dear Lou, don't worry about me and Clara and Ruth. They are my family, I know that. But Clara is a kindred spirit. She needs to be free of all this to work and her parents are helping us in this. And you, above all people, know me."

Squeezing my hand, he said, "Remember now our promise, Lou." For the first time I saw no peace in those luminous eyes but a kind of frenetic anxiety he was helpless to quell. No matter, I thought, it was the work, his work, he was telling me, that counted.

Rainer was expelled, sent back humiliated to a garret room in the slums of Paris, leaving Clara to fend for herself in Meudon. She would come back to Paris and they would live together just briefly and then apart. Oh, I think it was consensual, their parting. I heard nothing to the contrary and he would still see Clara and they would go together to visit their little daughter living with her parents.

They would go their separate ways and never need to legally dissolve that union. They may have tried once but Rainer's residency, his citizenship was in question. With Europe in turmoil he was fast becoming a man without a country. No, their parting was as natural as their coming together had been. And so they let it drop and sim-

ply outgrew the tether, she staying in the hold of Rodin's sculpture
and he eventually leaving, banished but ever loyal.

He cried his anguish in letters to me of Paris's assault on his
senses comparing that time to his nightmares of military school and
he wandered the city's streets and looked and touched in his looking, trying to shape the feeling. Rainer would press his face up
against the jailed fence of the Jardin des Plantes and peering
through its iron bars at the panther pacing within, he'd remember
the small tiger plaster, an antique Rodin kept in his studio, and he'd
think and think and turn it all over prowling for the words that
seized what he saw. The panther, his panther, would finally speak to
him a silent mellifluous vision:

The Panther

His gaze from constantly passing the bars
has grown so tired, it can hold no more.
To him it seems a thousand bars from afar
and beyond a thousand bars, no world at all.

The gentle gait of his strong and pliant strides
that pace the smallest circles he draws
is like a ritual dance around a source
in which a mighty will stands paralyzed.

Still sometimes, before his pupil, a curtain
rises silently—then an image is seized,
glides through the muscles tensed and uncertain,
enters the heart, ceases to be.

Rainer was free, unleashed to his own creation, and his *Ding-
Gedichte* (his thing poems) were nothing short of spectacular, published in two volumes, the *New Poems*, in that first decade. He was

sculpting words and I don't think ever a poet had done this before and he still did not see it, complaining that he could not make "things" out of his fear. He was still in anguish and once back then in those earliest days after we'd parted, I had written him a sharp cruel note in frustration: "Go with your dark God. Suffer if you must. I cannot help you. I have some joy . . . my own. No, we cannot meet."

Why such a harsh note from me? No, it wasn't altruistic or out of the blue. Frieda had told me just the day before that Rainer had been engaged to the dark sculptress and they would marry posthaste—with no small degree of pressure from the bride's family.

Had I been secretly trying to draw him nearer by threatening a break? My jealousy knew no words and no bounds. Was it that I simply could not allow another woman what I could not myself have? No, it was more than that—his departure was a bitter reminder of what I had already given up, the child I had abandoned— a life decision for which there was no earthly redemption. I may have castigated Rainer for his dark hours and his relentless demands on my time, my sympathies, and I did. But his every appeal to me to be the sounding board of his uncertainty echoed that faint familiar infant's cry in the hollow of my soul.

Rainer with all those years of our coming and going must have seen through it all. We had become expert in the art of enduring intimate distances. He made Clara his wife and he never ceased to return to me in his words.

Rainer never questioned my harsh words. Instead he would pull back and then gently confess his need to speak that anguish to me: "Forgive me for my petty worries . . . " he wrote. "You, Lou, are the doorpost against which I measure my growth. . . . You see, I am only a stranger and a beggar. And I will pass away. But everything that could have been my home, had I been stronger, will rest in your hands."

I relented of course and he was creating in those poems the beggar and the blind man, and Leda and the Swan, and so much else—all things that he had seen in those years in Paris—and the most beautiful poem of autumn that I have ever read and there is no autumn to this day in what surely must be the winter of my life that I do not think of it, speak its beauty and love him as I did then. Yes, he was right. It's what's left, all we have, all I hold of him:

Autumn Day
Sire, it is time. The summer was so huge.
Place your shadows on the sundials
and on the meadows, let your winds loose.
Command the last fruits to ripen on the vine.

Give them a few more southerly breaths.
Drive them to completion and press
their final sweetness into the heavy wine.
Whoever has no home, will never find one.

Whoever is alone, will remain so for a long time.
Will wake, read, write long letters into night,
will wander aimlessly up and down the streets,
while the leaves scatter from sight.

It was the autumn of our life together then, his and mine, and we would wander and he would become famous, though it did not seem to touch him (I was popular but he was to become revered). We would meet on occasion every year or so but we would always write and I would drink in slowly the verses he sent to me like a fine wine, and in writing long letters into our separate nights we would always speak to each other. The words, they were our hold.

ᴄᴑ

That first decade of our time apart, we became even more restless, the two of us on our separate paths. I spent really more time away from my home, though for the first time in our married life, Fred and I would truly have a home on the edge of the country where foxes would prance before our windows. Fred had finally secured a professorship in oriental languages in Göttingen and there on a hillside just below the woodlands, we bought a beautiful three-story stone and wood house built into the hill with its living room and study walls covered in a pale blue silk that bleached into a silver gray with the blaze of each morning sun and I decorated its interior with bearskin rugs and the brilliant red wall hangings and intricate wood furnishings sent to me from St. Petersburg. There was a garden with some forty fruit trees and wherever I might be wandering I always came back for the spring and for the autumn to walk through the blossoming and the falling of fruit.

I loved that as I do today. That is what I remember most and my only exception to my routine of spring and autumn in Göttingen was in 1905. I'd been to Russia in late 1904 to tend to my ailing mother who with Evgeny's death and my older brothers fighting (and losing) Russia's skirmishes in foreign outposts (Port Arthur) was now at the mercy of a household staff that had dwindled to a core few with the years. A "mercy" that became more and more tenuous with each demonstration proving the workers' cries to rebellion might be temporarily quelled but not expunged.

As a general's family, we were high servants to the Imperial Crown, enjoyed a noble status, but with each imperial defeat abroad and defiant strike at home, the entire line of command was thrown into question.

The ties that bind began to unravel and form a threatening noose for all those higher-ups within reach, those in the emperor's outermost circles. Sofya's prediction was coming to fruition—her peasant workers dropping their devotionals and raising a defiant fist. In all social and individual dealings, the human animal was unnatural, had the advantage of stealth. Its bearing and felling of fruit knew no natural cycles. And as I came more and more to understand, our human creations could be both miraculously spontaneous and cruelly extinguished.

I came away from that visit thinking that my mother's advanced age, her minor status within the crown, her clear workers' sympathies (taking to the streets herself during one demonstration of mill workers and seamstresses) would keep her out of harm's way. She would be safely looked after by her loyal maid, butler and coachman. But I feared for my brothers, because they and their families would ever be on the front lines representing the crown wherever they went. With the territories between Germany and Russia constantly shifting allegiances, travel to and from Russia was becoming ever more difficult. And since our move to Göttingen had added yet another day to the trip from St. Petersburg, I did not know when I would be seeing Mother Russia again and so I decided to take a brief detour and wired ahead to Fred that I would be making an overnight stop in Danzig to visit Johanna Niemann.

We had not seen each other for at least a few years. Our correspondence had lapsed but I sent her regularly a stipend to help with Cosima and there was always a cheerful card at Christmas. I don't know if Rainer had pursued the relationship since I had warned him so vehemently against it so many years ago. But I was curious, and arriving with so little warning, I did not know what to expect.

Johanna had gotten my wire only the day before my train arrived in mid-afternoon on Saturday. Karl, Johanna's husband, and Katya, the nurse, had taken the little one Cosima to Zoppot for the weekend to celebrate Opa's birthday that Sunday. "It's better for her outside the city," she explained. "Children get to be just children, not Poles or Germans or Russians. Just children." She herself had stayed in town to grade exams and would be going out for festivities tomorrow, she said, but had she known I was coming, she would have delayed their journey. She could call though, feign some excuse and have them return.

"No, no, Johanna, it's surely best so. Seeing her now would be too painful for me and too confusing for her. It's the last thing I'd want the child to know." I felt myself canceling out my presence with every word and offered the simple explanation that travel being what it was, and being so near, I'd just wanted to check in, perhaps only to spy her from afar as I did when she was an infant. I'd thought to take a room at a pension by the station. "No, no, Lou, you *will* come home with me now and stay the night. I am alone there this evening and you can at least see the home we've made for her. We'll both go to the station tomorrow and you can catch the Berlin train and I the local to Zoppot."

And so Johanna and I returned through the Jewish quarter to a section of two-story modest stone townhouses with wooden cross-hatching in the old city with a view of Danzig's harbor, not too far from the boardwalk. I stepped in through the doorway and stumbled on a small child's boot in the entryway. The culprit, a dachshund, whimpered and cowered, chewing the other boot in the pantry. This home brimmed with books and activity and you could see it in its plump chairs, its comfortable disarray—the desks overflowing with papers, the parlor with curtains pulled back, piano console open and stool askew, an open book face down, a pipe, tack with cleaners on the armchair table, and a bone lying near the dog's pillow beside a hearth still crackling with embers. This parlor was not there merely to receive guests in private. It was the hub of an activity momentarily suspended that would clearly resume. And I had stepped into its pause and captured its heart between beats as in a photograph.

Johanna took my suitcase and led me upstairs, down a narrow corridor past the master bedroom and a maid's room to a garreted back bedroom with silk walls covered with lichen- and salmon-colored flowers and one window that looked out to the harbor. "This is Cosima's room, Lou. I hope it'll be all right. Now I'll leave you to freshen up in the lavatory just outside the door. When you're done, come down to the parlor and we'll have a good long chat and some evening dinner. You must be famished from the long journey."

How strange, I thought. There on the wall by the head of the bed was a print of one of my beloved childhood friends: the blue gentian flower. I looked at the lace curtains, the white percale sheets and beautiful burgundy afghan crocheted by a nursemaid or Oma perhaps. I would never know. And there on a child's miniature wicker rocker in the corner of the room amidst an array of stuffed animals sat my doll of long ago—my Cosima.

I picked her up gingerly by her cloth arms and touched her cool porcelain cheek against mine, smoothing her lace and blue taffeta dress, and I suddenly remembered my mother at the lake, her pellucid skin, my wish that she drown, and Evgeny, my sick brother, and the sanctity of our hideaway—the garden gazebo. And I was there again amidst a flood of feelings. And I lay down hugging that doll on my little girl's bed and I felt at home. I'd found her. My Cosima. No longer mine. My Cosima.

Later on I sat with Johanna in the parlor and she told me what a good student Cosima seemed to be—inventive, always making up stories. That those first years Cosima had spent with Katya and her family, that Rainer had come, asking only once but did not see her and only later when Karl and she discovered they would not themselves have children did they take them both, Katya and Cosima, in as their family.

My eyes gravitated to a small studio photograph on the mantelpiece—of a girl with high forehead and long blonde curls swept back by a large bow on the top of her head, hands neatly folded on an armchair, and huge doe eyes that made her look as if she were peering through time. And I smiled as I thought of Rainer. I looked silently for only a moment and then closed my eyes as if to catalogue it in memory and then I rose to Johanna's suggestion that we retire.

The next day as we stood in the main hall of the station making our final farewell, a couple of blue feathers from the plumage of Johanna's broad rimmed hat became undone and looking for something to affix them back I pulled a hatpin, a pearl encased in a crown of tiny rubies, from my carrying bag. "This should do," I said, as I secured them back atop her nest.

"No, Lou, I can't. It's an antique—a lovely piece." "Don't be silly, Johanna. Take it as a keepsake, as a memento of these few stolen hours we've had together. I'm so grateful to you. Honestly, Johanna. You must know that. Her room brims with a fantasy life . . . and I can't tell you how it pleases me so to know she is thriving. All you've given her." And then with a teacher's raised eyebrow giving my hand a firm squeeze, she corrected me, saying, "No, Lou, it's quite the contrary. It's all you've given me."

I went home feeling a comfort wash over me that I had not felt in seven years. I had not reared my own child and never would. I did not even know her. But you see, I lived her absence nonetheless every day and I could never be fully content in whatever I might be doing however unrelated—calling Darwin home from our woodlands, looking for that hopelessly elusive last sentence, replacing lost buttons on Fred's coat.

No there was always the veneer of something missed, the here and now somehow needing to be perfected. And oddly only occasionally would I actually be aware of her absence and my fear of not knowing her whereabouts. But that day, that one day I did have a respite from it all. I did know and I could feel it in my quickened step as I stepped off the train onto the platform. I was at home in the moment and I could see Fred and his eyes fire into a smile as he caught sight of me and raised a bouquet of flowers in the air to beckon me.

We chatted all the way home about St. Petersburg, the unrest and uncertainty, my fear for my brothers' safety, my mother's magnanimous support of the workers and her disdain of the mystics—that ghoulish Rasputin who had insinuated himself into the tsarina's rather dim good graces . . . and on and on into the house where I was greeted with the slurps and the nips of an ever hungry Darwin. Some cervelat, fruits and cheeses neatly laid out like a still life on the kitchen table. Maria, Fred said, had not been feeling well and had decided to retire early.

Begging off on the food, I urged him to go on without me. I'd settle in, and as I whisked out the door Fred added, "But do join me later for a glass of port." To which I paused and smiling replied: "Yes, of course, dear. I'll be down in a few minutes." If I hadn't known our routine, my arrivals and departures like the back of my hand, I could have sworn he missed me.

But alas it was something more than that. That night in the sitting room Fred confessed to me that Maria, our maid, was pregnant with his child. It was such a moment that I wished to blot out from memory that I don't remember the exact words we exchanged.

I do remember knocking the entire decanter of port onto the Persian carpet, looking at the stain's blur and thinking of Fred's stabbing himself years back and me racing for a doctor before we were married. And no, no, I did not want this in my own home, I protested, not here, no.

Fred sat remorseful but calm, asking my forgiveness and only my forbearance with the girl. His hand reached out to mine. No, our marriage was his life, he said. He only pleaded that I understand him now and this circumstance within a marriage of long absences, such as we had lived it.

He would of course look after her and the child. She could go home to her mother. I stopped him, saying I wished only to sleep and would have a word with Maria in the morning. And with Fred at the foot of the stairs, I climbed up as if I would shake off a weight thrust on me, thinking how unwelcoming that pious home of hers was likely to be, and turning back spying through the window my grove of fruit trees like sentry on the horizon I said, "No, no Fred, it is her decision but she will not be cast out. Not by me. We have done that once. Not again."

And so it was. It was the only natural thing (though personally wrenching and surely improper in the eyes of some, though we'd never lived our lives deferring to that gaze). It was the least I could give back to Fred, the child I could not give him, the child I had not given myself.

I saw Maria through her confinement and birth. And no, life I knew was so much more than art. It was not just a hand in the magnificent space of mind. It was the hand of a daughter that reached out into the ether and seized onto my finger—her first human touch. That was what truly mattered. Nothing could replicate it. And feeling both sad and grateful on an early summer night in 1905 I delivered that girl-child into the arms of her mother.

꿍

Maria stayed with us through Fred's death in 1930 and then as we were lamenting on his grave I remember her—then quite infirm and aging herself—turning to me, leaning into my shoulder and saying, "It is probably my time to go and my daughter will take me in. I know that and I know Herr Andreas would want me to stay on. But I would want something more. I would want to look after you, Frau Lou, as you did for me, when I needed it most." And she did.

12

My Dear Professor

My God, those years were like no others before or since. I wore
them. It was as if I stood before a mirror greeting no one, nothing
but a fading countenance—my own. Those lines of demarcation I
had drawn through all my relationships began to surface into delicate rivulets on my face and I felt a certain terror of life that could
not be recovered, of growing older.

Oh, I wrote somewhat autobiographical novels of my Russian
past (*Rodinka* and *Ma*) and essays, but I was at sea that first decade.
Though Rainer had long fallen out of my conscious daily thought,
he was somehow too always just beyond the next door, and when
Rainer and I were no longer intentionally avoiding seeing one another, we were hopelessly just missing one another, once in Copen-
hagen, another time in Duino on the Adriatic. "I went there and
walked the beach but where were you? . . . No, no you were coming
to me? What, you mean we missed each other in transit?" The truth
is our plans for being apart were as aimless as our sporadic attempts
to see one another were fated to fail.

Years later there would be a meaning ascribed to such slips but then
we had no way of describing it other than as reckless self-abandon. We
were untethered. We'd lost hold of what held us together—Rainer spinning out into one doomed affair after another and I spiraling inward

into a psychic freefall of loss. I had a home I was all too eager to leave. I had a love I had turned away and a child I had left and never even succored, all by my own choosing. I had always been best at leaving, usually to defend against being left first, but now I felt something different. The pain of no excuses. The weight of nothing. I had no ballast.

I sailed through those years looking for a port, flailing, and I found it. Not surprisingly perhaps, in the hold of nothing physical but in the rapture of a community of mind. A small band of doctors and artists, brothers and sisters, was charting a new course of psychic investigation into the unconscious wishes, the dreams and the trauma that triggered our most innocent and aberrant behavior. It was a place perhaps to begin my own spiritual renewal. And their navigator was a neurologist crafting a technique of deep psychic diving and a surfacing release in conversation—the treatment of a talking cure. Their captain traversing that mind storm was none other than Sigmund Freud. "My dear Professor."

It was 1912 when in returning from Sweden on a visit to my feminist friend Ellen Key on what would be one of my last long journeys abroad, I was persuaded by a doctor friend to accompany him along with a young actress, Ellen Delp, a fan of my novels, to one of the early foundational psychoanalytic congresses in Weimar. I went along, committing to nothing, and there I heard about a method that sought to give credence to our most individual dreams.

I remember sitting there encircled by men unknown to me then but now famous: Carl Jung, Sandor Ferenczi, Karl Abraham, and so many others. And I remember thinking how my earliest dreams, my creations as a child, had been beaten out of me by my mother, ridiculed by my pastor and my teachers, spoken in privacy and shame to my only real confessor Gillot when that child in me knew all the while they were the spark that kept me alive.

I thought of Charlotte in her attic of yellow wallpaper and Nora walking out the door and winced at the scream of Munch's "man on the bridge." And there in the weight of my boa and furs and the rumor of my fame amidst this foreign crew of spiritual seekers I felt a secret thrill of some curious deliverance in the middle of my life. I felt the wish of a "yes," the glimmer of reclaiming the girl I was and all I had given up. I could not turn the clock back, could not touch, but at least I could know them again. I could know the *me*, that dreaming child, who had let go. It was the promise of a homecoming of the soul. Perhaps Tolstoy was wrong. Perhaps there was still for us all a worldly redemption. For me.

I went home ebullient in what I felt was possible and I immediately sent word to Jutta and Bettina to come to us in Göttingen for a few days. For once I was not summoning her to intervene in crisis. Jutta arrived, looking grayer but still strong, now nursing the much younger yet ailing Bettina who was somewhat under the weather with a cough, but they said the trip would be good for them and that they would both welcome the time to leave the city air and take walks through our woodlands. And after seeing Bettina into bed that evening the second night, Jutta came down to sit with me and we sat clasping each other's hands across the kitchen table.

"Jutta, I don't know how I can ever give back to you all you've given to me."

"Lou, my dear Louli, you needn't give anything to me. You seem so energized, so for once in your life happy. It's not someone else, is it? It's just you. Am I right now?"

"Yes, Jutta, you can see that, can't you? But it's you who have helped me through all these life changes and years back you saved mother and your brother. I just don't know how you did it alone, how you survived. You've always extended such a firm hand to me."

"I was there, Lou, yes, but I could do nothing else. Grampa's illness quickly spared us any further havoc. And the nightmares, which I did have, Louli, eventually subsided into a quiet of the river

Lethe, his death, and the delta of a woman who would hold me. That was what saved me."

"But now, Jutta, it's strange. I think I've finally found something, I really have, a way of fathoming sadness and turmoil, all that you did for me so naturally. They're a community with a method that reaches out to all that sad psychic abandonment, everything I felt so long afterward, all these years. I don't know but I think I can help others before it's too much, before all those losses that make life so impossible. I don't know how you did it alone, Jutta."

"Dear girl, I did not, I did it with the love of my dear Bettina. And I must go to her now. She's ill. I worry she's got a fever. I must look in on her. My dear, just know your mother will never understand this, never mind that, but your father is proud of his Louli in the middle of her life. Know that. And write to us about how this all goes."

We kissed each other's hands and I watched her as she unleashed her long gray mane and retreated to the upstairs bedroom. The next day they were up early and Fred had seen them off before I'd awakened. She left a note though: *"Louli,—Bett and I have had to go home. An early train. I'm so sorry, dear. Bett's not up to it. She needs to be home, with her horses in familiar surroundings. Don't look back now. That is all long done. Look only to those strangers you can greet there at your door. They will be blessed in that light I've seen in your eyes. Forward now to your own happiness and seize that moment.—Yours ever, Jutta."*

And I did just that. I began with my outlandish written request to the founding professor in Vienna, Dr. Freud, that I visit him and that I be allowed to be part of the inner sanctum of his Wednesday meetings. My eager presumption must have taken him by surprise, surpassed only by my shock when he responded that he delighted in my forthcoming visit, to introducing me to psychoanalysis "such as it is," that he would arrange with the others my presence at the Wednesday meeting (clearly a breach of some sort of protocol) and that he greeted it all, my visit, as a "good omen."

I arrived in Vienna on a Sunday in early October of 1912, and calling his residence the next day from my hotel I was told he could not see me until very late in the night. That night. He had patients. He hoped that would still be suitable. So soon, I hadn't expected it. But, of course. Would I come round at ten o'clock?

And so I did, arriving at Berggasse 19 at the unseemly hour of 9:45 P.M. I was ushered into the entryway and up the stairs into a waiting room of dark wood and books and burgundy sofas where I sat and I remembered how decades back in St. Petersburg as a child I had sat, palms sweating in white gloves, waiting for the countenance of Pastor Gillot, and how sadly vulnerable and shivering and humiliated I had felt then. And with all that life had taught me, I could hear my heart still bleeding, bursting with each beat. But that was St. Petersburg, I a mere child in a backwater, and this was Vienna, the open cosmopolitan home of art, music and ideas, an empire breathing its accomplishments, exhaling possibilities. And I, well . . . I removed my gloves and taking a bit of lotion from my purse I smoothed my veined hands and closing my eyes I sighed. I was that same girl. I felt no different.

But no, this was Vienna and a different time and space. I could not tell you then what Vienna was for me personally beyond the imperial splendor of the city's face juxtaposed to that quiet interior of tastefully appointed bourgeois walls within Berggasse 19. But I can now. The explosion of hindsight . . . the explosion of an empire that was unraveling, about to reveal to us all a world of percolating desires plotting very disparate agendas. As I came to know only later, it was all festering there. Let me tell you about it. . . .

∾

Vienna's heart had once been shrouded in a fortress that was dismantled in the 1860s, its cloak peeled away and replaced with the necklace of a Ringstrasse that encircled the inner sanctum of the city, making the interior still not accessible but visible, from inside and out. And as Vienna deconstructed its balustrades, it resurrected a walkway for its many parades. It was exposed for the displays of its military might—the pomp and circumstance of empire, the gleaming helmeted grenadiers atop prancing horses—and for the endless plaintive demonstrations of its unemployed working subjects with red carnations and black armbands plodding their anguish in their workaday dress on foot.

I saw it all. I did not understand it at the time.

Lenin was there that winter charting his single-minded Bolshevik rebellion of Russia's starving masses while, oddly enough, seeking medical advice from Vienna's finest doctors for his wife's goiter. Trotsky, his brilliant young rival of thirty-four, sat amidst the smoky milling of laborers, social activists (Karl Renner and Victor Adler), artists (Kokoschka, Schnitzler, Musil and Schiele) and nameless unescorted women caught in staves of cathedral light filtering through that pea-green den of iniquity, the infamous Café Central. And there he sat scribbling copy for Vienna's *Pravda,* railing against St. Petersburg's wimpish *Pravda,* calling for a socialist union of Mensheviks and Bolsheviks that would burst far beyond national borders. My God, Fritz would have cheered his anarchical fire.

Stalin (a pseudonym that stuck from his *Pravda* writings) arrived under yet another Greek-sounding pseudonym hobbling out of Vienna's Northwest Station with withered hand carrying a wooden suitcase and limping from a bike accident in the mountains on his way to the palatial apartment of his elite Viennese hosts, the Troyanovskys, just around the corner from the emperor's home at Schönbrunn. They were less than pleased with this crude yokel from Georgia with walrus mustache covering a pock-marked face, eschewing all social decorum and even the most innocent chess game—at which he excelled (no, no, there was work to be done!)—

doing his sleuthing of the socialist movement, forging the connections between Vienna and Paris and Kracow and St. Petersburg and writing his *Marxism and the National Question,* which would secure Russia's hold and yes, make Lenin smile. Who was this motley crew of exiled malcontents—my countrymen—plotting socialism's next strike in the heart of imperial Vienna?

Vienna's own socialist monarch, the dignified psychiatrist and founder of the Social Democrat Party, Victor Adler, was aging then but still planning the now traditional May Day celebrations which he had conceived years before in the very same sanctuary that would spawn yet another revolution—the outrage of psychoanalysis at none other than Berggasse 19.

The belly of Vienna's wants and needs, the belly of Vienna's imperial beast, was bursting, its mind always expanding and its empire large, magnanimous and dismissive enough to embrace it all. It was dancing its misery and parading its excesses, its delusions of grandeur, as if forever rehearsing a ball. Its social and psychic palliative hatched within those very same walls, the home of my "dear Professor."

◡◦

The door opened. "Frau Andreas, do come in." A weary bearded Freud in gray suit with a pocket watch and monocle took my fur wrap and laid it on the consulting couch across the dimly lit room, and lighting an oil lamp on his desk he motioned me to one of two leather chairs to the left of his desk. "Forgive me the wait. It was a long arduous session that did not want to end. May I fix you a whiskey, a glass of port or a red wine, perhaps?"

"A red wine, Herr Doktor Professor, please. Something that always warms me on these damp nights."

And pouring himself the same, he drew from the hands of a Chinese antiquity between two Egyptian lion bookends on a side table one of a few cigars that he said he had gotten just the day before in the Café Landtmann, his favorite haunt, but had not yet had the pleasure of smoking. Would I mind? Why, no, of course. The house was absolutely asleep. I wondered about his family. The only sound the metronome of the corner grandfather clock meting out our silence.

We quickly got beyond introductions, they having already been made in writing. How was my trip? I mentioned how I had seen a demonstration of seamstresses and laundresses on the Ringstrasse the day before from my coach while riding in from the train station. "Yes, there are so many unfortunates unemployed now, so much discontent brewing here in this civilized city. So many threats to one's bodily survival." And pausing he mused, "And there are psychic threats as well. What we do here really in our little circle, what I do, Frau Andreas, is nothing more than teach people to wash dirty linen."

I smiled. I understood but was stunned by the analogy. We quickly settled into talking of who I had met within the community, what I was reading and how he could ease my access to discussions that would enhance my studies.

I felt a kind of positioning going on, an exploration of what I did and did not know. I sensed a flush in my cheeks and a sweat beginning to form in my palms. I felt I must be abysmally failing, novice that I was, caught in the pauses of the tick-tock—I wasn't keeping up. And immediately stepping into a quagmire, I mentioned my reading of Alfred Adler and my intention to attend his reading group.

He drew back, blowing curls of smoke into the air and breathing a sigh, and said: "Ah yes, well you are too new to our circle to know, Frau Salomé, that there are unfortunate ones, whose clever hubris has led them to stray . . . to stray from the centrality of the sexual theory that is utterly foundational to the purpose and practice of psychoanalysis. Adler is one sad case, mired in feelings of inferiority which are his own and have become his cause. . . . This is a science of observation and analysis, not of imposition of feeling."

"Why yes, of course, Professor, that's why I've come, to learn that method," I offered lamely. "And there are others," he said. "Dr. Jung and his collective hogwash that may fire the cultural imagination, yes, yes, very seductive. But they will never speak to the pain that informs individual neurosis. Be warned now. I trust that you will never carry insights from our Wednesday meetings into Adler's gatherings nor his polluting imaginings into ours."

I blanched and confessed my ignorance and my need to understand the hierarchy of oral, anal and genital psychic experience—the words themselves stuttering off my tongue. I felt panicked and stupid and then finding a focus blurted: "Surely, Professor, you can direct me to your papers on the subject." He smiled and pulled from his desk an offprint of a paper, and realizing my embarrassment he began a brief survey of the theory, what he'd written and where it might be found, all the while puffing his cigar and stroking the head of an antiquity with his left hand. The theory which may have been dogma but then was far from hardening in cement. What little I knew of the subject I interjected tentatively.

Then far into the morning he looked at me with assurances that he would send me some papers and a book and then said: "Even after we've talked about the most terrible things, you look like Christmas is coming." I laughed relief because I was flagging. He said he would expect me that next Wednesday out there in the waiting room where they all convened and then he added: "It will be a breath of fresh air to have you, a 'Sunday' amongst all the dour analysts of our Wednesday meetings."

And patting my hand, he said: "Oh, I've gone on far too long. Forgive me, Frau Salomé. We'll continue this conversation and next time, we will talk about you. I have heard so much and I have much to discover. Let's plan on that. Perhaps you can come round again on

Sunday evening and we can continue this informal private conversation. I'll see you out now and secure a coach. It's so very late."

That was the beginning of our "Sundays" together, our weekly evening conversations there in his consulting room which were never an analysis at all, but in this twilight of my life opened my line of inquiry for others, hearkening back to the dawn of my own awakening with Gillot.

I went back to my hotel that would be my home for six months and scribbling a few notes immediately sank into a fitful sleep and a mad dream.

Rainer was there but far, far away, seated with scores of others at an infinitely long medieval table stretching for miles into a dark dungeon. It was lit by countless dancing torches like festive birthday candles, but who, but why? I kept on looking. Rainer sat laughing and gesturing down to the empty head of the table, as if he saw. He was looking intently at the woman beside him, kissing her arm up and down from fingertips to shoulder and she jumping as if on a pin cushion. My God, it was the emperor's consort, Frau Schratt. Did Rainer know? Of course, he nodded slyly.

And there across the table, a man in a floppy hat and amulet of silver cross and chalice with the mustached face of Fritz (Not Fritz, that's Wagner!), raising his goblet and squinting into the eyes of a beatific Cosima with porcelain face and hydra curls writhing snakelike out into air. There seemed to be thousands of people coming to the table, walking out of the darkness. The archduke was there with his Sophie on his lap. And a footman racing up and down the table crying out "God is not dead" and pouring something into the goblets. "God is not dead. We have saved him. . . . He's coming, don't you know? He's coming to our table." And there was a man with a bowler hat and tails. His pants were falling but he was just dancing round and round tipping his hat to collect the coins. "Let us not forget our guest. He who must be saved, survive, and we who obliterate, pay service and die. . . . " There was laughter and a nodding of heads and hoisting of glasses to that dark focal point at the head of the table. Everyone was nodding, seeing, and I saw nothing. I looked down the table and saw Rainer holding the detached arm of Frau Schratt as if an offering. And suddenly a face too close to see, but a familiar voice, roaring into smoke: "You are my Christmas." And his hand, his hand stroking Darwin, the dog nipping at his knees. . . . "He" is coming to our table. I can feel the tugging, being pulled forward and drawn into that dark hole. . . .

I awoke with a start. Rainer was so long gone. . . . I was alone now, had been so for a good long time. What on earth was I thinking, still feeling? It was too early to get up. I lay there tossing and turning, thinking of the newspapers I'd read the day before. How many of the royalty themselves were at that very moment also alone, tossing and turning in their beds? The widowed emperor with his consort, the actress Frau Katharina Schratt, a union reputedly not even consummated (something that did not trouble me in the least), and the dashing irascible archduke Ferdinand himself with his extraordinarily fashionable lowborn wife Sophie, enduring all measure of insult and imperial slight—bringing up the rear of a procession of royal toddlers, before she was even announced. As if the objects of one's passion, the true love of one's life, even those of the highnesses, were mere afterthoughts to court protocol. Everyone vying for position and power. And all along the way carefully proscribing the great leveler of us all, sexual desire.

No love at all was better than the indignity of that, I sighed, pulling at my pillows and the feather coverlet trying to bury myself in some comforting hold of solitude.

And the chivalrous Dr. Freud, what comfort has he? Remembering his words from the night before, "You look like Christmas is coming," and recalling my transcription in dream to "you are my Christmas," I blurted out loud, "Thank God, my dear Professor will never know my dreams."

No, Freud had much more on his mind than the analysis of an acolyte from the provinces. He was waging a silent war not unlike the Balkan quest for independence from the empire. He was isolating his detractors within psychoanalysis, staking out an empire of his own. He had so much as told me so the night before. And what I failed to tell him was that I had a date the following evening with one such rival, unbeknownst to me then, none other than that "blond headstrong fellow," Dr. Victor Tausk.

Freud had hinted at a self-destructive sadness in Tausk that he found menacing and as I tossed from side to side, I finally decided: "Go. This is not your war. You are a visitor, a guest at their table. You needn't choose sides. After all this is Vienna, the cosmopolitan hub of unlimited possibilities—the theater of modern empire. And you have always wanted to see the 'moving theater'— the cinema. Go . . . "

And as my dear Professor would confess only later, he was always "a conquistador with all the temperament and tenacity of such a man," and as with all conquerors, there were others who vied for the same territory. But Tausk, my young escort to the cinema the next day, fifteen years my junior, was not one of them. He was nothing more than ferociously vulnerable and I thought quite wonderful. No threat to anyone but himself. We saw Germany's first film star, Henny Porten, in *Love's Fortune for the Blind Girl* and she gesticulated, fell on ottomans, there was a spurning nobleman and we laughed and laughed, and later I mentioned Tolstoy's *Resurrection* and he screamed "*Parzival*: Is there ever any other story? It's contagious. We must do something about this. All these forlorn women." And his strong arm wrapped around my shoulder.

I loved that young man though I could not help him in his mad moods, could never be the comfort that he sought. But we were fast friends for the six months I spent in Vienna. Freud was ever dismissive of Tausk, increasingly so, perhaps, I thought, because he knew

I liked his abandon so much. It was an annoyance to my dear Professor but that was not the only thing that we didn't agree upon.

Narcissism, oddly enough. We came upon it at loggerheads really, that sore point—over his favorite dessert, *Marmorguglhupf*, a marble coffee cake—at the Café Landtmann, his regular haunt, late one Sunday afternoon when we could not meet for our evening conversation at Berggasse 19. We sat amidst the finery and the tingle of Rosenthal coffee cups and silver spoons at a small corner oval table and tried to make small talk.

I mentioned how I'd seen from my coach just a couple of days before so many people dressed in their black finery, some in shrouds, with white asters and lilies, top hats and workers' caps bobbing, walking the streets in droves making their way out to the cemeteries, and then the next day the tallying of the competition of graveside floral arrangements and wreaths: Schumann was down this year, Beethoven was winning and Mozart, I thought, where was he but in some undiscovered pauper's grave. Perhaps the lucky one, no longer in the count.

"Well, yes, 'All Souls Day,'" he said, clearing his throat. "Vienna celebrates its dead as it does its living, to the utmost. Civilized society here, such as it is, that makes our life's struggle to survive a game of commerce. Even beyond the grave. . . . " And then he quipped: "Anatomists used to rob graves for science, now we rob souls and sell them to the best taker as entertainment!"

"Professor, it does seem a contagion to my foreign eyes, but probably no more than elsewhere," I replied, trying to make light of my observation. "And by contrast to Vienna, Göttingen seems surely more naïve, not unlike the provinces."

"Well, perhaps so, Frau Salomé." He smiled faintly but wasn't convinced.

His fork stabbed into a large wedge of gooey cake before him. He relished it with a slightly audible smack, clearly enjoying it at least as much as the cigars he smoked during our evening sessions. I picked tentatively at mine, not wanting to paste my mouth shut in conversation.

"Yes, Frau Salomé, I seem to remember Dr. Jung telling me of a paper you sent to us last summer for publication. But I must confess I've not read it yet. I'm afraid Dr. Jung didn't send it on to me, though he did write it was strange but amazingly powerful all the same. . . . What was it called?" He paused for a moment, his index finger gesturing that I hold my tongue. Squinting his eyes, he looked up at the ceiling's squares as if searching its patterns for a clue. "Oh, yes of course"—he'd found it. "Yes, yes," he said intoning deeply and too loudly like a bell pealing through the din for silence, as if announcing dinner: "'The Anal and the Sexual,' wasn't that it now, Frau Salomé?"

The woman at the next table peering out through the gauze of her black veil under her wide-brimmed peacock-plumed hat promptly let her teaspoon drop to the floor, as her eyes squinted at the Professor, then widening seized on me, and dipping in a semicircle, continued a stealth escape to breathe in the better air on the other side of the table, aided by the lucky stroke of an ivory fan held delicately in her all-too-bejeweled plump hand. Coughing to swallow a guffaw her gentleman partner bent down to retrieve her napkin and then turning to my dear Professor, he gave him a knowing nod of recognition. Or was it a wink?

I should have been humiliated, though it was ludicrous. I felt the corners of my mouth pinching, fighting an irrepressible urge to laugh, and leaning over to Freud, I piped up: "My dear Professor, I do believe I'm taking the fall here, as seems to be the way with all my sex. May I make something clear though? 'The Anal and the Sexual' may be *my* paper but it is *your* theory!" And Freud, wiping away his smile behind his napkin, and nodding to our neighbors, now hastily departing the adjacent table, whispered to them: "Yes, she's quite right. It's *my* theory."

Relieved of our audience, the professor and I relaxed into idle chatter. What was this he'd heard about Tausk encouraging my exploration of narcissism? I must take care not to be led astray by someone who may simply be compensating for his own weaknesses. I felt I must defend my friend, and my own theoretical scribblings, preliminary as they were.

"My dear Professor. I think you judge Victor unfairly and prematurely. Tausk is tender at heart and fierce in his thinking and so very socially concerned. Oh yes, perhaps more open about his personal troubles than most of us and well, more vulnerable to criticism, now isn't he? . . . He's led me nowhere I haven't wanted to go. . . .

"And as for narcissism, if I can be so bold—you, Professor, seem to regard it a negative instinct to be contained, a stage to be overcome. I think it's quite natural to us all—an expression throughout life of a primal relatedness, a state of oneness with the world. Of course it must find its limits in conscious adult life but basically it's something innately good and human. Tausk simply calls its manifestations in the world—in art, for instance—'elaborations.' That is what I have from our dear Tausk—the core thinking is my own—raw as it is!"

"Yes, my dear Frau Salomé, I can see how narcissism, its idealization and coming to love oneself is all part of each individual's humanity. But the notion of narcissism as the expression of a primal unity with the world has never really interested me. Your interpretations of my writings, I must say, tend to extend my theses, seeking some grander completion. I so rarely feel the need for synthesis. . . .

"It's the separation, the breaking up into component parts of what would otherwise revert to an inchoate mass—that's what attracts me to the work of psychoanalysis." My head was spinning. He continued: "You see, I am a doctor and I have a notion of psychic dynamics, of conflicts with shared themes that fester in our unconscious life, and a technique for bringing them to light and releasing the afflicted from the knot of their hold." He dug in for another giant piece and swallowed it whole.

"But the story—the story of that unraveling will be as different as your face is from mine." His fork now circling at his plate to continue his thought. "We share the same structure with traits inherited from our families, the light sensibility of your father's blue eyes and your tendency to migraine, and those traits worn from experience, the stutter I carried away at age six from my cousin's drowning perhaps. So then the story that releases us from the psychic knots that hold us back will always be individual and our own."

He threw back his head as if shaking off his own questioning muse. "Oh yes, some have disparaged psychoanalysis as 'the talking cure' but indeed if it is anything, it is just that. A cure born of telling the story of one's life. . . . So you see, Frau Salomé, I would no sooner prescribe a philosophy to cure psychic illness than I would a pill. One might just as well pick out one of those tonics they sell in the back of catalogues—the 'Heidelberger Belt' perhaps—that wonder strap that fires the libido and cures men instantly of impotence."

We both laughed and bowing my head to him I said: "I fear, Professor, you are making light of my philosophizing and I admit my tendency to abstraction is the bane of my existence and a real stumbling block to close relationships. But, still, Professor, isn't it funny though how we've imagined a belt for men that frees to match the same old one that constrains women, the chastity belt! Strange but somehow typical, don't you think? . . . "

"Frau Salomé, your philosophical vision and clear intelligence will bring you far in your theoretical writings. But what I wish merely to point out here is that in the actual practice of analysis, I can only minister to the poor psychic soul in its specific torment and I cannot invoke a collective unconscious to explain that suffering. My task as a doctor is to find a psychic cure for the troubled individual mind before me and not a religious panacea for all."

I felt I was on the edge of some forbidden territory, and only less than a year later upon Jung's break with Freud would I discover how volcanic that terrain actually was.

And motioning for the waiter, he ordered us both a cognac, and raising his glass, he toasted our future. "To Frau Salomé, whose piercing inquiry is bound to bring me and analysis to places we otherwise might never go and perhaps to send others running for cover," he said nodding to the now empty table. I grasped for my napkin patting my lips, thinking of that ghost of a woman who escaped with her fan. "No, really now, Frau Salomé, you will send me your writings on narcissism? Particularly as you say they relate to that still dark continent of the female psyche. A mystery that I admit to my embarrassment has yet eluded me."

And hoisting my glass, I countered: "And to you, my dear Professor, that you may tolerate my blunderings in the next few months of analytic study and that with you as my guide I may become ever more mindful of psychoanalysis's promise and its pitfalls."

"Agreed, then. May I be up to the challenge of being your guide, Frau Salomé, and may we never bore you with our banter."

We were instantly up, fetching our coats and out the door hailing taxis and kissing cheeks, back to our routine of Wednesday evening meetings in the waiting room at Berggasse 19 and our Sunday night discussions amidst cigar smoke curling through the dim jaundiced light of his consulting room. In between I would occasionally go to the cinema with Victor Tausk and his two small sons with our hilarious dancing reenactments of what we'd seen while walking home or I'd go to dinner at the Schnitzlers or occasionally visit one writer or another.

But for the most part that time in Vienna was confined to my pension room and its downstairs parlor sitting room where I would study the books and papers Freud had lent me, my eyes always wandering to the sentry of the linden tree outside the window. That initial afternoon in Café Landtmann was etched in memory as momentous, never to be repeated, though at the time I could not know what an aberration it had been.

We had come so close to exposing fault lines that afternoon, fault lines that we knew were there between us, we knew were there within analysis, we knew were there within the mores and the politics of all those clustered in that room, randomly brought together by a common taste for that gooey *Marmorguglhupf*.

For the time, we yielded to the ritual, to the harmless masquerade. We skirted the fault lines. The world would present them to us soon enough. I had found a mighty teacher in the twilight of my life, one who listened, corrected my wanderings, firmly but not without humor, and I was content to be led. Vienna was about to bare its soul, to unmask its fear and show its true face.

I was not the only one showing the weariness of age.

INTERLUDE

February. Beginning to look like a winter of no return. It's not so much the snow, unremitting and sometimes blinding, that gets to you. It's this total abandonment in the wild. Even the resident moose seems to have flown this coop. Is there something in Dylan about her not buying valentines? Well, this girl would like one right now.

I open the door to a gust of below-zero wind and pull some logs stacked beside the chimney; Dar escapes for a ten-second call of nature and I discover yesterday's paper jammed between the logs, probably left there by the mountain man who occasionally drops by to replenish the supply of firewood on the porch.

I bang the door shut, throw the latch, stoke up the fire and collapse onto the couch, devouring the paper, hungry for any news of the outside world. The quilting competition—missed that, too bad. The snowmobiles back out on the lake—thrills, a few accidents, ice solid. The wolves are back the experts say but nobody has seen one. Bad for the experts in these parts.

Stats—More snow and more snow! Alert level—orange. Up here, whatever for? Two thousand young soldiers fallen and still counting. No asylum up over the border for a twenty-five-year-old conscientious objector. Canada's declared the war illegal; the soldier still has to prove a prior aversion to war. I think of my son. No exit this time. Well, couldn't do the draft again, could they, not in this country? Austria did back then. Complained but they still did as did all the others, when push came to shove. When it comes to Empire.

Another piece on local textbooks being stickered with "evolution" as a mere theory and not fact of science. And "evolution" banned down south in IMAX theaters outside the park—to protect market share. Evolution won't be safe til it's a cereal brand we eat for breakfast. And what's this, no, did someone really say that—pronounce evolution with a devilish "i" on the second syllable before congressmen seeking funding for the NSF, no less. It's a joke, right, or a slip? A kind of "nucular" moment. Contagious. What is this chip, chip, chipping away?

No we don't see the body bags anymore but we see some real hits and always collateral damage. . . . WMDs. That's the scary thing. The ones we know and the ones we don't. But bottom line, they're there. Terrified by what we don't know. Eclipsing freedom right and left. Preempting ourselves . . . "It's a hard rain gonna fall."

And who of us can hear the cries? Distant as we are, distant as our smart tech allows us, not yet in the middle of it, safe in our huge SUVs with our little yellow ribbons bounding forward into the American night, . . . me in my cabin. That old jeep tank of mine in the barn.

"Come writers and critics / who prophesize with your pen / . . . The chance won't come again." It's a great song, Bob, but some quill technology—the pen. In an age when all we do is push "send" and the message is delivered before we know it around the globe. Before we've had a chance to read it over. How do you roll that back?

Let it rest for now. Get back to her story. The isolation's getting to you. Do something later, when you come off the mountain. The WMDs will wait. What did they do back then before them? Another world maybe. No, they didn't think so, their individual lives . . . so torn and trivialized as the whole world that first time erupted around them as they'd never seen before. . . .

13

◦❧◦

Leaving Vienna

1913. It was a turning point. A turning point for us all. And like all turning points we moved toward it with the simple trust of the ground we stood on that our footing would not falter, that we would be held by our experience and our time-worn beliefs. But the ground was moving and we could not see the cliff.

"Face-work is over / now do the heart-work," Rilke had written that year, commanding himself to plumb his own desire. He was turning away from what he saw outside—the surfaces—to the images that incubated within. But his words to himself were nonetheless a clarion call to us all, as another poem of that time warned:

> *Exposed on the cliffs of the heart. Look how tiny down there*
> *look: that last village of words but higher*
> *and still so terribly small, one last*
> *farmhouse of feeling . . .*

Rainer had imagined something threatening in his own "turning point" at the time and indeed in our greater cultural alienation from feeling—the image of a sheltered bird flying around a peak of pure denial, sure-footed animals milling around below—and then leaving us (as Rainer was wont to do) in suspension he cried: "But without shelter, here / on the cliffs of the heart . . . "—inconclusive, ever questioning a much larger collective fate.

I'd just kissed Victor's giggling towheads and hugged him at the pension door scaling the steps up to my room, still feeling the crazy whimsy of our night out at the cinema. I turned the key, eager for sleep, and found a note slipped beneath my door. It was a telegram from Jutta: "Louli, sad, sad news, your mother has died. . . . Don't come, dear. I'll go. Travel to Russia now too dangerous. Fred knows, expects you home. Courage, now . . . —Jutta."

I sank onto the bed but did not wail, just felt the trickle of tears rain like a stream throughout the night. I remembered the last visit of months ago when mother had been confined to her bed, shrunken in her pillow, and she called to me and I found her standing in the shadow of her canopied bed like some strange ancient doll dwarfed in her long lace nightgown, that porcelain face now framed by cascading snow white curls, her piercing blue eyes that I remember a friend once saying would cast shame into any slightly guilty conscience, suddenly looking plaintive. Arms outstretched, she beckoned: "Louli, it's been too long, come here my wild girl, at last to feel my arms around you." And I fell into her embrace, feeling only the bones of her frail body, and she said, calmly stroking the back of my head: "Louli, my passionate one, my wild rose." "Mushka, yes, I was always that, wasn't I? All that trouble. And you, my mushka, mushka," holding her gently trying to keep her together. It was the same pain, the heartache of a lifetime together we both held at that moment and let go of. That was our gift to each other, how we parted life. Beyond forgetting . . .

Her death was a real turning point for me. And though she was old and I was middle aged and it was the natural course of things, that rationale offered small comfort to how I felt then. It was as if some cataract, some thin veil of difference, had fallen to slightly blur my vision. Mama's passing was very simply a final break from my origins held now only by thin strands of memory and in my heart I was now an orphan in the world.

I thought of her "wild rose" and "the passionate one" and I sighed. "Yes, she was right. I was headstrong and I sought out like-minded kindred spirits." All those loves, my loves that troubled her so, yes it was like placing my hand right smack into a thicket of roses and pulling back over and over again. I couldn't seem to learn: There were always thorns but oh the glorious brilliant wild ones with petals that fell to the ground and a scent that never died. She was one herself. I suspect she knew that but she would never let on. That was our hold. And in her dying I did not feel freed from her, as I had so often wished to be in my youth, but somehow now reconciled. . . . Life may want endings but not death. Death only wants more. . . .

⁓

I did not tell them of my loss, my fellow analysts in that Wednesday group of some thirty people, mostly men. I simply said it was time to go, I must return to my home to perhaps begin a practice of my own back in Göttingen. They gave me, oddly enough, a bouquet of white roses, wild ones I thought they must be. And Freud, his eyes heavy and his mouth somewhat slanted, looking weary from the dissension that no doubt plagued him within the international ranks of analysts, simply thanked me for my "singular presence" and then delivered an invitation to all to share our papers with each other, adding that he hoped we would all meet at future international conferences.

Taking my leave and returning their toast, realizing how silent I mostly had been at all their meetings, I simply said, raising my cognac: "Women thank and men squabble." And Freud pressed my hand firmly and laughed: "You are so right, Frau Salomé. You do know us. I will miss you. I always take such comfort with you there in your center front seat. That space will not be filled. Let us write now often. I'll long to hear your voice and to meet again when time allows. My regards to your husband. . . . I'll be looking for some patients to send your way." He kissed my hand and I choked up, saying barely audibly, "My dear Professor, I am honored. For now then." There were no farewells.

It was a gray afternoon in April with large low cumulus clouds threatening a downpour when I looked out my window at the linden tree one last time and thought how that linden would survive generations of admirers like myself and remembered the words of my father, "Everything wants to live," and slipping the key on a hook inside the door I set off to Vienna's train station with my few bags packed to the gills with papers and a couple of books I had on loan from Freud for my return trip to Göttingen.

It was early, my train not yet ready to board, so I walked over to a kiosk in the station to kill some time and rummaged through a stack of small postcard sketches and paintings at a makeshift table attended by a Jewish vendor. They were skillfully rendered pen and ink drawings, some watercolors of mostly bucolic scenes interspersed with a few sketches of Vienna's sites, so I plucked from the offerings one postal card of the opera house and another of the Franziskanerplatz, thinking to possibly write some cards on my way home.

And suddenly a tap on my shoulder from behind. I nearly jumped out of my skin and turned to find an excited breathless Victor. "Oh, Lou, I thought I wouldn't get here in time. Traffic was terrible. I wanted at least to see you off, my dear friend." He looked disheveled and distracted, with a sad smile.

"Where are the boys?"

"With their mother out in the country for the weekend," he said, shrugging off the question.

"And what have we here?" he asked, motioning to the table and the cards in my hand.

"Oh, just a couple of cards for the trip back." He looked at them smiling. "Not bad but a little ordinary I'd say, but I guess they'll do. And they'll put a few morsels on the table of some struggling young artist. So hard to make a living these days."

"Well, Victor, you're making me feel guilty. Perhaps I should buy more then." I pressed a few coins into the vendor's hands. "Thank you, ma'am," he said, tipping his worker's cap to me, "and the artist Herr Hietler thanks you too."

I smiled at what I assumed "must be a country name" and stuffed them into my cloth carrying bag, thinking nothing more of it then.

The loudspeaker called out my train and Victor made a sad face.

"Now Victor, you must take care of yourself and those wonderful boys."

"Oh Lou," he said feigning drama, "Now I've driven you away like all the others."

I laughed and said, "I won't fall for that, Victor. You have a brilliant life ahead of you and you'll get it together and find your happiness. There's no better heart than yours. We'll write now."

And looking still forlorn, he pinched my nose and said: "Well, yes, maybe a postcard if you're good." Walking me down the platform to the train, he gave me a hug, and hoisting my bags to me, he blew me a kiss and shouted as the train began to pull away, "But, Lou, Lou, who will take you to the cinema?" And we laughed and waved as the train slugged out of the station. Victor, a mensch with a heart that embraced everyone but himself.

The trip was long and uneventful. I pulled one of the postal cards from my bag, the one of Franziskanerplatz, and thought to write a note to Johanna. I don't really know why, but it was a need I had to forge what family connections I had left.

Dearest J.—Mushka has passed away and I am returning home to Göttingen. I wanted you to know. Travel's too difficult to make the trip to St. Petersburg now. But perhaps, before too long. Take care of yourself and Karl and your dear sweet daughter. As ever—L.

I felt relieved; I had made contact however meager and settled into a deep sleep, awakening hours later at my connection in Munich where I posted the card and continued on to Göttingen, only a few hours away.

At home Fred was solicitous, Maria careful to tend to small creature comforts to make me feel better—warm milk at night, cut flowers on the bedside table and breakfast of homemade jams and fresh-baked brown bread with tea served out on the garden veranda. "Mariechen," by then a little girl with Fred's big black eyes, could be heard running and shrieking at the top of her lungs beyond the garden wall with Darwin in tow, brown ears flapping and his distinctive beagle howl.

The second morning after my return I sat in the garden, still in my nightgown and robe inhaling that musky earthen smell of early spring, and looking at the array of budding sprouts and the blue and white crocuses poking through the earth. I imagined the wild roses I would plant at the garden's open back periphery so that their full shaggy heads of petals could bend and wave out against the wild grass of meadows beyond.

And whose head should crane from behind the front wall but Rainer's and stepping through the gate he laid a sprig of forsythia on the table. His eyes, always slightly bulbous, gave off this air of expectancy or foreknowledge, as if they'd seen something that did happen or was about to but were sworn to secrecy. He cradled my head and sighed, "Oh Lou, my Lou," and settling into a chair he simply took both my hands in his and I don't know for how long, we just sat together caressing each other's fingers and looking through a trickle of tears. No words were necessary.

Rainer stayed with us through those days of mourning, til I was up and planting and writing again. Fred had called him, I knew. It was the comfort he knew I needed. We all ate together; Rainer and I took long walks through the woodlands—he showed me new poems and I was speechless, they were so strong. And he said, "It's so good finally to be able to give something to *you*, Lou."

And when I was myself again he prepared to go back to Munich and walking to the gate he said I must come soon and meet his new love, a painter, he'd mentioned, whom he had just begun living with. "Well tell me, what's her name, Rainer?" I asked.

"Her name's Loulou. She really wants to meet you, Lou."

We burst out laughing. "Oh, yes, I can imagine that. Take care, my dear friend, and send me more poems."

I watched as he sauntered down the hillside road, stopping once to pluck a few wildflowers, turning to wave them to me on his way to town and his train.

෴

Vienna was roiling. There were comings and goings whose truth would only surface much later.

The painter in his early twenties fled from that May Day parade in 1913 and boarded a train to find his fortune in Munich, where a few days later he was picked up by the military police and charged with having evaded the draft of a neighboring state for nearly four years. He pleaded poverty, hunger, his meager wage from street sales of postcards and sketches to support his training, and threw himself on the mercy of the court as a starving artist.

233

In truth he'd been turned down twice by Vienna's Institute of Art and his pan-German sentiments absolutely prohibited any association with the multiethnic Austrian army. He had turned his passions to writing: "If social democracy is opposed by a doctrine of greater truth but equal brutality of methods, the latter will conquer." He was let off, judged "unfit . . . too weak to bear arms." His failure, his cowardice, the belief in his lie had served him well. He would peddle it elsewhere.

That same day in May, Colonel Alfred Redl, general staff chief of the Prague Corps, had sauntered into Vienna's Hotel Klomser in dapper civilian attire, scaling the steps to room number one, the package he had just retrieved from the General Post tucked neatly under his arm. "Good, they always come through," he thought. "My Stefan, he's so expensive. But oh, he'll know the risks I take. I'll chastise that bold boy for this." Redl, his fantasy cut short, was charged by Vienna's imperial security with selling secrets to the Russians, of border movements and armaments. Redl's chains and pink whips and women's black garter belt were quickly removed from the Hotel Klomser's room number one and Redl having signed a paper was promptly handed a Luger. A shot discharged and Redl was given a full military funeral, his national secret exposed via Bosnia to the German press weeks later.

There was another nationalism brewing at the time, one that wanted to ally itself with my homeland. That very spring a young eighteen-year-old man in Sarajevo, Gavrilo Princip, sat with friends in a café reading Maxim Gorky, translating Poe and Whitman, and taking solace from Fritz's verse:

> *Everything I embrace becomes light*
> *Everything that I leave becomes coal*
> *Flame, that I surely am.*

Literature, words were a palliative but they wanted action, relief from the hegemony of Austria.

His friend, Sima Donatich, a tall gangly twenty-something fellow and member of the outlawed Young Bosnians, just freshly returned from his studies in Vienna, was regaling Princip and other young cohorts with tales of imminent insurgency. They should cede from the empire, take Albania, merge with Montenegro and form a south Slavic state. He had seen and spoken to Leon Trotsky just recently, he bragged, in the famous Café Central and apprised him of the plight of Serbia, the will of a youthful band to break free of church and empire, to adhere strictly to the precepts of socialism and a sexual abstinence that would embolden them all the more for the assault on the giant. Trotsky, as he told it, lifted an eyebrow in disbelief and said, "No reason to carry the revolution too far."

"No, no, even our brethren are unwilling to make the sacrifices necessary to slay the giant," he claimed. "But we can show them the way and because they, our enemies, and even our comrades least expect it from us, our will can be lethal if we strike at the core. . . . Are you prepared to turn those words of yours into action?"

Gavrilo listened and nodded, picking up the gauntlet that the older wiser Simi had dropped, and swilling his beer he murmured, "But where and who, the imperial guard in Belgrade perhaps?"

"The Austrian Governor in Belgrade is too small potatoes. Besides he's a puppet," Simi snapped. "And the emperor in Vienna is too well protected, virtually a phantom . . . "

"Simi, who then?"

"The archduke, of course. Now in him lies all the unrealized potential of the empire—that insatiable appetite for conquest and more. Are you *in* then, boy? Will you swear on the Black Hand of Serbia?"

The boy could not know Franz Ferdinand's sympathies for the Slavic cause, his warning to the crown against alienating Serbia. "If we go there we will spend millions better spent elsewhere just to keep them down, we'll lose far too many good men and we'll still have a horrible insurgency." Princip never heard the archduke's pleas for restraint, made behind closed doors. He knew only the challenge to his manhood that had been laid before him.

No, Franz Ferdinand was simply the heir apparent, a sniveling young buck's opportunity to soar within his circle of peers. Franz Ferdinand was the future, the future who had become the target and who would come to them in time. And Princip was the man of the present, the man with the gun, the messenger, whose trigger would be the cue unleashing a world war on reason—unmasking the pretense, exposing the fault lines, testing the bounds of empire's indifference.

の

The emperor Franz Josef was suffering that entire year, down with influenza that saw the ancient monarch confined to his bed for months on end, leaving the imperial governance in limbo and the heir apparent, according to the predatory press, plotting a swift and seamless succession.

It sold newspapers. The truth is nobody penetrated the cloak of secrecy surrounding the imperial court and in fact the squabbling cousins—King Georgy in England, Tsar Nicky in St. Petersburg, Kaiser Willy in Berlin—were more likely to know the emperor's condition before any mere commoner in the Austro-Hungarian Reich, not to mention the next room. It was bad enough that the obstinate Crown Prince Franz Ferdinand himself had already compromised the sanctity of the Hapsburg crown through his marriage to the far lesser-born mere countess, Sophie von Chotek. Bad enough the insurgency from within. What would become of monarchy?

And my dear Professor, the conquistador Dr. Freud, suffered a relapse of his colitis that year as he prepared to enter the fractious arena of the International Psychoanalytic meetings that September in Munich, where I would meet with both Freud and Rilke in the

Parkhotel. Altogether it was a cordial but strange, or should I say, stressful meeting. And I fell ill under the strain of those two meeting for the first time. Franz Josef's fate would remain precarious throughout 1913 until his miraculous recovery was hailed by the press early the next spring, while Freud would cede the presidency of the International Congress that fall to his arch-rival Jung, and then retreat to Rome to consider his options.

There he would make daily visits to Michelangelo's *Moses* in San Pietro (the Basilica of St. Peter in Chains)—where he would sit sketching before the very same statue that had utterly sickened me on my visit with Paul Ree so many years ago, and there my dear Professor saw a Moses I barely recognized.

His Moses with his stone tablets at his side was not a man of anger but one of reconciliation. Having descended Mt. Sinai with his Law inscribed in stone, ready to impart to the faithful only to discover the Jews worshipping false idols and dancing around a Golden Calf, this Moses does not strike out in anger but internalizes his own wrath. In Freud's view, in neutralizing his anger, Moses had wrestled down his vengeance for the sake of a nobler cause to which he was fully committed. No need to break tablets, confirmed as he was to contain his rage and persevere serenely. I smile when I think of it, this modern Moses of Freud's invention, this Moses who mirrored all Freud's frustrations with dissenting analytic factions at the time and this Moses who sanctioned Freud's composure as strength and not capitulation.

As for myself, I looked again and saw indecision as I had years before where my dear Professor saw only resolve. . . .

That restraint was short-lived. Spring 1914 found the emperor feeling better and reinforcements were sent to the Balkan borders and Freud himself began to have misgivings about his mode of passive resistance. "I'm weary of my tolerance," he wrote. "I fear I've outgrown my own kindness." Responding to that signal, his sentries from far and wide launched such an offensive in the international journals against his young interloper that Jung ceded the presidency of the International and became instantly an apostate, losing the right of succession.

That June 28th the archduke, inspector general of the Austrian Army, traveled to Sarajevo to observe troop maneuvers. Beyond the reach of court protocol he rode in an open Daimler with his lovely wife Sophie by his side, for once not behind him, for this day, their fourteenth anniversary, they would celebrate, leaving the Austrian security behind, protocol be damned—celebrate their union amid other revelers of the Serbian holiday, St. Vitus' Day, the patron saint of actors and the protector against storms. A bomb would be tossed, deflected by the archduke, leaving others wounded on the way to city hall—a speech making light of it, "Vienna will give the would-be assassin a medal of honor," he quipped to friends—and then off to the hospital to visit the wounded, a wrong turn, and a shot rang out on Franz Josef Street.

Gavrilo Princip had found his destiny . . . a walk-on on the world stage. Calling, calling all the royal cousins back from their extended vacations to bring out the toy soldiers and play war in a quest for empire.

∽

Rainer wrote, "God can't take the war back because people won't let him. . . . Avaricious human beings hang on to it with all the weight of their guilty consciences. . . . One has no right to give up one's future for a communal one."

I wrote to Freud, "The Big Brothers have all gone stark raving mad. They cannot be psychoanalyzed."

And my dear Professor responded to us all,

I don't believe that after all this we shall ever really be able to be happy again. The world is too hideous and the saddest thing about this is it's exactly what we should have expected given our knowledge of psychoanalysis. . . .

My secret conclusion has always been: since we can only regard the highest present civilization as burdened with an enormous hypocrisy, it follows that we are organically unfitted for it. We have to abdicate, and the Great Unknown, He or It, lurking behind Fate will someday repeat this experiment with another race.

I know that science is only apparently dead, but humanity seems to be really dead. . . .

WE all hunkered down during those first years of war—Rainer in Munich, Freud in Vienna and me in Göttingen. I drew inward, trying to make a living wage from my few patients that Freud had sent to me. My stipend from St. Petersburg was cut off. The German mark had plummeted. My brothers, both in the military, were now moving targets for the opponents to the tsar. One would fall, the other would cede his home and live in one room together with servants and workers of the new order. Travel was now perilous. Freud sent me money, large sums, and one lump sum I promptly spent to replace the moth-eaten fur coat I had been wearing for decades.

Vanity is the last stand . . . of individuals as well as empires.

14

～o

Surviving Death,
War and Empire

War does funny things to people weak and strong. Amidst lightning night sky, crack of gunshot just beyond the horizon and troop maneuvers closing in on the town periphery it signaled that shock of recognition that this was neither celebration of past feats survived nor rehearsal but a test of the real. And its threat sent us all scrambling for some last vestige, some sanctuary of home.

One does not see so much of war as hear its warnings. What we saw were the preparations, the scarcity of flour, sugar, coffee, men to work the farms, and the aftermath, the rubble in a schoolyard, young men returning without limbs, young uniformed faces peering out from cameo portraits on headstones, Iron Crosses, women and children digging graves. What we heard was the sound of our own fear—what we could not see—a constant arrhythmic throbbing within, beating its own time. There was no predicting anybody's fate. You could go around the corner and your heart could stop.

We all took cover during those years—Rainer in his modest apartment at Ainmillerstrasse 34 in Munich and my dear Professor in his consulting room at Berggasse 19 in Vienna. And I with Fred, Maria, Mariechen, Darwin and a stray terrier, Druzhok, I had newly

241

adopted at "Loufried," my home in Göttingen. My few patients kept me at home. I did not travel much and only within Germany when I did. Trains were canceled, delayed for hours, sometimes days. I traveled in my thoughts though, meeting my good friends in correspondence, a daily ritual, letters that crossed, were often inspected, arriving weeks beyond the moment. That is how we all talked, writing with an urgency and waiting indefinitely for an answer.

My dear Professor sent me papers, his dreambook, his book *Totem and Taboo* and word of his son Ernst in the military. He'd been shot but not seriously, two bullets, one deflected off his helmet, the other grazing his shoulder, but his father awaited word of his condition for weeks. He sent his teenage daughter Anna to stay with me one of those summers and there I forged a relationship that would last my lifetime. She told me truly how her father was feeling. "He's depressed, Frau Lou. Our summers in Bad Gastein haven't relieved him at all. He's in pain, his stomach and his jaw, but he does not tell us. He doesn't complain at all, except to lapse into melancholy. Perhaps you can help. Perhaps he would tell you. . . . "

Rainer in those years had been called up for military service, as he had back when we first met almost twenty years before. It was mid-war and they needed more men, regardless of past deferments. This time he was assigned to the War Archives in Vienna and there, through the swift intervention of the princess Maria von Thurn und Taxis, he was relieved of his duties, released as "unfit" and delivered into the care of his royal patroness.

That patronage came not without costs. Maria was a great lover of Rainer's lyric poetry, had translated his work into Italian in fact, and she was nothing if not bluntly maternal about preserving the treasure of his gift. She called him her "Dottor Serafico" and chided him for allowing his energies to be diverted by the string of ardent young women who pursued the now famous author of *Cornet, The Book of Hours* and *The New Poems*.

"Rainer," she said, "I heard one of those young ladies called you a 'trickster of misery.' Now, now, you mustn't let yourself be so compromised. Promise me, Rainer, you *will* come and I'll secure a place for you to work, that magnificent verse you began back in Duino."

Yes, the beginning of Rainer's epiphany, the *Elegies,* the two he'd written before he fell silent. She knew that. Rainer nodded and properly chastised took leave and paid a visit to my dear Professor before retreating back to Munich.

"I've had the pleasure of a visit from your wonderful poet, Herr Rilke," Sigmund wrote, "who bears such a resemblance to my son Ernst. He took pains to tell me though that 'no lasting alliance could be forged with him.' As cordial and delightful to our entire family as he was, I dare say we will not see him again."

And I promptly responded, "My dear Professor—No, do not misinterpret Rainer's attitude. It was not due to any estrangement on his part, but only to his shattered state of mind. I know quite well his esteem for you. . . . "

"Trickster of misery," not mincing words, was one woman's bitter complaint, the truth of a lover scorned. "Shattered state of mind," I had said, trying to explain it away. No, Rainer was simply Rainer. In matters of love, which he seemed constantly to pursue, he could never decide, never commit. At the time he had moved on from his Loulou and would be courting two women in Munich, the actor Elya Nevar and the poet and political activist Claire Studer-Goll, not unlike his earlier simultaneous courting of Clara Westhoff and the painter Paula Modersohn in Worpswede. Elya and Claire were substantial women, one pursuing him directly by quoting from *The Book of Hours*—"Poverty is a shining from within"—and the other indirectly through the shadow of a rich fiancé who would eventually intervene. But Rainer moved between them, approaching each totally and always retreating.

One would say he made a "sacrament of separation" and I can see that. And my dear Professor seized on it instantly from his briefest acquaintance reading into Rainer's words his resistance to any "lasting alliance." No analysis for him. Despite the analytic insights that I poured into all my correspondence with Rainer during those years, insights that he took into himself, and folded into his interpretations of his own childhood in our letters, my Rainer was never game for the couch.

He would later explain that he feared while it might expunge the demons, it might expel the angels as well. It was his intuition, the commandment of his heart, and that homelessness, that "sacrament of separation," he wrote into his poems, finding there the only safe haven from his wayward spirit.

REVOLUTION in Russia in 1917. Two of them. February. Mensheviks, Bolsheviks. October. Provisional government, then overthrown. St. Petersburg up in arms. Bolsheviks prevail. Property confiscated. Armistice. My brothers scrambling for cover. Reds and whites. There was no real end to this war. And sometime at the beginning of 1918 a letter from Danzig.

Dear Frau Salomé—Our dear Johanna has passed away due to the influenza that has cruelly taken so many here before their time. She knew she was going and wanted me to tell you.

C. is strong, a major help to her father, who is so distraught. She has followed the path of her mother into teaching, holding up as best any of us can in these perilous times. (We never know these days whether we wake to Polish, German, or Russian control but have faith that Danzig has always been a "free city." . . .)

I will watch over C. as I have from the beginning. We all mourn our dear Johanna's passing, as we know you do too, but take comfort that she must now be in a better place. Yours—Katya Wolensky

No one can rob the heart, I thought. No war, no disease, no body whose life's expired. Life may end but like blood coursing through the tree of life, love survives never-ending in its connections.

Dear Katya—She resides now in all our hearts helping us beat through these terrible times just one more moment. . . . Take care of our C. She has had in her mother the most remarkable teacher. Perhaps one day when all the horrors of the war are past, I'll once again be able to visit on the way to my homeland.—Lou

∽

War did not end, in name only. National pride receded into momentary relief and then national humiliation. The military technology's machine of destruction was now matched by the citizenry's silent resolve to reconstruct a homeland stone for stone. Conceding defeat we had swallowed our pride, taken our wrath inward where it did not neutralize but infected us. . . . (It would rear its ugly head again in time.)

Rainer invited me to visit him in Munich in the spring of 1919 and I seized the opportunity to see him and reconnect with the cultural world such as it was, that had all but gone underground during those war years. Trains were beginning to run again and then a general strike and my journey at the end of March that would normally take just a half day now lasted three! No matter, milk and eggs, a *Bauernomelette* (farmer's omelet), a luxury, and flowers greeted me with friends at Rainer's apartment.

Rainer had arranged for my friend the actress Ellen Delp to put me up in her garden house just around the corner from Rainer's place and I would then be able to spend my days working with him in his study. Rainer was busy with arrangements but he was in personal turmoil as well. I worried for his physical safety and his emotional

245

well-being. Rainer's dilemma seemed to revolve around his poet friend, his "Liliane," a pet name he'd given Claire Studer-Goll, who had recently returned to reconcile with her fiancé, Ivan, in Switzerland only to discover that she was pregnant with Rainer's child:

Dear Herr Rilke,—Thank you for your note acknowledging this most difficult situation we now find ourselves in. Your willingness to cover the expenses is commendable as is your yielding to Claire's wishes. But since a child would be an impediment to us both at this time and this child would only be a reminder of a painful period of separation in our relationship, it's best for all to end the pregnancy. Claire agrees.

I'll send you an accounting of costs when the procedure is done. Otherwise, in putting an end to this matter, your suggestion that we burn this exchange of letters meets with my full agreement. There need be no record of this most regrettable mistake, for Claire's sake.

Yours, Ivan Goll

"Claire agrees," I thought. Had she really, I wondered. Paternity decides. Rainer told me about this in the quiet of his study and together our eyes dropped, I thinking only of Danzig. There was nothing to say—the nameless child conspicuous by its absence.

Freud had written me in response to my anguish about the chaos in my homeland that "revolutions are acceptable only when they are over." But the revolution, though proclaimed as victorious in St. Petersburg, had its repercussions in a crackdown throughout Germany and Austria, quick to eliminate any suspect pockets of a possible Bolshevik insurrection.

I stayed aloof from any political wrangling, making my way to the theater, the galleries and mostly wanting to talk and work with

Rainer during those two months of April and May. He showed me the raw forms of two more elegies, the third and the sixth, and I was hugely happy that beyond the translations he seemed to be writing his own original verse again.

He would usually give me a few pages and leave me to read them in his study, claiming he had some errands to do, and when he came back he'd sit hunched over on the edge of his easy chair as if about to bound up and be gone. And he'd rest his chin on his hand with those soulful expectant child's eyes staring out into space, waiting for my reaction. And when I told him what wondrous verse this seemed to be, how it so moved me, lifted me, he was surprised and then a glimmer of terror in his eyes, as if he'd surpassed himself and was destined to fall off the summit.

And though my Rainer had never been a political man for all the years I'd known him, I realized all too soon in Munich that he had come under suspicion for harboring leftist writers. Claire and all her contacts, many now dispersed, had been a central focus in this. The reds had passed his apartment by years earlier. Now the whites were in control and prowling.

Ellen knocked at my door one late May morning. "Lou, they have taken Rainer's apartment, stormed in at five in the morning and trashed his study, looking for God knows what. Come, my dear, we must go to him." Both of us throwing off night clothes and dressing in whatever was at hand, we arrived at his door shortly after nine.

Rainer was milling about through the chaos of his study. Books and manuscripts thrown about, drawers pulled out and overturned. "I'm just trying to collect what is important here. My God, Lou," he said, falling into a hug, "They took so many things. I just don't know what. I'm to appear before the local magistrate at eleven o'clock. But I just want to see what's missing before I go."

"Rainer, what on earth are they looking for?"

"Something subversive, I'd think, what can they find—a few poems and some stray angels . . . ? Elyar is coming with me. We'll find out then. You stay here and do what you can with this mess."

"Of course, Rainer. Now collect yourself, it has to be some ridiculous mistake. They will surely realize that."

Rainer went off to return many hours later, saying he'd have to go back again; they'd found his photograph in a random cache of photos with the outlawed leftist writer Ernst Toller. He looked at us frazzled in the doorway as we took his wrap that evening and sat him down to eat something and he said: "Well, I just don't know. In times like these, I guess, we must all take care not to have our picture taken."

Rainer was let off, only to have them storm his study a second time. Whether it was incompetence or harassment, a guest retreated amid gunfire one evening and it had its effect. My stay was nearing its end in early June and Rainer was beginning to think of moving on from all this, his safe haven, what he thought would be his last domicile. But no, he prepared for a lecture tour in Switzerland just a couple of months later, a journey that would make him a refugee again.

"Now it is over," I wrote Rainer shortly after in 1919, "and I don't see you anymore. I must always remember that I'll retain the pleasure of our subterranean connection even when we aren't aware of it. . . . But I haven't even told you what it meant to me that for a while this sense of connectedness, of knowing you were only a few blocks away, lifted me strangely into the bright light of day, into an hourly reality."

And my dear Professor was writing at the same time: "Dearest Lou—If things keep progressing . . . if the tempo of change continues for some time as it is now, then the restoration of communication and the possibility of seeing you will be no mere Utopian dream." I wrote to him of a child I had in analysis in the first stages of exhibitionist repression (yes, that's how we spoke then), who looked aghast at Christ on the cross and said: "Fancy, having let himself be photographed in that position." We were all under assault.

And Victor, my Victor, he too but not in the war but also its aftermath. Victor, being the strong socialist analyst he was, had worked in the front lines, tending to the new hysteria suffered by shell-shocked men and then coming home to a fiancée, his own shell-shock set in and he delivered a bullet into his brain the week before his wedding.

"Successful suicide seems to me a proof of sanity rather than its opposite . . . " I wrote to Freud, and he responded: "Poor Tausk, I confess I don't much miss him . . . his high-flown sublimations. I would have clipped him in a moment but for your high regard of him."

And Victor, I did not defend you but cowered and deferred to my dear Professor's better judgment, saying that your act of violence must represent "a supreme subliminal satisfaction" because I believed he knew more, but no, he did not know you. And I did. I must live with that. Where, where was the feeling?

Rainer went to Switzerland where he wandered. Oh, he took a lecture tour and he moved through various loves, finding some final solace in the painter Baladine Klossowska—his Merline or "Mouka" as he called her—divorced from a count with two sons. He embraced those two sons, helping them in their studies, more so than he had his own daughter Ruth. They celebrated Christmases together.

Merline was his last true love and I believe that she must have truly loved him and he her, but always with the proviso that he could not commit. She would find perfect words to express her complete devotion and frustration with that damnable epiphany that always required the renunciation of love.

No, Rainer could never commit and her financial circumstances dire, Merline finally retreated to her brother's care in Berlin, returning one last time to Switzerland to find Rainer his final haven, the Schloss

Muzot—not a castle at all but a small primitive stone turret on a hill-side surrounded by a garden with a couple of arches. Leaving her sons in Berlin, she returned to secure the rental of this small three-storied tower without gas or electricity and only outside plumbing, to furnish it, to have a couple of stoves installed for some warmth, and all the way fighting Rainer's reluctance to commit to anything, even to sign-ing a lease. And staying with him there for some six months and en-gaging a housekeeper, she knew she was in the way, a stumbling block to the silences, and so she took leave mournfully.

She was crazy about him and she'd been insanely drawn, when she would call him back from their separations. She must have known her rival was nothing other than the complete abandon to his poems. He needed isolation and she finally ceded to that.

My life during those twenties was also sheltered, in the calm pro-tected space of my consulting room in Göttingen, negotiating the peace of tortured individuals. I awaited the stranger to come through that door and I soon found myself faced with a patient Freud had sent me. Freud chided me for charging only ten and not twenty marks.

She was a Czech woman who found herself in her third pregnancy deeply depressed, suffering from agoraphobia, with her marriage in shambles, her husband wanting to leave her. They would wait it out through the six-month trial of her treatment. Mid-analysis her hus-band announced he was leaving her for another. I recoiled and sent to him a firm no: "No, I have a responsibility to the commitment I've made to see this analysis through and you to wait it out, a responsi-bility to protect my patient's rights to her children, her lifeline, and you, you have a responsibility to honor our agreement."

I turned to Freud for help in this, sending him my proviso, and he wrote: "Step back from this. The contract is broken. You must declare the contract null and void. . . . It's not your business to prepare Frau E. for her divorce. You are neither legal advisor nor universal aunt, but a therapist who can only do her work, if the agreed conditions are adhered to. . . . Do not regard this advice as cruel, it's simply correct."

I wrote back to Freud, "No, no, the contract is not with her husband. It's with her father. He is footing the bill. He can quarrel with the lawyers. The analysis can go on. Yes, perhaps I was too emotional and elated with the progress I'd seen. The poor girl is now in hospital with rheumatoid arthritis—swollen wrists, ankles, knee joints and temperature." I'd rescued the analysis on a technicality, saved face with my dear Professor, thanking him for his line of "demarcation."

We would not speak of it again. But I thought of my Aunt Jutta, what she would have done. What I did do. I loved my work. I felt alive in it. I had dissembled because I needed my dear Professor's advice, and more so his admiration and love too much, craved his letters beginning "Dearest Lou." That "demarcation," our own, was something we'd never discuss.

I THINK of war and the sometimes easy conclusion that the world would be better if it were simply run by women. And I think not. We imagine some sanctified notion of "maternal endurance" but that is not the half of it. . . .

You see, motherhood entails in its very essence extreme partisanship in love and hate—a stubborn intolerance and even destructive rage whenever what we bring into being is involved—a part of ourselves we have released which is nonetheless inalienable. The maternal instinct bequeaths its devotion and its brutality alike to every child, the inexorable limitations of who we are. Our nature.

Think of it, we, not unlike the primitive, wage war with lethal weapons and then are quick to assuage treating the wounds we inflict on the enemy. We wage war because we are at war with ourselves. . . . Mankind engages in such a double life, emotional and rational, that we can hardly imagine it's one and the same person involved in this necessary struggle. Except that we have the resources within ourselves to strive for a third possibility: to reconcile things so that the two get along. . . .

Psychoanalysis was nothing more than warlike in identifying those impulses which rage within us, rooted in the very foundations of the soul. Nothing took us so far beyond the state of war—two individuals a foot apart upon the borderline of peace—exploring the basic nature of the human soul.

But you know the individual's personal life in the larger scheme of things may be far less important than we think. Lives of the seemingly insignificant may loom large in the public eye, while lives of the truly exceptional may fast fade.

Existence remains such a picture puzzle; important or not, we are all included within its open secret. We can't escape who we are but only try to contain that rage against its ending.

༄

February 11, 1922, from the dank hollow cavern of Muzot: It was pitch dark outside but for the moon casting a sheath of blue light, silhouetting the little chapel's spire just up the hill on the horizon; the oil lamp lit a low halo glow inside the tower's study. Frau Wunderly, the woman who looked in on him, her bread and wurst, barely eaten, the potato soup she'd left, simmering all morning til noon, now cold on a side table, a carafe of water, a little Rotwein should he want something to warm him. And water trickling through the veined walls, the musky smell of earth seeping in, a swirling of snow like a pointillist painting framed in a window of night, a whirling siren song, ever higher around the tower, and the baying of dogs, the ones that stalked the crest of the hill: "Who if I cried, would hear me in the order of angels?"

And he sleeplessly pacing, sweating, a little feverish now, peering out through the window to the moon's half-face, remembering the gray horse with the wooden peg in his foot galloping toward us in a

252

Volga meadow, leaping through the years, and he cried out loud: "What is time? What is the present?" He talked to himself, talked to it all. Casting in one log after the other, the ones she'd neatly stacked for him, and pulling a shawl over his shoulders he sat back to his desk and an inkwell, one of two she had left for him, and wrote some more and finally laid his head on a sheaf of scribbled paper.

A voice arose in that storm announcing a victory of words, brilliantly cast in the fire, the great bell assuming its form, hardening, and resounding the birth of the *Elegies* and the *Sonnets to Orpheus:*

Lou, dear Lou, this Saturday, on the 11 of February around six o'-clock, I lay aside my pen, having completed the last elegy, the tenth—Just think! I have survived to this point.

What a miracle. Everything in a few days. It was a hurricane. Everything in me that was fire, texture and framework has cracked and bent— . . . Now I know myself again. It was really like a mutilation of the heart that the elegies were not there. And now they are. They are!!! . . .

Next morning, he opened the door to the first light glimmering on blue and taking a fistful of snow, he washed his face. Too cold to go out to the well. And closing his eyes and leaning his head against the doorpost, he gently patted the firm wall of his Muzot, as if it were our horse, that mythic horse of old. Could they really have finally arrived after so long? Yes, yes, he kissed the wall.

And I wrote immediately:

Oh, thank God—How he has showered you with gifts and you me. . . . I sat and read and wailed with pleasure and it was by no means just pleasure but something powerful as though a curtain had been lifted, torn and everything was once again quiet and sure and existing and good. . . . They were so many years on your lips, a word that one can not remember but is: in the beginning was the Word: oh, how they now live in my most secret heart, the extraordinary unsayable suspended, in immanence, spoken. . . . I sit at my kitchen table amidst my birthday cards and flowers but this, this is truly the birthday of all birthdays that has come to you and from you. Dear good Rainer, how my heart leaps gleefully in gratitude to you.—Lou

LOU, only with your deeply understanding letter could I truly acknowledge that they, so long in coming were truly there . . . and oh yes, I know of the possible reaction but I fall now into the spring and want only to thank you that in the midst of all your work you have so quickly responded.—Your old Rainer.

❧

Some two years later, he wrote to say the relapse I had warned him of back then had set in with a furor and now he "lived in the middle of his terror." We wrote regularly those years after the elegies and then I think he found his way to a brief excursion to Paris and then back with a vengeance to the familiar hollow of Muzot. And then a span of almost a year, a stay of some months in a sanatorium, and finally a letter on December 13, 1926, from his tower:

Oh, Lou, I don't know how many hells there are, Lou. You know how I've always regarded pain as a way into the Open. But no, now, it unloosens me day and night. . . . You know, there is an air of harm in this year's end, something truly threatening.
—Proschai, Dorogoya moya. [Farewell, my darling]

Nanny Wunderly and his doctor, Dr. Haemmerli, had been in touch with me, telling me the situation was grave and that Rainer did not want anyone by his side. I was beside myself. I did not want him to know it was the end, but short of being with him, I thought I must, I must write to him daily. I penned letters always open-ended, anticipating a response, trying to recreate the banter of our lived conversation. I wrote about who we were back then and what he had become to me, how he had never left me, how no, I would never believe that.

My love, my dear Rainer—if you must go home, then come home into this heart and take me into yours and Rainer, Rainer, remember always what you used to say to me, our oath that I now deliver back to you this day and always: "You Alone are real to me."

And in another I wrote:

My dear Rainer—remember that night when we sank into a pillow of leaves and the cypresses above and you looked up at the twinkle through the canopy, telling me there was no place we were truly alone, no place we could hide. Once as a girl I looked through a telescope and I remember my teacher directing me to those stars, reminding me: "they float in the chill of the heavens like us. But we feel them. They are still burning." Feel that Rainer. There is the lived pain of distance. We two have known that. But keeping that star in sight, the two of us are always united. We two survive. Love knows no loss, for we live in that distant tiny light. She shines beyond our lifetime. Dear Rainer, Would that I could cradle your head as I did then.—Your sad Lou.

Rainer died at three in the morning on December 29. It was as he'd predicted at year's end. And I carried on. Frau Wunderly later returned those dozen or so last letters I'd written him, saying only that at the very end Rainer had said to ask "Lou" about this: "Perhaps she will understand what this is about." And I lived with those letters for a time, living with their questions as if an answer might come. And when I needed wait no longer, I one night laid them on the coals and burned all but a couple of them, and the most intimate ones from the earlier period of our love affair. Letting all those questions fall to ashes in Rainer's keep—our love a secret held by that star.

And then I sat down and conjuring his face, our words, his pain and our laughter, I listened to the stirrings, the advice that arises from tranquillity, and one dawn early in that New Year I began to write:

> *Mourning is not as singular a state of emotional preoccupation as is commonly thought: it is more precisely an incessant discourse with the departed one, in order to draw him nearer. For death entails not merely a disappearance but rather a transformation into a new realm of visibility. Something is not just taken away, but is gained, in a way never before experienced. In the moment when the flowing lines of a figure's constant change and effect become paralyzed for us, we are imbued for the first time with its essence: something which is never captured or fully realized in the normal course of lived experience. . . .*

It was a memoir of the birth of his poems, the beginning of an afterlife we would share together. Rainer's last gift to me that I would publish on that first anniversary of his death. Receiving the first copy, I folded those two last letters into the little volume's bookends and tucked it neatly into the bookcase like a secret I would keep, knowing these words would succeed me, thinking to send them on one day, that they would breathe comfort to a lost star.

15

∽

Letting Go

The years after Rainer's death were work years for me. I spent the days closeted in my country home outside the town, mornings walking the dogs through the hillside meadowlands with their long staves of cat-o'-nine-tails, pruning the white roses that now grew with abandon in my garden, and seeing patients, young and old, in my upstairs study throughout the afternoon into the early evening. I could feel age whining its lament in my bones each morning, climbing the stairs with me to my consulting room. But I would emerge energized, with an almost giddy excitement over uncharted territory in our many-storied lives so rich, so worth telling, and that hunger for discovery quickened my step down those stairs each evening.

I came to know my husband Fred in that last decade, in his last years, as the loyal companion he had ever been, with the difference that now we talked eagerly at day's close. I had finally come home to him in our home—and sitting together in those evening hours, our chatter was such fresh comfort, two old people who had come together to discuss their distant travels—our married life finally converging on the same destination. I loved my work then—it was my sustenance—and he chuckled and laughed out loud saying: "I've always loved your joyful single-mindedness, Lou, then when you pursued it fiercely and especially now, when you share it with me. To see you now, stubborn as ever, that's the best." He'd smile at my psychoanalytic terms (cathexis, id, ego—all borrowings from dead languages) with the same respect he always had for foreign tongues as human artifacts of distant worlds and then he'd surprise me with insights into some odd cranny of lost languages he had studied that would immediately bring that world to life.

I remember being fascinated with his pictographs of Egyptian hieroglyphs, because these simple images, inscribed on headstones, were the sole remains of cries and hopes and dreams of a people who obviously wanted to be remembered, the only clues to their language now dead, its sounds forever muted. . . . A language that now lived strangely enough in a netherworld of metaphor—bridging two worlds between the first written record of an ancient people, long dormant, and one lone inquiring mind trying to piece it together, to reconstruct the meaning of it all, to give voice to origins.

Fred would nod and say that what he did in his excavations of ancient languages trying to fathom the wishes and the desires of the dead is what I did for the living in analysis. Here I was trying to assign meaning to those newly found objects, those just spoken words. And there he was trying to divine a melody from these ever silent symbols.

He showed me the hieroglyph for truth depicted as a feather, and the word for soul, a bird's body with a man's head. It seemed woefully right that this soul that takes flight from us forever when we die should be the human mind. But what fascinated me most about this lost language was that they also had a word for "spirit"—quite distinct from the soul that leaves us for all time.

This symbol invoked another soulful spirit of the dead that seemed to want to stay, to survive on this side. Or at least generation after generation wanted to believe so. This word was depicted as a pair of human arms, bent at the elbows, with forearms and extended hands pointing upward—a kind of human "u"—and it was inscribed not only on gravestones but on doorposts of homes. I think I loved this word because Rainer used to call me his "doorpost" on which he marked his growth and I wanted to believe that his spirit had come home, was inscribed in my heart.

This "Ka"—as the linguists called it—was in any case the real thing to my mind, the only soul worth knowing. Because this lingering soul was the living memory of the departed one, beckoning our imagination, pulsing in the lifeblood of our continuing story. I wanted to believe that those words did hold an entire civilization's spirit, and ours, my Rainer's spirit too and eventually would hold my own and that millennia hence, some poor questing mind would find solace that those anonymous hordes that had preceded him or her had the same needs and desires and wishes to be known, handed down and spoken again and again on human lips.

Our language then was the only real afterlife, the only record of a communion of souls truly preserved, because our words held on with desperation, they did not give in. They loved life too much and holding life's lost spirits in the sarcophagus of memory, they impart the wisdom of the departed to the newly born.

I don't think Fred ever quite knew the gifts he gave me in those last years when he would smile at my newfound scientific language and he'd explain to me the meaning of his lost ancient words. Like me, trying to piece together shards of individual shattered minds, Fred had always been mining the remains, the languages of entire lost continents of people. Speaking always in foreign tongues and across vast distances, we now found ourselves for once on the same continent of a marriage that had lasted for decades.

⁓

I spoke to my dear Professor mostly in letters during that last decade. He wrote of the disturbing experience of growing old, calling the "detachment of old age" quite bluntly a process of becoming inorganic. He complained about a lack of "eruptions." All the while not wishing to be assuaged. He called things for what they were and said he simply lacked a kind of resonance, likening it to no longer using the pedal of the piano, as if the two instincts he had postulated (of life and death) had somehow become confused.

Of course, I understood, he was sexually and physically failing. He said he felt ashamed. I tried to bolster him, writing of my own experience of old age as a way into the clearing of a much more inclusive wisdom. Youth, I said, was an exclusive sexual cul de sac, accommodating only two, but now, there was truly something else, yes a hardening around the fruit but something much more rewarding, a shedding of superficial experience to something much more essential and vital. . . . "And yes, my dear Professor, you have a right to feel angry because the kernel of your fruit is so large. . . . "

I can't believe I wrote that but I did. I was ever mindfully stroking his ego. And he would counter calling me his dear "indomitable Lou," with an enviable old age: "You and your old man, still enjoying the sun. But with me crabbed age has arrived—a state of total disillusionment comparable to a lunar landscape. Perhaps the central fire is still there, sterility affecting only the layers and if there is time, another eruption may come . . . " I wrote back about Rainer, the truly departed, of my pain and grief and how strangely real he was to me now in the moment, how impossible too that Rainer could not know my lamentation. It was a piece of experience he would have connected to. I think I was simply telling him to be thankful for life itself.

There had to be an end to this. I had to see my dear Professor and I did that last time in Berlin, 1928. He was at Tegel sanatorium for more painful work on his cancerous jaw. The outdoor café on the palace veranda at Tegelhof outside Berlin—our meeting place.

Freud arrived with a bouquet of pansies he had picked from the palace garden, producing them suddenly from his back like a young boy. His eyes heavy, his mouth locked in a slant. He sat down awkwardly as if in pain, laying his cane on the adjacent chair and resting his one arm gingerly on the table as if favoring it, coaxing it into cooperation. I was struck by his visible infirmity now, his jaw with a prosthesis, his hearing failing and his speech somewhat halting. He was slower, more deliberate in his responses as if the words had a longer distance to travel. The burned hole on the sleeve of his tweed jacket, I realized, his poor eyes had not seen.

He caught me looking aghast at him and said, "So my dear Lou, now do you still think this ossified carcass of mine has a few eruptions in him?" We laughed and held hands. I remember feeling how different he was, we were, from that time fifteen years ago in the Café Landtmann in Vienna when I was a new acolyte and he was still plotting out the conquests of his theory, his empire. Now his pain was a present reminder of imminent loss and he was looking back wanly surveying the landscape of his accomplishments.

Once again I turned to my experience of nature and Rainer as the saving grace of my old age. I told him that I felt closest to Rainer in nature and that I experienced Rainer adapting to the changing light and shade of nature's surroundings, enduring now as an essence unaffected by his or my own subjectivity. In a sense, Rainer, standing right there under my trees, weathered all life's seasons—summer, winter, autumn, spring. He'd become "mature" like those trees are for me, evoking life's innermost emotions—the way our impressions of external nature symbolize the deepest feelings within us. "Professor, I don't know why I've wanted you to know this ever since Rainer's death. It's just I feel it's somehow connected to what you've taught me to see and recognize and experience. . . . "

Freud looked at me and patted my hand. "You know, dear friend, you can't help yourself, can you?" he said. "You have an insatiable urge to imagine, to embellish, to complete. Sometimes I must confess in the past it actually annoyed me when you took some bit of our scientific theory and gave it back again in rather fuller distorted form. But in the case of your Rainer, he is so lucky to have found you and to find himself today reflected in your eyes. Old man that I am, I confess. I'm a bit jealous. We should all be so blessed."

He sipped a rum tea, not interested in the plate of condiments left by the waiter. Then scanning the distance he stopped, lighting on an afterthought, and said he'd just recently read my Nietzsche's "Hymn to Life." Not realizing that I had penned those lines so long ago and Fritz merely set them to music, Freud said, "Just think of it, that ending. 'If you have no more joy to squander, then give me your pain.' I can't go along with that silly sentiment of his. It's nothing that a good bout with the flu wouldn't cure."

I looked up at him, trying to make light of his pain and he so obviously in decline and my eyes welled up, saying: "Professor. I have a confession to make. Once again, I embellish life, trying to ward off its losses. . . . I wrote those lines, not Fritz, some forty years ago and they were pure drivel then and now, without an ounce of experience behind them. The bizarre thing is that you, that you, my dear man, have lived those words. It's you who extended your hand, accepting the psychic pain of forlorn, desperate souls with no more joy to give." And I broke down and sobbed because I knew I could not turn back his pain. My last memory of Freud was not at all visual but the hold of his arms on my shoulders as I wept.

Freud had developed a language for that lived individual pain, making it bearable, and I embellished it with a belief in its ultimate release—in nature. Words were the key, the language, all the afterlife we need know.

I would not see Freud again. But a year after our last meeting in Berlin, he wrote to me chiding me for neglecting to tell him of my seventieth birthday. He said: "I would have wanted to tell you how much I value you and love you."

No pretenses, no exaggeration, no embellishments. Conquistador by his own calling, empire builder to be sure, conqueror of this heart. When I thought of a world without him, I thought nature must resonate all the more profoundly in the hollow of his absence. He would then surely be playing the pedal.

∽

It begins with a *for* and *against* that tolerates no nuances.

For moral discipline in family and state. *Against* decadence and moral decay. WE name . . .

For devotion to people and state. *Against* cynicism and political treachery. WE name . . .

For awe of our past. *Against* the denigration of our history and its great figures. WE name . . .

For veneration of the national spirit. *Against* arrogance and presumption. WE name . . .

For the nobility of the human soul. *Against* the filthy exaggeration of man's animal nature. WE name . . . *My dear Professor. No, not you.*

And before you know it, there are elections and officious unknowns ushered in to wild applause, venerated as saviors, liberties falling like so much messy indecision on the wayside, laws enacted to exalt state and family values, entire government departments created to purify information within, to censor the evil assault from without. To cleanse society of it pollutants. Creation is invoked as mystical; evolution is condemned as mundane. Science cedes to the spiritual. And after each incantation of a by now unquestionable ideal, it feels so good to be one of the folk again, it feels so right to be pure and protected; to be a patriot and let that blade fall. To salute the commando in charge. Names are named. Individual writers, artists, political theorists and "the entire Freudian School," in one fell swoop, and the presses of their Jewish conspiracy, the journal *Imago* too. All their questions. Burn them.

The Irish poet was right who wrote in those years: "The falcon cannot hear the falconer; / Things fall apart; the centre cannot hold." It is precisely that moment when tyrants are born. And so it was with us in postwar Germany during those years. The mark was worth nothing. We were hungry and humiliated. A natural order that was flailing and falling apart was seized by a most unnatural command of thugs predicated on fear and destruction.

This was only the beginning and there were many casualties but their common victim was simply the word. Mann, Einstein, Brecht, Marx, Remarque, Freud. May 10, 1933, on Franz Josef Platz in Berlin, ten, no twenty, now fifty, a hundred, a veritable herd of brown-shirted students out for a rebellious good time, sacked the book stores and the libraries and the private collections of surrounding homes, carrying the books on manure carts into the square, accompanied by fire engines and following upon the incantatory rant of their *Feuersprüche,* their fire chants, they set those words aflame to the roar of throngs, some forty thousand, around them. Why read when we need only believe, they said. "Reading is instinctual," their Führer had said. "—A spark to action. Reflection, be damned." WE shall create, create anew, tear down the old.

The German poet Heine in writing of the purges of the dark ages had said only a century earlier: "There where one burns books, one eventually burns men." We did not heed him then and certainly not now.

A FURIOUS rapping on the bedroom door. Eleven o'clock, one late spring night in May of 1933. "Frau Lou, Madame, you must get up. It's me, Maria." I opened the door and saw Maria's plaintive eyes caught in the flicker of the candle she held just below her face, her gray hair tangled in the shawl about her shoulders as if rousted from sleep. "It's my daughter, Mariechen. There's trouble in town. She's down in the kitchen. Come now." I threw on a robe and lighting a small oil lantern, I trundled down the stairs after her, looking out the stair window into the pitch dark, no moonlight, save for the occasional clouds of smoky mist billowing across the meadowlands. Not a night to be out walking.

Mariechen, Fred's child, now a woman in her late twenties, herself with child, stood anxiously in a cloak soaked from the rain and trembling. "Come, come in, dear child. Get those wet clothes off. You'll catch the death of you. Come in here to the fire."

I groped for a blanket to warm her down and Maria fetched a robe and some slippers from my closet. "Maria, something hot now and some brandy." The girl was in tears, her dark eyes looking out with a fear of the hunted. "What is it? What's happened to you? Where's Jakob?"

"He's coming. He said I should walk the road alone. He'd come the back way through the fields. He was afraid that if he'd come with me, they might follow." Maria threw two more logs on the fire, and the flames suddenly catching, Mariechen seized up and cried out, "No, no."

"What on earth is it, child? What is it? Followed by whom?"

Mariechen stared into the flame with those dark black orbs blinking, the eyes of her father, widening then squinting in retreat. My Fred, now dead three winters, lived in those eyes. She warmed herself, now rocking back and forth ever so slightly, stroking her belly.

"Frau Lou, it was horrible, so humiliating. It was dusk when people were making their way home through the square. They began with the university library and they just pushed their way through, plundering whatever struck them, pulling out volumes and journals and papers, bursting out the doors and throwing them onto their carts outside and then they banged on the doors of the square's apartments, forcing their way in and ransacking and coming out with more and then they ran through the streets, pushing people aside, rummaging through the kiosks and the bookshops and Herr

265

Rosenberg's bookshop on the square where Jakob works and they went at it with a ferocity pulling down whole shelves and shoveling them into their carts. The church doors were locked, so there was no place to escape to, to hide.

"Oh Lou, poor Herr Rosenberg, he was transfixed, irate, screaming that he had paid his taxes, he would speak to the burgermeister and he cried, trying to scoop his books up in his arms like his own children. And they pulled him and others out into the streets throwing them face down on the pavement on all fours beating their hind sides with whips calling them *Schwein,* throwing yarmulkes into the fire. Herr Rosenberg crawled over to a heap of books and tried to retrieve them and then with a gun leveled at his head they told him, he must let go, throw them back into the heap and he wouldn't. And two thugs came up to stronghold him, the books dropping at his feet and with two billy clubs they broke his arms. And the fire, the fire, Lou, was huge and the cheers and a ridiculous chanting as if it were a sacred offering. All those words rising up in ghostly spirals of smoke, a sacrifice to appease some dark, dark god. All *our* authors. *Ours,* Lou—the passion of our German soul. You would know them all. Your Freud was called out too. . . .

"Jakob was beat up in the fray. I was making my way to him from the dress shop on Bismarkplatz and we were caught, detained by some lieutenant or other. I thought for sure I recognized him, Marianne Becker's older brother—my classmate from Gymnasium, you remember. But his look was steely cold, not wanting to see me. 'You're a dark one, look at those eyes,' he said. And Jakob defended me: 'No, no, she is the daughter of the university professor Frederick Andreas,' and he let go with a shrug and a scathing look at Jakob: 'You, now *you,* are not our kind.'

"The truth was spoken, Lou, I had to. I'd said it, that Herr Andreas was my father, and worse he dismissed it with such scorn:

'Professor's daughter. Hah! You think you've fooled us with elitist connections—what, with those black eyes, you, just a *Zigeunerin* [gypsy-girl] with her Jew-boy? Don't worry. We will get to you in time. Your days are numbered.' My dear dead father had saved us. We slunk away. I felt like such a coward, Lou, but we just wanted to survive it. At the square we turned our heads away from the students painting 'Jude' in large white strokes on Herr Rosenberg's bookshop window.' In one hell-fire night, all our words dissolved to white ash."

A rap on the back door. Jakob. "Come in, my son."

"Frau Lou, we can hide in the cellar. It's not good for you and Maria if they find us here."

"Jakob, it'll be a cold day in hell, when I have my kin cowering beneath the stairs. . . . Come now; look after your wife and that soon-to-be grandchild. Maria, show them to their room. Yes, my dear Fred is gone now but this is still his house and he would have it no other way for his children. You need sleep now. Your mother and I will keep watch." And they did not come for the moment.

MARIECHEN and Jakob stayed with us for only a few days. Jakob, going into the university, had discovered there'd been some uniformed man nosing around the Near East and Oriental Studies Department asking questions about the late Professor Andreas and so Jakob and Mariechen both went on to the neighboring village to stay with Jakob's relatives.

They returned that fall to spend the last weeks of Mariechen's confinement with her mother and me and once again amidst all the distant noise, the radio rants, the clipped commands, the edicts nailed on public walls, the symbols, the Hakenkreuz and the Star of David delineating our fears and beliefs, one fall night an infant boy breathed out into that darkening world its cry for life, for life. They

267

named him "Friedrich Abraham" and that wail of his that grew stronger and stronger with each new dawn became a barometer of just how far they would go to silence that cry.

✍

It was all around us. We could not read the signs, the full meaning of their symbols, their rhetoric, their language. Though we'd seen it clear as day, in the ashes of the book-burnings that spring of 1933. We could not believe how dire our situation was. We couldn't believe that we cultivated Germans, the world's cultural heart, that we could kill babies. No, no, it was posturing, intimidation, politics, power-play. It need not concern us. We let it happen.

Even the best of us—my dear Professor too, himself a marked man, could not believe it, could not bring himself to imagine where it was going. He quipped wryly when he heard of those book-burnings: "Just books? . . . In earlier times, they'd have burned us with them." It would take another five years and the love for his daughter Anna—her future—for him to see through the masks of our culture, to look into that conflagration and to know that they would not stop at setting minds afire, that bodies would soon follow.

No, no one knew. We all knew. We just couldn't believe—not us. Before they left to take refuge with his family that winter, Jakob took me aside and said that they—the brown shirts—would surely come again, that some people were taking the books they valued most, burying them or burning them before they fell into mischievous hands. I looked up at the shelves to my library, to my *Rilke* with those two last letters wedged into its covers nestled there between Darwin's *Origins* and Freud's *Civilization and Its Discontents* and I said: "No, no, not yet, Jakob. I speak to them daily. They are my comfort, my sole surviving companions in this world."

And I kissed their little boy's forehead and looked into Mariechen's black eyes and said farewell to Fred. I smiled at the irony, thinking of this Persian-German girl now being sheltered by Jews. I pleaded with them to stay in my house but Jakob merely tossed it off, saying: "Within these four walls maybe, but out there it's no longer safe for us to be here. Especially now with the baby. It'll attract too much attention. . . . We'll go first to my parents and later when the baby's stronger we'll move into a community with others where we're less visible. I'll find work and take up my studies later."

Maria went with them returning just a few weeks later, saying they had moved on further into the country, into an inner migration of Jews who would protect them. They wanted to remind me to hide or get rid of my books though. "No, Maria. No, not yet, those books, they are my life, those words bear witness to imagination's force in the world. I need their presence. And that is protection enough in my old age."

❧

Death is a stalker, insatiable to one and all; she doesn't discriminate, we can't elude her. Just how we face that most certain of fates is only one measure of our character. But in these most unnatural of times, when so much of death is manmade, inflicted by our war-mongering machine—death by hunger, losing one's livelihood and support for family, death by humiliation, marking outcasts as a larger conspiracy, death by chance of having been near and seen too much death, death as a rational means to a greater end of a superior race and empire—that other death, the individual one, the one by natural causes, seems an ever more rare and precious blessing.

And so it came to me. Oh, I never gave into it willingly. But when in discovering a tumor not too far from my heart, the doctors cut the mutant cells from my body, taking with them my left breast, I knew

I would never be fully whole again. That death could not be too far off. It was a beginning. My eyes had become too weak to be fixed and so I had to be read to, though I still wrote occasionally to my dear Professor in those last years, writing to him of his *Moses* and sending him an awful picture from the now obligatory identity card that I told him I procured because they were a necessity to any future printing of my literary remains. *"Forgive me this little souvenir. I didn't actually look like that but I must say I look no better. But oh, how instead, my dearest friend, I might for just ten minutes look into your face, into the father-face that has presided over my life.—Your Lou"*

I would heal but pain would now be the constant reminder of life—automatic like breathing. Freud in his seventy-ninth year with fifteen years of excruciating pain behind him still had five analyses with him and I now only one, a man who had returned blind from the war. We sat there in our separate dark forging through life's struggling impulses, unearthing the light of a peace that made it all worthwhile. I could go on for another day. Freud had once written that it is necessary to love and work in order to live and now I understood the full weight of his complaints of old age and an amazing mind that still yielded so much. My loved ones had passed on. I had only my lone patient. I knew my days were few.

And then a cold and a fever and one evening I hobbled down from my room into the library against Maria's protests, and stoking the fire, she wrapped a shawl about my shoulders and threw a blanket over me. I asked her to take my *Rilke* down from the bookshelf and to pull out the letters and read them to me. *". . . those stars . . . they float in the chill of the heavens like us. But we feel them. They are still burning. Feel that, Rainer. There is the lived pain of distance. We two have known that. But keeping that star in sight, the two of us are always united. We two survive. Love knows no loss, for we live in that distant tiny light. She shines beyond our lifetime. Dear Rainer, Would that I could cradle your head as I did then.—Your sad Lou."*

And feeling the frayed parchment of those letters in my fingers and seeing only the haze of fire, I kissed them and cast them into the flame to Maria's "no, Frau Lou."

"I don't need them anymore, dear. I'll be there soon. . . . Now Maria, remember how I stayed with you in your confinement thirty years ago. You must do this for me now. You must write a note to Katya Wolensky, the address is here on this pad, when it's over. Tell her, I thought she should be the first to know. So much we wished to do. But life is simply too short, too short when it is over."

Another day and night of fever with Maria by my bedside and I awake suddenly, asking her to pull those heavy velvet drapes aside to a night I could no longer see, look outside the window to tell me if she saw a star.

"Frau Lou, yes there are just a few but one way out there quite strong."

"So many stars falling, Maria. I dream of him, I dream of her— that one, our star . . . burning. In the morning, the morning, I'll tell you, that star . . . in the morning . . . "

૭

A young woman in her mid-thirties in stylish plumed hat with ruby and pearl pin is running down the platform in her loden cape with brocade trim, new leather lace-up boots, clip-clip clop, clip-clip clop, racing against the clock. Dragging a brown leather-strapped suitcase and a large quilted cloth carrying bag. We must hurry. They have held her too long reviewing her papers, checking identity cards in customs. A scrutiny of her picture, eyes lifting up and down and up again, seizing her alarm, catching her escape and then a slow sly smile, enjoying the hold, her squirming discomfort: "Okay, all is clear. Danzig to Berlin, Berlin to Bremen, Bremen to Stockholm. Auf Wiedersehen. Gute Reise, Fräulein. Warm greetings from Poland." And the stamp like

271

some loud indelible footprint of yes, of no, of origins that will follow. Passport slipped closed. A plaintive nod. Taken.

It is the beginning of a deep winter freeze, late afternoon in December, and the darkness has already begun to set in. There is commotion in the station, children crying, a stray vagrant hand held out here and there, a screeching of wheels against track and giant puffs of steam breathing a mist and the smell of burnt tar. Turning to the old hunched woman in headscarf struggling to keep up with her: "Why all these people? So many, where are they going?"

"Inland, south to Warsaw, Krakow, to family. But you are going out to an adventure you must write us about. We have a map, Cosima."

The old woman presses a small book wrapped in brown paper into her gloved hands saying her mother had wanted her to have it but fallen ill before she could give it to her. She said these words, a book of hours, would comfort the lone traveler. She tucks it securely into her carrying bag. Her suitcase is hoisted up. The girl now reaching down from the railway car steps to grasp her Katya's hand one more time, the conductor now pulling her in, "Fräulein, it is verboten. You must take your seat now. We are departing." She falters a moment. Her bag opens and her old doll spills out, caught. The doors compressed shut. She pulls, it gives and the doll is lost on the track. She winces stroking the cloth arm with porcelain hand, its tiny bloodless fingers, folding it into her bag. One of those children. They will find her. She takes her compartment, peers out the window. One last clipped view of Katya, a smile and a fistful of kisses thrown out like invisible birds into the cold wind. And the train chugs slowly deliberately into the dark, gradually picking up pace. She needn't worry now. She looks out into a rain of crystal snowflakes extinguished on the pavement, rests her head on the window and thinks, "like so many stars falling into night."

Epilogue

Stunning stillness, a chill against my cheek, the cedar smell from em-
bers of the fire in need of stoking, and another foot and a half of snow
outside my mountain cabin now beginning to resemble an igloo. Spring
nowhere in sight. I awoke to a hint of dawn—that grayness that could
also be twilight—and suddenly saw in the freshly coated red pine just
outside my window the arms of a dancer twirling her silk scarves and in
the icy knives that hung from the gutter glistening tears that could not
fall. A distant cascade of whites and blues and grays scrolling those coal
black high peaks. How could anything so beautiful, so serene, just be
there. So magnificently, damnably physical. How could it not speak its
simple truth, pulsing out, moving far, far beyond this moment? To the
waves of the ocean, to the rippling desert sands, to the Arctic wind . . .

The heart-work was done. The imagined world complete—my words,
Lou's story safely stored in the memory of my laptop neatly shut on my old
maple school desk. What now, I asked? Time to throw on some Dylan,
"It ain't no use to sit and wonder why, babe, . . . don't think twice, . . . "
an antidote to unanswerable questions. He asks them and moves on.

Was it really just me now? No, no chance of that. My baby beagle
whimpering his chimp sounds, letting go a huge yelp in the back
kitchen. I bounded out to feed him, to let him out. Distracted I fed him
twice, maybe three times, catching myself, thinking with a few slips of
memory, this beast might eat forever. Wet sandpaper licks on nose and
forehead, his thanks, I let him out tying him to his long, long leash on

273

the porch, watching him leap brown ears flapping into the deep snow. One last tentative look back and then off, attacking the porch's cedar posts. My little bark eater. This was his turf. Dog heaven. I needed that howl, now more than ever. A few more logs tossed on the fire to hear its crackle. The whispering of water trickling through the pipes. That's better. Familiar ghosts. The house was waking up.

To the kitchen, firing the leftover coffee already on the stovetop, I poured myself a large mug and made my way back to the bedroom study and plopping into the armchair, I pulled out from under my desk that old hatbox, the one that had jump-started this all, thinking now that the story was done, I'd rummage one last time through its contents. A kind of inventory. A leave-taking.

"Oma," I said out loud, because you talk to yourself in the North Country. It's healthy, the only company there is and no one there to commit you. "Grandma, my Oma, I found your Lou . . . I brought her back to you. But now she's silent again like you." She in that machine, you in these things. And tracing with index finger the flourished script "Fields" on that fifties hatbox, I pulled the frayed ribbon loose, releasing its top, to what remained of the bits and pieces of her life.

What would she say now, how much had she really known or only suspected? The arm of the doll with its delicate hand (carried so far from Russia and Poland, what had she looked like, when had she lost her), the exquisite hatpin (I have to make a brooch of it, wear it when I come off the mountain), the postcard of Vienna's Franziskanerplatz by one A.H. (don't want to imagine what that would bring on today's ungodly market), The Book of Hours with its intimate inscription from the great poet to Lou (priceless as a heartbeat).

But I remembered back then when she gave me that book, there'd been something more. She'd said that. Something still missing. I rummaged through it all, marriage license, snapshot of her looking like a flapper smiling up to her Carl Lippe, the grandfather I did not know, corsage of dried white roses, baby pictures of my mother, teaching certificate, Mom's

4-H ribbons, and at the bottom of the box a German-English dictionary with random words underlined and circled in pencil. I read them all, thinking when she'd needed to use them, needed to know, and coming to the very end, I read circled in pen "Zurückwerfen-reverberation, echo," and neatly folded into that page what I thought was maybe the bookshop's receipt. No, this was something else. A small folded note. It read:

Dearest Johanna—

Rainer's book. For C.
May she know through these words
from whence she came.

—Yours ever, Lou

It was such a flood of emotions, incredulous joy at having found it, anger at it being too late, a pleading ache to tell her, to tell someone. "Oma, Oma, you were hers and I too." A fear of being alone. A sobbing stream of tears and weeping through smiles for I don't know how long and then a rocking release . . . letting go, letting go. It was over. Put it all back now. Time to go forward, time to join the living.

A yelp on the porch, a scratch at the door. A tearing at something. What's he gotten himself into? I don't want to think of what eviscerated poor creature awaits me. I open the door. There's a package torn open—UPS from Saratoga to Anna Kane—paper strewn all over the place. There's a card I pick up. And look to "Dar" on the edge of the porch—a stuffed bear with tiny insignia heart firmly clenched in his jaws. Whatcha got there? Come on now, let's have it, let's go in. Here's a bone now. I'll give it back. I always lie to my dog.

We sit before the fire and I open the card. It's a picture of a glistening stream in snow and one stone heart glimmering from the riverbed. And inside—

My dear A.—A valentine a full month late but I've got an excuse—been in the Arctic. Thought you might like the bear. You won't see a real one for a few months yet. I'm back now. I'll be up tomorrow. Want you to read me that story.

Til then a few lines from a poem (William Stafford) I liked about a river speaking through ice—says it better than I would or maybe I just know you:

Some time when the river is ice, ask me
mistakes I have made. Ask me whether
what I have done is my life . . .

I will listen to what you say.
You and I can turn and look
at the silent river and wait . . . We know
the current is there, hidden; and there
are comings and goings from miles away
that hold the stillness exactly before us.
What the river says, that is what I say.

From this heart to yours—J.
p.s. Hug that bear.

Yes, I smiled. I'll bet she'd have liked that. It was the beginning of a story. One I would not write. No, this one mine. One I would live . . .

Author's Note

On the Truth and Fiction of Lou

This novel may follow the arc of a life, but it is wholly imagined, creating an inner voice for Salomé herself and giving context, character and emotional cohesion to details as varied as a gesture noted in passing in a memoir and events discussed exhaustively in correspondence. All its characters, whether bearing familiar names or not, are creations of fiction.

The pregnancy with Rilke's child that is pivotal to this novel is extensively noted in the scholarship, but never confirmed or denied, with most scholars assuming Lou must have aborted and only one younger but contemporary female critic, Cambridge professor Eliza M. Butler, asserting that Lou most probably bore the child. Much of the critical correspondence from this period was burned, presumably by Lou. However, Rilke's *Florentine Diary*, written to Lou on his studies in Italy during this time, is conspicuous in its effusive celebration of motherhood. Finally, toward the very end of her life, Lou in explaining her relationship with Gillot and her primary contract with God did say that she astonished someone once in saying she had not hazarded the risk of a child and went on to add that she had failed in all bonds of consummated love: marriage, motherhood and eros.

This novel does not attempt to make a definitive claim on the historical truth of a child. It simply follows the evidence of a life and derives from that life's questions the inspiration of an answer in fiction.

Sources

In reconstructing this fictionalized life of Lou, this novel has drawn from the correspondences of Lou Andreas Salomé with both Rainer Maria Rilke and Sigmund Freud. With the exception of Lou's last two letters to Rilke, which were indeed burned and lost to us, all other references are the author's renderings of existing correspondence. The translations of Rilke's poems are the author's own, as are the translations of Lou Andreas Salomé's "Prayer to Life" and "Volga." All other poems by Lou are the author's own creation. The author further wishes to acknowledge the lyrics of Bob Dylan, the lines from W. B. Yeats's "Second Coming," and the lines from William Stafford's poem "Ask Me."

In addition to the primary writings of Lou Salomé, Friedrich Nietzsche, Rainer Maria Rilke and Sigmund Freud, a large body of secondary work was consulted in researching this novel. The author wishes to acknowledge a few outstanding sources as inspiration: Matthew Battle's *Library* (2003); Rudolf Binion's *Frau Lou: Nietzsche's Wayward Philosopher* (1968); E. M. Butler's *Rainer Maria Rilke* (1941); Curtis Cate's *Friedrich Nietzsche* (2005); Ronald Clark's *Freud* (1980); Ralph Freedman's *Life of a Poet: Rainer Maria Rilke* (1996); Ian Kershaw's *Hitler* (1998); Angela Livingstone's *Salomé: Her Life and Work* (1984); and Friederic Morton's *Thunder at Twilight: Vienna 1913/1914* (2001).

Beyond the general works mentioned above, I provide here a few additional source notes, principally to specific quotes from the correspondences cited in the novel for those readers curious about this novel's historical underpinnings and for those interested in pursuing the legacy of Lou Salomé and her circle.

Notes

vii *All life is poetry . . .* : Adapted from *Dank an Freud: Offener Brief an Sigmund Freud zu seinem 75 Geburtstag* (*Homage to Freud: An Open Letter to Sigmund Freud upon His 75th Birthday*) (Wien: Internationaler psychoanalytischer Verlag, 1931), p. 14. Also cited in *Looking Back* by Lou Andreas Salomé, translated by Breon Mitchell (New York: Paragon House, 1991), epigraph.

5 *All the soarings . . .* : "Letter to a Young Girl," July 1921, in *Wartime Letters of Rainer Maria Rilke,* translated by M.D. Herter Norton (New York: Norton, 1984).

57 *The story about the madman:* Adapted from Friedrich Nietzsche, *The Joyful Wisdom*, paragraph 125, cited in *Nietzsche* by Ronald Hayman (New York: Routledge, 1999), pp. 3*ff.*

65 *You blocks, you stones, you less than senseless things . . .* : Adapted from Shakespeare's *The Tragedy of Julius Caesar,* Act I, scene 1.

91 *Lou's aphorisms and Nietzsche's revisions:* From *Frau Lou: Nietzsche's Wayward Philosopher* by Rudolf Binion (Princeton, N.J.: Princeton University Press, 1968), p. 91. For more on Nietzsche's pruning of Lou's aphorisms, see Angela Livingstone, *Salomé: Her Life and Work* (Mount Kisco, N.Y.: Moyer Bell, 1984), pp. 47*ff.*

106 *Behold, I am that which must always conquer itself . . .* : Nietzsche, *Thus Spake Zarathustra*, cited in *The Portable Nietzsche*, selected and translated with an introduction by Walter Kaufmann (New York: Viking Penguin, 1982), p. 227.

107 *Of all that has been written . . .* : Ibid., p. 152.

108 *Every philosophy conceals another philosophy . . .* : Nietzsche, *Beyond Good and Evil*, paragraph 289, cited in Hayman, p. 38.

109 *Solitude is . . .* : "The Last Days of Nietzsche" by John Banville, *New York Review of Books* 43, no. 13 (August 13, 1998).

110 *I would believe only in a God who could dance . . .* : Nietzsche, *Zarathustra*, p. 153.

115 *Put out my eyes . . .* : Rainer Maria Rilke, *The Book of Hours* (Frankfurt: Insel Verlag, 1905). (Author's translation.)

117 *Those are my animals . . .* : Adapted from Nietzsche, *Zarathustra*, paragraph 10, p. 137.

122 *Oh maker of the material world . . .* : *Avesta: Vendidad*, a collection of holy texts in Zoroastrianism. *Fargard 3: The Earth*, English translation by James Darmeister et al., http//www.avesta.org/avesta.html.

133 *Koepenicker Blutwoche:* Based on a massacre of socialists, communists and Christians by the Nazis on June 21, 1933.

148 *Who if I cried . . .* : Opening line to "First Elegy," Rainer Maria Rilke, *Duineser Elegien* (Frankfurt: Insel Verlag, 1923). (Author's translation.)

155 *Lines from the song "Falling in Love Again":* From the film *The Blue Angel*, 1930.

157   *How shall I hold my soul . . .* : "Love-Song," Rainer Maria Rilke, *New Poems* (Frankfurt: Insel Verlag, 1907/1908). (Author's translation.)

163   *Heart burning before her mercy . . .* : *Rainer Maria Rilke—Lou Andreas-Salomé Briefwechsel*, ed. Ernst Pfeiffer (Frankfurt: Insel Verlag, 1955, 1975), hereafter cited as *BW*. Rilke to Lou (June 9, 1897), p. 20. (Author's translation.)

163   *I am yours just as the last tiny star . . .* : *BW*, Rilke to Lou (June 8, 1897), p. 18.

167   *My struggles are your long-won victories . . .* : Rilke, *Florentine Diary,* cited in *BW*, p. 35, and in *You Alone Are Real to Me*, by Lou Andreas-Salomé. Translated with a foreword and afterword by Angela von der Lippe (Rochester: BOA Edition, 2003), p. 8.

167   *I am like a little anemone . . .* : *BW*, Rilke to Lou (June 26, 1914). See also Salomé, *You Alone Are Real to Me*, p. 80.

167   *I question myself so often these days . . .* : *BW*, Rilke to Lou (June 1897), p. 21. See also Salomé, *You Alone Are Real to Me*, p. 36.

180   *So the hour bows down to me . . .* : Opening lines to Rainer Maria Rilke, *The Book of Hours*. (Author's translation.)

181   *What will you do, God . . .* : Rainer Maria Rilke, *The Book of Hours* (Frankfurt: Insel Verlag, 1905). (Author's translation.)

182   *I saw her that summer of 1900 . . .* : Fiedler quote on Lou and Rilke in Russia cited in Angela Livingstone, *Salomé: Her Life and Work*, p. 109.

185   *They were kindly people . . .* : Adapted from Binion, *Frau Lou,* pp. 275–278.

193   *If he forms a hand . . .* : *BW*, Rilke to Lou, p. 93. See also Salomé, *You Alone Are Real to Me*, p. 51.

194   *I used to think it would be better . . .* : Salomé, *You Alone Are Real to Me*, p. 45.

214   *Analogy of psychoanalysis as a form of "washing dirty linen"*: *Lebensrückblick,* by Lou Andreas Salomé (Frankfurt: Insel, 1968), p. 168. See also *Looking Back,* by Lou Andreas Salomé, translated by Breon Mitchell (New York: Marlowe, 1991), p. 104.

221   *I so rarely feel the need for synthesis . . .* : Discussion of the role of psychoanalysis in individual psychic healing, from Sigmund Freud and Lou Andreas-Salomé, *Letters* (New York: Norton, 1972), here-

after cited as *SF and LAS Letters*. Freud to Lou (July 30, 1915), pp. 32*ff.*

227   *Exposed on the cliffs of the heart . . .* : Rilke, 1912/1913, from *Uncollected Poems (1911–1920)*, cited in *Ahead of All Parting: The Selected Poetry and Prose of Rainer Maria Rilke*, edited and translated by Stephen Mitchell (New York: Modern Library, 1995), p. 136. (Author's translation.)

234   *If social democracy is opposed . . .* : Adolf Hitler, *Mein Kampf* (Boston: Houghton Mifflin, 1942), pp. 40–43.

234   *Everything I embrace becomes light . . .* : Nietzsche, *Zarathustra*, cited in Frederic Morton, *Thunder at Twilight* (Cambridge: Da Capo, 2001), p. 155.

236   *What would become of the monarchy?* The dramatic unfolding of events leading up to the assassination of the archduke is discussed from the dual perspectives of Princip and Franz Ferdinand in Friederic Morton, *Thunder at Twilight*, pp. 242–264.

238   *Vienna will give the would-be assassin . . .* : Cited in Morton, *Thunder at Twilight*, p. 247.

238   *God can't take the war back . . .* : Ralph Freedman, *Life of the Poet: Rainer Maria Rilke* (New York: Farrar, Straus and Giroux, 1996), p. 396.

238   *The Big Brothers have all gone stark raving mad . . .* : *SF and LAS Letters*, Lou to Freud (November 19, 1914), p. 20.

238   *I don't believe that after all this . . .* : *SF and LAS Letters*, Freud to Lou (November 25, 1914), p. 21.

243   *I've had the pleasure . . .* : *SF and LAS Letters*, Freud to Lou (July 27, 1916), p. 51.

248   *Now it is over . . .* : *BW*, Lou to Rilke (June 6, 1919), p. 409.

249   *Successful suicide . . .* : Adapted from *SF and LAS Letters*, Lou to Freud (August 25, 1919), p. 99. See August 1, Freud to Lou, for further discussion of Tausk.

250   *The case of the Czech woman:* Discussed in *SF and LAS Letters*, pp. 147*ff.*

251   *You see, motherhood entails . . .* : Adapted from Salomé, *Lebensrückblick*, pp. 184*ff.* See also Salomé, *Looking Back*, pp. 113*ff.*

252 *Existence remains such a picture puzzle . . .* : Cited in Salomé, *Looking Back,* p. 115.

253 *"Lou, dear Lou, this Saturday . . .* : BW, Rilke to Lou, p. 444. See also Salomé, *You Alone Are Real to Me,* p. 134.

253 *Oh, thank God. . .* : BW, Lou to Rilke (February 16, 1922), p. 446.

254 *Lou, only with your deeply understanding letter . . .* : BW, Rilke to Lou (February 19, 1922), p. 447.

254 *Oh, Lou, I don't know how many hells . . .* : BW, Rilke to Lou (December 13, 1926), p. 482.

256 *Mourning is not as singular a state . . .* : Salomé, *You Alone Are Real to Me,* p. 27.

259 *On old age: SF and LAS Letters,* Freud to Lou (May 11, 1927), and Lou to Freud (May 20, 1927), pp. 165*ff.*

264 *There where one burns books . . .* : Heinrich Heine, *Almansor,* 1821.

Acknowledgments

I am especially indebted to the late Liz Maguire, publisher of the Counterpoint/Basic group at Perseus Books for championing the life of literary historical fiction and for the wit and sharp intellect she brought to editing this book. I also wish to thank the following people for their critical reading of parts or drafts of this manuscript and needless to say, I take full responsibility for any infelicities or howlers that may remain in the text: Willis Barnstone, Amy Cherry, Nancy Condee, Kate Kaplan, Betsy Lerner, Vanessa Levine-Smith, Robin Morgan, Caryl Morris, Israel Rosenfield, Martha Serpas, Lauren Slater, Kathy Streckfus, Christopher von der Lippe, George von der Lippe, and Peter Whybrow.

Finally, the writing and publishing of this book have been greatly enhanced by the steadfast and wise guidance of my agent, Kim Witherspoon, by the sensitive publishing direction of my editor, Amy Scheibe, and by the invaluable support of my first reader, Jim Jordan, who has been an enthusiastic accomplice on this imaginative journey to Lou and her all but vanished world.